Knox

A Merrick Brothers Novel

by
PRESCOTT LANE

TABLE OF CONTENTS

PROLOGUE

THANK YOU NOTE:

Knox—

I'm sure you've heard the saying "you don't get anything in life for free." Well, I don't agree with that. I think you just have to know where to look.

I'm talking about a post of a kid in uniform on his first day of school. A cute monogramed school bag. A stick figure bumper sticker of a family and pets. A sign in front of a house celebrating a new baby or a child's birthday. A selfie and a tagged location.

They tell me where someone lives, where their kid goes to school, his name and rough age, how many kids are in the family, their hobbies, whether family pets may bother me if I came by, unannounced, for a house visit.

These are things us "normal" people do. All such innocent information. All given away for free.

For me to use.

Now let's talk about you "Hollywood" types.

You all are even worse—pretentious attention whores.

Knox, I've heard you say you try to avoid the spotlight, that having a social media presence is just part of the job. That made me laugh. We both know that's not true. You post everything so freely.

I know where you've shopped, when and where you're on vacation, which hotspots and fancy restaurants you're at, what you drive, your favorite workout routines, who you hang out with, what kind of phone you have, what certain rooms in your houses look like.

You may not post quite as much as some others, but, like the rest of Hollywood, you crave the attention, seek it out, thrive on it. And you've given me more than enough to use.

So congratulations on a job well done.

You've got my attention. I'm watching.

Consider this a thank you for all the free information. I'll make sure to use it!

CHAPTER ONE
THREE WEEKS EARLIER

Mae

"Welcome to *The Breakup Bible*. Ring the bells! Your Sunday night service is in session. Consider me the Mother Superior of broken hearts," I say into the microphone of the radio booth that will be my home for the next two hours.

For the past couple of years, every Sunday from ten in the evening until midnight, this has been my gig. I give advice on how to break up with your boyfriend or girlfriend in a compassionate way, and how to handle being dumped without going off the deep end.

My personal experience with both has turned *The Breakup Bible* into a nationally syndicated radio show. In a time when streaming television and podcasts reign supreme, I've managed to bring people back to the radio. Of course, you can stream audio of my show on a radio app—we don't live in the Stone Age. A little luck and the world's epidemic of broken hearts made my show the success it is.

I hit the button on the switchboard to take the first caller. "What's your name? And how can we break you?"

That's my usual way to address a new caller. I don't "break" people. That catchphrase started back on my very first show. I was nervous, and my words came out wrong. Somehow, it just stuck. It was my senior year of college, and I was doing an internship. Normally, I got coffee and took messages, but when the regular Sunday night DJ didn't show one time, they put me in front of the mic. Before I knew it, I had my own show.

"Mother Superior," the caller starts.

Most callers refer to me as Mother Superior or sometimes Sister, but my true identity remains a secret. Only those closest to me, my inner circle, know who I really am. Keeping my identity a secret started out as a way for me to maintain my privacy. After all, I *do* talk about some pretty private things. Anonymity also allows people to open up more freely, like talking to a stranger in an airplane, but the secrecy has become part of the draw of my show. There's a mystique surrounding it, but I'm also a private person by nature, so it's a win-win.

My show is syndicated, meaning that people across the nation listen to me. I don't like to know how many people are actually tuning in. And unlike most radio personalities, I don't make appearances. There can be big money in those side hustles, but my privacy is more important to me.

"Hi, my name is Sally."

There is no way this young woman's name is *Sally*. No one actually names their daughter Sally anymore, but I'm not using my real name, so I don't expect my callers to, either.

"Confess," I say.

"There's this guy."

"There always is," I say, grinning to myself.

"We've only been seeing each other a few weeks. I really like him. I think he's the one."

Oh dear Lord, she thinks she's found the "chosen" one. Where's the holy water? This one might take an exorcism.

"I don't usually feel this way about guys. I've never slept with a guy this quickly before."

Yes, my callers give me all the details. Anonymity also makes for loose lips. It used to surprise me what people would call in and tell me, but not anymore. I've pretty much heard it all, but even after almost four years, it never gets boring.

"Things were going great, and then last night, he tells me that he wants to take a break. He says he's got some work to do on himself.

Can't devote himself to me one hundred percent."

That's the modern man's version of the *it's me, not you* speech.

"I told him I'll give him all the time he needs, but I'm wondering if that's right. Should I wait around?"

Normally, I might ask some follow-up questions, needing more details. Things like the exact length of their relationship or how they met, but sometimes the answer is obvious, even if the person on the other end of the line can't see it. It's often hard to see what's right in front of us. We're too close to it. That's why people call me. It's an honor, really.

I'm just a twenty-something single woman. I'm not a psychologist. I'm not a relationship expert. I'm just someone who's been there, too.

"You should praise God to be rid of his ass. Hallelujah, the devil has left your bed," I say.

"But I think I love him."

My show is fun, but I also try to speak from my heart. "Sally, I'm going to let you in on a little secret I've learned. Following your heart is never wrong. It's just the heart doesn't always have a good sense of direction. At least mine doesn't. My heart needs a GPS!"

She giggles a little. All she really needs is to know she's not alone, because nothing feels lonelier than having your heart broken.

"I don't know if you're anything like me, but when I sleep with a man, I start to catch feelings."

I hear her start to cry, and she asks, "Why aren't men the same way?"

"That's one for a higher power than me."

CHAPTER TWO

Knox

Lola, Lula . . . I look over at her naked body in bed next to me. Christ, what's her name? I know it starts with an L.

Luna?

She arches her back, her full tits presenting themselves. Who gives a fuck what her name is? Her head turns, giving me a smile that makes her look a little too full of herself. I've seen it before. It's why I don't feel bad that I don't know her name. She knows mine.

Knox Merrick.

She's seen my name on movie posters, theater marquees, sexiest man alive covers. She wanted to bag a movie star. I wanted to fuck. She gets to spend the rest of her life telling everyone about the night she slept with a Hollywood movie star, but I'll forget all about her by tomorrow. Seems to me she gets the better end of the bargain, so her name is a minor detail.

If she's looking for round two, she'll have to look somewhere else. She wasn't that good. She's got all the right equipment—a killer body, but no idea what to do with it. Give me a woman with a real body who knows how to use it over one of these model types who just lay there any day of the week. I should've known better, I've been burned before.

"What time is it?" I wonder aloud, looking for a clock. Hotel room clocks never seem to have the right time. They're either twenty minutes off or still on daylight savings time.

She rolls over on top of me, her black hair falling around my face and grabs the clock. "Oh my God, it's after ten?"

"So?" I ask.

"So!" she screams, messing with the clock, turning the radio on. "It's Sunday."

"Late night Bible study?" I joke.

"Sort of," she says, still searching the radio channels. "Mother Superior is on."

"You aren't serious?"

Playfully, she tries to kiss me, but I turn my head. "She's not a real nun. Well . . . No one really knows who she is. Her show is called *The Breakup Bible*. Have you not heard of it? She talks about all her bad dates. People call in. She's totally awesome. I never miss it."

Seems like as good an excuse as any for me to make a getaway. Shifting her off me, I get up, reaching for my clothes on the floor.

"Found it!" she says, sitting up straighter in the bed, the sound now coming in clearly.

"I'm going to go," I say, pulling up my pants. "You stay, enjoy the room."

The woman with the mysterious L name grabs my hand. "Listen with me. You'll like it. I promise."

"Our caller brings up an interesting point."

My heart starts to race. I'm frozen, unable to even finish zipping my pants. Her voice stops me dead in my tracks. I'd know her sassy tone anywhere, even after all this time apart. I can't remember the name of the woman I just banged, but I'll never forget that voice, her name.

Mae Sheridan.

My Mae. The one I let get away.

"Some heartbreaks haunt you. You think you're over the person, but then bam! You break down all over again."

How my dream woman turned into the love that haunts me, I'll never know. Well, I do know. I fucked it up. It's the classic story of man who doesn't know what he has until she's gone. Let me tell you, the pasture isn't always greener on the other side.

Prime example: the "L" named woman before me.

Mae keeps talking, and the hair on the back of my neck stands on end. She's on the radio? Is this really her? I look over at my one-night stand. I can't have Mae's voice in my head, and a different woman's tits in front of my face. It feels wrong, even though it's been five years since I've seen Mae.

It makes no sense, but I imagine this is what infidelity feels like. I wouldn't know firsthand. I've never been married, and I've never cheated. I've had a romp or two or twenty in my trailer on movie sets and one-night stands aplenty, but if I'm exclusive with a woman, I don't stray.

"Got to go," I say, throwing on the rest of my clothes.

"Call me," she says as the door slams behind me. I don't bother with a response. We both know I won't call. Why lie?

When the door closes, Mae's voice disappears. It's almost like losing her all over again.

~

My first memory of Mae is the day my mom died.

Haven's Point, Colorado sits just forty-five minutes outside of Denver, but that day, no haven could be found. I had just finished kindergarten two days earlier. I was sitting on my front porch across the street from her grandmother's house. People had been coming over all day, dressed all in black, carrying flowers, cards, and casseroles. I was crying because my dad wouldn't let me kiss my mom goodbye. I was six years old. I know now it was because he didn't want me to see her lifeless body, to have that image burned in me forever, but back then, all I wanted was to kiss her one more time.

Mae walked over, all knees and elbows in a navy sundress with red flowers on it. Her light blue eyes looked almost clear, and her brown hair was pulled up in pigtails, except for a few loose strands hanging around her face and neck in little curls. Her grandmother and parents walked inside the house, and she took one look at me and ran back towards her grandmother's house. I thought it was my shaved head that scared her off. My dad, older brother, and I all did that for my mom. But Mae wasn't scared.

I learned that about her early. Mae Sheridan doesn't scare easily.

She came out carrying a pair of scissors. Looking me right in the eye, she cut one of her pigtails right off. Her lopsided haircut made me smile. Even at six, I already knew how important a girl's hair was to her. My mom losing hers taught me that. There Mae was, just six herself, and she cut her hair off to make me feel better. This kid she never met. That's who she was.

That day began a fifteen-year relationship, most of which we spent as friends and pen pals across the continents that separated us. Me, living a quiet life in Haven's Point, and her, the military brat shuffled around the world from base to base. Then there were the years we were together. Those teenage years when everything feels so damn intense. It's now been five years since things ended. We spent more time apart than we ever did together. Maybe that's why five years hasn't changed my heart.

I'm used to loving her from afar.

She became my best friend that summer so long ago, my partner in crime. She knew when to let me be sad about my mom, and she knew when to make me laugh. But it was only a couple months, that was it, then she went back overseas with her parents. I didn't know it then, but I'd just met the first girl I'd ever kiss, make love to, fall in love with. Sometimes I wonder what that means about us.

Our friendship was born in sadness. Is that why things went so wrong?

Cassette

Mae to Knox

Age Thirteen

Knox, for your information, I've heard of email. I don't live in a cave. I'm a military brat. Yes, military bases have Wi-Fi, even in Germany. I know handwritten letters take a long time, but I find them more personal. Besides, we've been pen pals since we could barely write. Do you remember that? I still have all your letters, even the drawings we used to send to each other. Still, I offer this cassette as a compromise. You can listen to my voice. That is, if you own an old-fashioned cassette player. Personally, I think all thirteen-year-olds should own one. They're vintage. You know how I love anything old. People, movies, songs. Everything gets better with age, except maybe food. Come to think of it, day-old pizza is surprisingly good, too.

I'm rambling. This is why letters are better. I don't ramble in letters, but since you insist we modernize our communication, your punishment is that you have to listen to all my unedited diatribes.

That's a word from my ACT vocabulary book. I'm already studying. Some of the kids on the base call me a nerd. I call them morons, so we're even.

~

Cassette

Knox to Mae

Age Thirteen

Mae, you're so old! I had to go to a thrift shop to get a cassette player. Cost me five bucks. But it's worth it to hear your voice.

When is your dad getting leave again? Will you be visiting your grand-mother in Colorado when he does? Haven's Point is so boring without you.

By the way, I know the word diatribe. I have the same book. I've learned all the words through E, so I guess I'm a bigger nerd than you. Who are these kids calling you names? Make me a list, and I'll come all the way over to Germany to kick their asses. I'm the only one that gets to call you a nerd. Just kidding.

I see what you mean about the rambling thing. But I think we should promise each other to always listen to the tape, no matter what. Even if we are in a fight or something. Also, when we are recording, we should never stop the tape then continue recording, or start over altogether. It's better this way. The ramblings feel more honest. And honestly, I miss you.

It's Sunday night, less than a half hour until Mae comes on the radio. It's been a week since I first heard her. I left the hotel that night, sat in my car in the parking garage, and just listened to her voice, trying to convince myself it wasn't her.

Since then, I've downloaded and listened to every old show of hers I could find on the internet. For hours and hours, I've listened to her voice. It's like binge-watching a show without video, but it doesn't matter. I can imagine her. The image of her is clear in my mind—her brown hair with those wispy curls that frame her face, her blue eyes, the way she moves, tastes, the feel of her skin next to mine. It's all still real.

It wasn't always easy to listen to her show, hear about her dating life. I shouldn't be jealous after all this time, but I still am. I've tried to Google her, find a picture of her, but I've come up empty. I know her show airs out of Denver, but there aren't pictures of her anywhere. There's nothing to connect her to the show. It doesn't matter, though.

I know it's her. I know it deep in my bones.

The lights are low in the bedroom of my Malibu home. Memories of Mae surround me. Running my fingers across the cassettes, I've kept every one, storing them in an old Nike shoebox from when I was thirteen. I loved those shoes, begged my dad for them for months. They were custom made with my initials on the back heel, blue and green, with glow in the dark laces. Wonder what happened to those? Some fan would probably pay big money for my old, sweaty tennis shoes.

Mae and I never started a new tape until the old one was finished, so each tape sounds more like a continuous conversation. Whoever had the tape when it was full, kept it. Not long after I broke her heart, she sent me all of hers. No note, no card, just the cassettes. All the places I've lived, all the moving around, these tapes have always been with me. For a long time, it was the only piece of her I had. I used to listen to them over and over again, but it's been awhile. I still keep a cassette player on hand just in case, though.

Her voice.

Even now, it calls to me.

CHAPTER THREE

Mae

"Men are like libraries. You hope you're checking out a romance, perhaps a thriller. But occasionally, you end up in a tragedy, or if you're anything like me—true crime. In the library of men, be careful not to get overdue fines," I say into the microphone, looking up at the clock.

The station broadcasts several different shows, but it's late on a Sunday, so it's pretty empty. *The Breakup Bible* has a producer who monitors the show. Given the subject matter, we have to be careful we don't violate any rules of the airways. My call screener sits right outside the booth in a plexiglass cube. We can see each other, but of course, I can't hear her. It's her job to make sure the calls stay on topic, the callers are over the age of twenty-one—that kind of thing.

It's nearly midnight, but I have time for a couple more callers. "Hey caller, what's your name and how can we break you?"

"Monica," the female caller says.

Generally, we get about as many male callers as female. I'd say the breakdown is sixty/forty female. The business of heartbreak does not suffer from sexism. Having a penis does not make you immune to having your heart broken, but most of tonight's callers have been female.

"I'm so pissed," the caller says.

Pissed or completely devastated tend to be the emotions I hear most often. "Spill," I say.

"My boyfriend just dumped me," she spews. "He said my orgasms are too quiet! How fucked up is that?"

The F word got bleeped, but we all know what she said. "You don't sound too quiet right now," I say.

She laughs a little. "I swear, I don't know what men are looking for. We get judged on our boobs, our butts. We get judged on our clothes, our hair. And now the decibel level at which we orgasm is up for debate!"

I bust out laughing. This woman deserves her own show.

"I mean, what am I supposed to tell my mother when she asks why we broke up?"

"Tell her you aren't the only one," I say.

"You've heard this before?" she asks.

"Well, not exactly," I say. "I'll tell you something that happened to me once. I've never told this story on the air before. In fact, I've never told anyone."

"I'm listening," she says eagerly.

"I had the opposite situation," I say, clearing my throat. "One time, this guy I was seeing was . . ." I pause for a second to think of the least crass way to say it. "Was paying me some lip service down there."

"Got it."

"Let's just say, he was very skilled. My legs spasmed, and I kicked him in the head."

She cracks up. "You're joking?"

"Nope, he had to go to the ER. He had a concussion." I start laughing myself. "He ended it with me a week later. He said it had nothing to do with that, but I have my doubts. I think he was afraid of me."

She's now laughing so hard, she's snorting. "Oh God, I feel so much better."

"Glad I could help, and good luck," I say, ending the call. "Looks like we have time for one more call." I look down at the board, hitting the button to answer. "Hey caller, got to make this a quickie."

"Mae?" a male voice asks.

I freeze. That's me! *My real name.*

And I know that voice. *His* voice! I'd know it anywhere. The rough texture that somehow sounds sweet. The man who broke my heart.

Quickly, I slap the button to disconnect the call, my hand shaking. I do some quick thinking, thanking God my name isn't Sophie or Natalie, but Mae. Mae can be a noun, like the month of May, or a verb like *May I ask you a question?*

I'm banking on my listeners thinking the caller was going to start his question that way.

"Looks like we lost the call," I say. "And I'm afraid we're out of time. That's it for this episode of *The Breakup Bible*, where getting on your knees has a whole other meaning. Until next Sunday."

I hit the button to start whatever commercial or music that's queued to play, then push my seat back from the microphone, my heart pounding. Maybe I was wrong. No, I know I'm not. It was him. It's been five years. I was barely twenty-one last time I saw him or heard his voice. I don't even watch his movies. I turn off the television when trailers for them come on. I painstakingly avoid even looking at magazine covers he graces—not at the grocery check-out line, not when they are online, never. And if I happen to be channel surfing and see him on the red carpet, I quickly change the channel— to maybe something about puppies to clear my mind. I have a complete blackout on Knox Merrick.

My ex. He's not just any ex. He's *THE EX*. The shouty caps ex. The one that still haunts me. The one who still makes my heart sting.

Very few people know that I once dated the sexiest man alive, according to nearly every popular online poll and magazine. A few friends remaining from my high school and college days know. My dad and my grandmother know, some locals in Haven's Point, but I don't volunteer the information. What's the point? It's old news.

The phone screener for my show sticks her head in. Amy has the most beautiful strawberry blonde hair you've ever seen. No bottle or salon in the world could mimic that color. She's one of those women that are just universally pretty—tall, thin, and always eager to help.

She's a good bit older than me, maybe ten years or so, but technically, I'm her superior. It's a weird dynamic. I don't like thinking of myself as anyone's boss. But she's a whiz with anything technical and constantly updates our website and social media outlets, and handles the app, which really helps me out, since those are not my forte. She was even able to bring our computer system back to life after it crashed a few weeks ago. She our own personal Genius Bar.

"I'm so sorry. I don't know how that guy slipped through," Amy says, looking down at some papers in her hand. "California area code. Gave the name Knox. I thought that was so funny. Who has the name Knox and lives in California? Besides Knox Merrick. Like he's going to be calling our show! Although, Knox is from Colorado, right? I think I read that somewhere. Maybe he's a fan. You don't think . . ."

"Don't worry about it, Amy," I say, gathering my things and walking past her. She's relatively new, hasn't been here long. She's going through a divorce, which makes her kind of a perfect fit for the show, not that I'd wish that heartbreak on anyone. I don't want to make her feel worse than she already does, and the damage is done, so it's best to let it go.

I promised myself a long time ago that I wouldn't give Knox Merrick any more of my time, and I'm not about to break that promise.

CHAPTER FOUR

Mae

Why do they call it "beauty sleep" when you wake up looking like death? The dark circles under my eyes could pass for black holes, and my brown hair is flat on one side and crazy on the other. Clearly, I didn't hit the beauty REM cycle of sleep. Having tossed and turned all night, I splash some warm water on my face.

Knox? Knox called my show last night!

Nope, not going to think about it.

Was that really him?

Yes.

Why would he call?

Stop it.

What could he possibly want?

Who cares?

Why now?

Enough! I grab my hairbrush, pulling my hair up into a ponytail. Colorado in the summer can be hot, but so far, this summer has been pretty mild. The ponytail is on every list for simple summer hairstyles, but it's not as easy as it looks. You can do a high pony, a low pony, a side pony, a teased pony, but this morning, I'd settle for getting my dang hair up. The thing about a ponytail is, you have to get it in the right spot on your head, or your head won't rest on your car headrest correctly, or you won't be able to lay down right on your yoga mat. Not that I do yoga.

You know the day is going to be crap when the hair tie on your ponytail isn't right. Two loops around is too loose, and three loops is too tight. The day is doomed.

My eyes close, and I can feel his finger twirling the little wispy curls around my face. My brown hair is thick and straight except for a few pieces around my face and neck that always frizz out in little curls. I hate it. My mom said they are my leftover baby hairs. Apparently, I had curls as a toddler. Well, I'm in my mid-twenties, and I'd think my baby hairs would've grown out by this point. Maybe that's what I'll call my extra curves—baby fat that I still haven't outgrown.

When I was little, my mom used to call my crazy curling tendrils my "koala ears" because they stuck out so far. We'd laugh. I miss her. She passed away a little over a year ago, just got pneumonia and died. She was still young, healthy, and the doctors didn't have any answers for us. She and my dad were stationed in France at the time. My dad's still there. I'll never forget that call. His *voice*.

Seems I'm haunted by a lot of voices these days.

Solution for voices in your head—play music as loud as you can! Turning on The Bee Gees' "You Should Be Dancing", I follow the lyric's advice and start a dance across my little house. Instead of having motion detector lights on my house, I should've installed a disco ball!

I've lived all over the world, but nowhere is better than Haven's Point, Colorado. It's a suburb of Denver, about a forty-five-minute drive to the radio station. It's good that Haven's Point is close to a big city, a major airport, nightlife, but still quiet and peaceful. It's not so small that everyone is up in your business—except, of course, my grandmother and her friends. They pride themselves on knowing everything about everyone, especially me. But this town is home. In fact, her house has always been my true home. And now I have my own little place here.

My cottage sits on a crystal blue lake. I own enough land around my place that you can't see any other houses from mine. My place is small, just two small bedrooms and an office space, but every room has a view. I can soak in my tub or stand in my shower and stare up at the mountains in the distance. To me, it's the best view in the whole world.

The house has a stone and wood exterior with planter boxes on each window. My Gigi, Imogen Sheridan to everyone else, always says you are either a plant person or not. Not quite sure what she meant by that, so I asked her one day. Does that mean one type of person cultivates life and the other doesn't? One kind is patient, the other isn't? She simply laughed and said, "Some people like to play in manure!" She's wise like that.

Gigi doesn't like that I live "out here" all alone. It's literally ten minutes to her house, but she makes that ten minutes sound like a trek across the Serengeti. I learned a long time ago not to argue. We see one another a lot, and always meet up on Monday afternoons. She likes to analyze my Sunday night broadcast.

Only a select few know my actual job at the station, and Gigi is one of them. Most people know I work for the station in Denver, but I'm always vague about what I do there. No one in Haven's Point would suspect I'm on the radio, broadcasting a national program from Denver! My cover story has always been that I work from home, doing research, social marketing. It's not a total lie.

Gigi is my biggest fan. She never misses a show, but I'm really hoping she didn't catch Knox's voice. I've overanalyzed that relationship enough in my lifetime.

~

Cassette

Knox to Mae

Age Fourteen

I got it! I got the lead in the school play! Mrs. Smith said I'm a natural. My dad isn't thrilled and asked me if I'm gay! Can you believe that? Does he think Sean Connery is gay? Or Harrison Ford? I can't wait to get out of this house, this town. Anyway, at least my brother was happy for me. I called Ryder and told him. He's in Nashville trying to become a musician. Wonder if my dad questions his sexuality, not that they are speaking. I wish I could do what Ryder did and just drop out of school, get my GED, and live my dreams. Maybe when I'm seventeen, I'll do that, what he did. Follow in my big brother's footsteps. Not music, but acting. That's what I want to do. It's the best feeling in the world to make the audience happy. To get to be someone else for a little while.

The only bad part is, I have to kiss Josie Miller. Do you remember her at all? Looks like she's gone to the tanning booth one too many times? Anyway, as soon as they posted the parts, she asked me to practice the kissing scene. I really don't want to kiss her. My friends are never going to let me live that down. Plus, I've never really kissed a girl. You know, really kissed. You're the only girl I've ever kissed. Shit, shouldn't have said that. I wonder if you remember that kiss?

～

Cassette

Mae to Knox

Age Fourteen

YAY! I knew you'd get the part. I had no doubts. You'll be great. I wish I could be there to see your debut.

Don't you dare think about dropping out of school to become an actor. You know I like your brother, but Ryder had other reasons for leaving. I know you don't like to talk about it, so I won't, but stop thinking that way. You're too smart. You can go to college and study acting.

As for Josie Miller, I don't think they expect you to ram your tongue down her throat or anything. Just close your eyes, and think of someone else. Pretend it's not her. That's what acting is. Act like it's someone you'd rather be kissing.

Hmm . . .

I do remember our kiss. It was my first. My only so far, too. It was just a peck on the lips the summer we met. The day I left, actually. We were only about five or six. I was leaving with my parents to go back overseas. I came over to your house to say goodbye. I was crying, which was so unlike me. I don't cry when I leave places, usually. I've been leaving people and places my whole life, but for some reason, leaving you that day had me really upset. You told me not to cry, that I was your best friend, and you loved me. I said, "love you, too," and asked you to kiss me goodbye. You did.

CHAPTER FIVE

Mae

Haven's Point is a collection of young families with children looking to escape the expense of big city living and retirees looking to slow things down. The only twenty-somethings living here are either living with their parents or already married. The dating scene is practically non-existent. Most of the guys I've dated recently have been from the Denver area. Not having to worry about running into any ex's is just another benefit to living here.

Riding my Tiffany Blue cruiser bike through town also goes into the plus category. People love to walk and bike here, so there are paths everywhere. It reminds me a lot of many European cities in that way. When the weather is nice, I like to ride my bike or walk places. Driving back and forth to Denver for work makes me want to change my address to Audi Q5. I had to cave and buy a new car after my beloved old VW Beetle died on me. I hated buying a new car, but with all the commuting, I had to get something reliable, even though I hated being all practical. Adulting sucks sometimes.

Strict local ordinances keep the integrity of the town square architecture intact. I've always thought the town name should be changed to Haven's Village instead of Haven's Point. We aren't at the point of any river or mountain, but this place looks like a quaint village you'd find over in Europe with its intricate wood latticework, fences, and mom and pop stores. Of course, bigger businesses have moved in, "progress" invading our little neck of the woods, but the center of town remains the same, seeped in small town perfection.

The town is set up in a grid pattern, with little parks or green spaces at the center of each square. It's common for people to picnic there, walk their dogs, or just read a book. My destination is slightly different. I'm headed to The Tune Up. My best friend, Everly, and her husband, Timothy, own it. Everly's parents owned it forever before passing it on to her. We used to hang out here a lot. It's slightly different now. Back then, it was just a coffee shop. Now, it's a coffee shop and bar! Yep, you can get any type of coffee you want all day long, but if you need a liquid tune up of a stronger variety, alcohol is served from five until midnight. Not much happens in Haven's Point after midnight.

And since I know the owners, I've been known to have my morning coffee spiked once or twice in emergencies. Actually, that's probably more Gigi and her gang than me.

Placing my bike on the rack, I tighten my ponytail. Dang thing, I'm sure my "koala ears" look more like Minnie Mouse ears after the ride. I glance up at the sky, and it looks like a storm could be heading our way. I should've checked the weather before I decided to ride my bike.

Opening the door, I find the coffee shop pretty full, and the smell smacks me right in the face. I love the smell of coffee. I don't actually like the taste of it, but I love the smell. It reminds me of my dad. My mom was always a tea drinker, but he drinks straight up black coffee, no sugar, no cream, and none of that frilly stuff, as he calls it. The smell of coffee filling the house in the morning always meant dad was home. Even though he wasn't on the frontlines most of my childhood, when you grow up with a father in the active military, you live with the fear that something could happen. You know kids who've lost parents, so coffee meant he was home, he was safe. It's funny how something so simple as a smell or a sound can bring back memories like that.

"They're in rare form today," Timothy whispers, nodding in my grandmother's direction and handing me my usual, an entire mug of homemade whipped cream. Yep, I just eat the cream that comes on top of the coffee—a whole mug full. "Everly will be here in a bit."

Timothy gives me a little wink before disappearing behind the counter. He's adorable, a total hipster in his glasses, which he doesn't need because he has perfect vision, and his knit beanie. I think the only time I've ever seen Timothy without a beanie was on their wedding day. Everly told him if she started down the aisle and saw that on his head, she would turn around. So Timothy got beanies for the all the wedding guests instead. When the doors of the church opened, Everly saw a hundred and fifty beanies, but Timothy's dirty blonde hair wasn't covered. She laughed the whole way down the aisle. It was classic.

Sticking my spoon in my mug, I spot Gigi and her crew. They are at their usual table in the back corner. There's about a dozen of them here this morning. Get this—my grandmother started a variety group called the Silver Sirens. They do comedy sketches, dances, all kinds of things. Gigi had several friends that were widowed pretty young. They had a lot of living left to do, so Gigi decided to help them do it. At first, it was just four of them. They did some singing at local churches, nursing homes. Before she knew it, membership grew, and they started getting requests for gigs. They even went to Mardi Gras this year and marched in a parade and performed at a ball. All the money they earn, they give to different charities. Since women usually outlive men, they are mostly a female group, but there are a few older gentlemen, as well.

Two years after she started the group, she lost my grandfather. The Silver Sirens were all there for her. They even sang at his funeral. They took turns staying at her house for weeks after his death. That's what they do for each other. It's an amazing group of women. They are spunky as the day is long. Some have taken to dyeing their hair purple, blue, or pink. Others think fishnets are a wardrobe stable. And we won't even talk about their choice of undergarments.

"Mae!" Gigi calls out to me, as if I didn't know where she was sitting. All the other ladies wave to me. They are my self-appointed grandmothers.

"We were just discussing your grandmother's birthday," one of them says. "Come on, Imogen, tell us how old you are."

They've been trying to figure out Gigi's age for as long as I can remember. Her birthday is coming up, so I guess that has reinvigorated the debate. I doubt her doctor even knows it. Whenever she's asked her age by anyone or on any form, her reply is always the same.

"Vintage," Gigi says. "I'm not one hundred years old, so I can't be classified as an antique, but I'm over twenty, so I'm vintage."

God, I love that crazy lady.

She pulls out the seat next to her, the one she always saves for me. One look from her and I know she recognized my caller from last night. She doesn't say a word, simply giving my hand a little squeeze.

She did the same thing the first time Knox Merrick broke my heart. We were fifteen. I hadn't seen him since we were around eleven. My grandparents always came to visit us at the base, so we hadn't been back to Colorado. Knox was my best friend. Though the extent of our communication was exchanging cassettes, he still knew me better than anyone, and I was thrilled when my parents had agreed to let me spend the summer in Colorado with my grandparents. But my trip lasted only a week.

Knox ignored me, barely even looked at me. I remember sitting in Gigi's window seat. I wasn't crying, but she knew how I felt. She sat with me and held my hand, just like she's doing now.

❧

Cassette

Knox to Mae

Age Fifteen

I came by to see you today, but your grandmother said you'd flown home. I thought you were staying all summer? She gave me the cassette you left for me. I couldn't understand most of it. You were crying so hard. I caught the "I hate you" part. Please don't hate me. I was a jerk. I know. Shit! I was so looking forward to this summer, to seeing you.

I know what heartbreak feels like now. Listening to you cry. I am your constant friend. No matter how many times you move. Please believe that. It kills me you don't believe that now.

I hope you're still listening. The last day of school, I knew you'd be coming, you'd be at my house when I got home. When I walked off the bus and saw you, I immediately knew it was you, even though we haven't seen each other for four years.

God, I've never wanted to turn the tape off like I do right now, never wanted to lie as much as I do right now, but we promised we wouldn't ever do that, and I don't ever want to hear you cry like that again and know I'm the reason.

I saw you, and suddenly I couldn't think of a damn thing to say to you that wouldn't sound stupid. I've been talking to you for years through the mail, but one look at you in person and I was struck dumb.

Mae, you went and got beautiful on me—and suddenly, I didn't want to be your friend. I mean, I wanted to be more than that, and I wasn't sure what to do. Shit! I can't believe I'm telling you this.

Now you're gone, and I've screwed it all up. Our friendship and . . . It's a lot easier to talk to this damn machine than look into your blue eyes. I got lost, Mae. It sounds stupid, but I got lost in you—how beautiful you are, how deep your eyes are, how soft your hair looks. That's the only explanation I have.

I got lost.

~

I forgave him back then. I was young, and I'm glad I did, because we fell in love. I think we'd been falling for years. And I don't believe in regretting love.

Love is not something to regret.

Even if it doesn't last, you should never look back and wish you didn't love someone. Even if they hurt you. Because taking the risk to love is an act of bravery.

Over the next year, our tapes to each other changed. Now people sext, have phone sex. Knox and I invented cassette tape flirting. We were inexperienced teenagers at the time, so it was pretty PG. It wasn't until a few years later that things turned X-rated!

"Don't look up," Gigi says, tightening her hold on my hand.

Of course, that makes me look up, right into the sexy blue eyes of Knox Merrick. He's standing by the entrance door, staring right at me, like he's just as shocked as I am. It must've started raining, because his dark blonde hair is slightly wet. The storm I thought was coming has arrived.

"Breathe," Gigi says, reminding me of what should be instinctive.

Five years. It's been five years since I've laid eyes on him. Five years since he broke my heart – the second time. What is he doing here? First, he calls my show, and now this? After all this time, why would he make contact? And he could've emailed or sent a . . . cassette. My heart warms at the thought. I used to love getting mail from him.

He smiles first.

He's a total scene stealer with that smile. That smile has made him one of the most sought-after actors on the planet.

A woman has two choices in this situation. She can completely freak out, or she can act totally unaffected. My heart, my stomach, my mind are going for the first option, but I'm not going to let them win. Freaking out, yelling at him, or crying means he still gets to me, and I *will not* let him get to me.

Totally unaffected coming right up.

I smile back. He takes a step my way, and I get to my feet. Refusing to reach for my hair to try to straighten it, I can't help but wish

I'd put a little more effort into my tank top and athletic shorts.

His blue eyes leisurely stroll up and down my body, meandering, like he's got all the time in the world. The muscles between my legs clench like my vagina is literally calling out for him. Damn it!

We start toward each other. I've got exactly fifteen seconds before I'm face-to-face with the only man I've ever loved—fifteen seconds to get my shit together.

"Holy crap!" Timothy cries, coming out from behind the counter, walking towards him. "You're that actor. Knox Merrick." He steps right in front of Knox, blocking his path to me. "You were awesome in that action movie with . . ." Timothy keeps talking, and Knox shakes his hand, being friendly, but he keeps looking over at me.

Despite what happened between us, I am proud of him. The little boy I met on his front porch has turned into a world-wide phenomenon. Timothy's verbal distraction gives me a chance to really look at Knox. He's tall, tan, with those blue eyes and dark blonde hair, but he's a little more muscular than he was in his early twenties; he probably has a trainer. Of course, he has to show up here looking good. God forbid he let himself go. Nope, my ex has to be Hollywood's hottest thing since Brad Pitt.

Knox always had an ease about him. The way he'd sit in a chair is a perfect example. Most people just plop their butt down, but not Knox. He tosses his leg over like he's straddling . . . Well, better not think about that.

"Can you excuse me?" Knox says, motioning in my direction.

"Sure," Timothy says, glancing at me, his eyes full of questions. Guess Everly never told him who my ex was. "Can I get you anything? Coffee, muffin?"

"No, thanks," Knox says, looking at me and grinning. "Found what I was looking for."

Obviously, he's still a flirt, but I'm not going to fall for it. A couple other customers come up to him, wanting pictures and autographs. He's friendly to all of them, but mouths *sorry* to me. I shrug like I don't care.

Gigi appears by my side, handing me my purse. It's raining out-side now, but I don't care. I'll ride my cruiser through a tsunami to get out of here. She motions to her comrades not to even think about asking for an autograph, and I'm not sure whether that's so I can get this meet and greet over with, or because she's still mad at Knox for breaking my heart all those years ago.

Knox signs every autograph, poses for every selfie. Thank God the coffee shop isn't that big, or we'd be here for hours. When his fan club has dispersed, Knox and I finally head toward each other. The closer I get to him, the harder my heart pounds, the weaker my legs get.

"You hung up on me," he says with a grin, leaning in to hug me, but I place my hands on his broad shoulders, forcing him to give me one of those awkward side hugs.

"Technical difficulties," I say with a smile.

He grins at me again, his eyes holding mine. "You look . . ." He doesn't finish his sentence, instead he reaches out, taking one of my crazy strands of hair and twirling it around his finger. He used to do the same thing when we kissed, and then later on when we were in bed together.

Taking a sidestep away forces him to stop, my gentle reminder that this isn't who we are anymore. This time, there's no grin on his handsome face.

"Ms. Imogen," he says, as my grandmother appears at my side. "It's good to see you again."

She barely nods at him, giving me her silent support.

"Knox," Everly says, appearing out of nowhere, standing at my other side.

I look over at her. She still has her keys in her hand and her purse on her shoulder. She must've just walked in, seen this train wreck in the making, and took her place by my side. At five-two, she's even shorter than I am. Somehow, her red hair looks even brighter today, like a phoenix ready for battle.

I feel like I'm pretty strong on my own, but with these two women flanking me, there's nothing I can't do, including what comes next.

Adjusting the shoulder strap of my purse, I say, "I have to get going. Goodbye, Knox."

CHAPTER SIX

Knox

I know when I'm outnumbered. Two women and me—that might normally be appealing, but not under these circumstances, especially when one of them is literally old enough to be my grandmother. Imogen motions to the group of women behind her. "Ladies."

Like wolves, they descend upon me, all talking at the same time, asking for pictures, hugs, for me to sign their boobs. Imogen just sits back and smiles. This was her little trick to keep me from following Mae. She's a sly one.

When I flew to Denver this morning, the only thing I knew was that I wanted to see Mae. I haven't been able to stop thinking about her. I had no real plan. I just jumped on a plane, rented a car, and drove to Haven's Point. Mae isn't listed in the white pages. It couldn't be that easy. I could've called the radio station and asked, dropped my name and gotten her home phone number, her address. I could've had anyone on my PR team do this for me, but the fame, the business destroyed me and Mae, and I couldn't use it to see her again.

But I had to see her again. Of course, I wanted more than the thirty seconds she allowed, more than that awkward, uncomfortable hug. She's all I've been able to think about since I heard her on the radio a little over a week ago. I haven't been back to Haven's Point in a long time. My dad died from a heart attack when I was still in college, Mae and I were over, and my brother lives all over the damn place, so there was no reason to come back here.

That's not entirely true. My dad and mom are buried here, and I pay to maintain their graves, but I've never really visited the cemetery. I don't like thinking about them in the ground. I still talk to them, even to this day, but not there. That place represents their deaths, and they are very much still with me. Unfortunately, my parents' headstones have also become sort of a tourist attraction. I've seen more than one fan post a selfie in front of my parents' place of eternal rest. Makes my stomach churn and blood boil every time. The cemetery has been alerted to the situation, but one or two visitors seem to slip by every year.

I figured her grandmother was a real long shot to help me, and judging by the mob of women around me, I was exactly right. My only other option to find Mae was Everly. If anyone would know where Mae was, it would be Everly. They were great friends, and I figured they still were. I knew Mae's show was based in Denver, so I guessed she still lived close. I wasn't sure if Everly would help me, but it was my only card to play. So I just showed up here, hoping to talk to Everly, get whatever information I could. I didn't expect to find Mae at the coffee shop. I wasn't even sure whether Everly's family even still owned it, or if she'd tell me where to find Mae.

I was shocked as shit when I walked in and the first thing I saw was Mae, as shocked as she clearly was to see me. Damn, she looked incredible—her brown hair even longer, her skin glowing, her curvy body still every man's dream, her eyes looking even bluer than I remembered. I'm not sure what came to attention first: my cock or my heart. It was a close race.

The band of women Imogen sicced on me has finally started to thin out. I guess Imogen figures Mae has enough of a head start that I can't follow her, so it's safe to disband her army.

"You never told me you know Knox Merrick," I overhear the guy in the beanie say to Everly. I'm assuming he's Everly's husband based on their matching wedding bands and the little girl between them, holding one of each of their hands.

She's a pretty little girl, blonde, with big beautiful eyes, and I've done enough charity work now to be fairly certain that she has Down

Syndrome.

"I don't *know* him," Everly says, and everyone in the room except the little girl realizes they're taking about *knowing* me in the biblical sense. "Now, Mae *knows* him."

"Really?" the beanie guy says. "Mae and Knox Merrick?"

I walk over to the counter and extend my hand. "Knox." He slowly reaches out to shake it. "You can drop the Merrick part. Just Knox."

It's funny when you become "famous," people all of a sudden start using your full name. That's one of the signs you've reached a certain status. I hate it, but oddly enough, I usually introduce myself that way. I'm not so conceited as to automatically assume that everyone knows who I am.

"And your brother is that country singer?"

"Ryder Merrick," I say.

"Timothy," he introduces himself. "And I guess you know my wife, Everly."

I glance at her. "Know, but not *know*."

"What are you doing here, Knox?" she says, full of attitude and clearly done with the small talk.

"Daddy, who's that?" the little girl interrupts.

He picks her up. "Gracie, this is Knox."

"He sounds like bear in the movie . . ."

"That's right. He played the bear," Timothy says, turning to me. "She's really good with voices."

Timothy boosts her up on his hip so we're all on the same level. Gracie asks me. "Were you really him?"

"Yep."

"The bear is my favorite."

"Thank you," I say. "It's nice to meet you, Gracie. How old are you?"

"You *do* sound like him," she giggles.

"She's five," Timothy answers.

"Knox, what do you want?" Everly asks again, clearing having no patience with me.

"Mommy," Gracie says. "You sound mad."

Everly releases a deep breath. "Not at you, honey."

"She's mad at you," Gracie whispers to me.

"I know," I say.

"Why?" she whispers back.

Everly motions for Timothy to remove Gracie from this conversation. "Can you help Daddy refill customers' cups?"

She smiles broadly. "Remember what they teach us at school," Gracie tells her mom, walking away with her dad. "It's always better to be kind."

"Hope you follow her advice," I say, as Everly draws another deep breath, watching them walk away. "She's five, but last time I saw you was about five years ago, and . . ."

"She's adopted," Everly says. "Timothy and I got married a few years ago, and he had a special needs sister who passed away young. So we always wanted to give a child a home who might not be adopted otherwise. Gracie was two when she came to us."

"And the coffee shop is yours now?" I ask.

"Yes," she says. "We are a bar, too. Stay open later."

"That's . . ."

"What do you want?" she asks again. "Because Mae has a really good life. She's successful and happy, and I don't want to see that get messed up."

"I don't, either," I say, wondering if Mae's happily attached or happily single.

"Then leave her alone," she says. "You broke her heart once already."

She broke mine, too, but I don't dare admit that to Everly. When you live your life in the spotlight, you learn to keep most of your personal feelings hidden. I didn't realize when I became an actor, I'd be acting in my personal life, too.

You get your heart broken, you still smile for the cameras. You don't feel well, you still show up for work. You have a death in the family, you issue a statement asking for privacy and don't leave your house until you can face the public eye.

You get threatening letters, stalkers, crazy messages—you don't complain, at least not publicly. No one has any sympathy when you're living in the limelight, making millions of dollars.

There are only a few people that really know me. My brother, Ryder, and Mae. Mae knows me the best. The whole world knows my name. They all *think* they know who I am. That's why it's called acting.

"Look at you," she says, waving her hands in front of me. "You got everything you ever wanted—money, fame. You have it all."

"I didn't get everything," I say softly, my eyes glancing at the door that Mae disappeared through.

"You only have yourself to blame for that," she says.

"So you won't help me?" I say. "Give me Mae's address, phone number?"

She just rolls her eyes. I stopped trying to figure women out years ago. Why they cry during movies? Or go to the bathroom in pairs? But I get this. I understand that Everly is Mae's friend, and she can't betray that. I knew this was a long shot, but Haven's Point isn't that big. I can find her.

Reaching for my keys in my pocket, I head toward the door. "Bye, bear," Gracie calls out, now coloring at a small table.

I give her a little wave, catching a glimpse of Imogen and Everly talking at the far end of the counter. I don't have to guess who they're talking about. I'm used to people talking about me when I'm around. Used to the whispers and snickers when I enter a room, but usually those people are happy to see me. That's not the case with these two.

"Come by anytime," Timothy tells me. "Gracie's going to make a sign that reads 'Autograph Free Zone,' so you won't be bothered."

Gracie gives me a little thumbs up. God, she's adorable.

"Appreciate it," I say.

He leans a little closer to me and whispers, "Mae's not seeing anyone."

"Really appreciate that," I say with a grin, suddenly realizing I was looking in the wrong place for help. Of course, women stick together, but so do guys. "Do you happen to know where I could find Mae?"

He glances back at his wife. He'd be breaking about a hundred husband rules if he told me, and he doesn't seem like a stupid man. "Can't tell you that," he says with one more glance. "But I *can* tell you that you should definitely go check out the lake. It's pretty out there this time of year."

There are a shit ton of lakes in Colorado, but I know the one he's talking about. I'll never forget it. Mae and I spent a lot of time out there as kids. It has to be the one.

～

I've listened to enough of Mae's radio shows to know she was faking her response to me at The Tune Up. She's given the same advice over and over again to callers. *Don't let him see you sweat.* That smile she gave me when I walked in—that was faker than half the tits in Hollywood. She's never faked anything with me before, and I'm not about to let her start now.

A slow rain falls as I head out toward the lake. My rental car is a simple four door sedan, not luxury, not a sports car. It's just a normal, everyday car. I have a few cars back home in California. Every single one of them is just like this one. Simple. I don't want a car to get me noticed. I want a car to get me from point A to point B, help me move something, and not cause a riot when I drive down the street. A red Ferrari cannot go undetected, but a black Toyota blends right in. And I prefer the latter.

The one exception to my practical car rule is a vintage blue convertible. My dad, my brother, and I rebuilt it together one summer. The last summer that Ryder lived at home. I hardly ever drive it. When dad died, I wanted my brother to have the car. Their relationship wasn't always great, but this car represented the good times they had before it all went to shit. Still, Ryder wouldn't take it. So I've kept it. I kept it for him. You'd think losing our dad suddenly and our mom when we were young would have made us both realize that you have to hold on to the people in your life, but I still screwed things up with Mae, and Ryder . . . well, his demons run deep.

My houses are another story. They're not necessarily huge. I don't buy them to be flashy. I buy because they are very secluded—private. I have a beach house in Malibu, a penthouse in New York, and I still own the property in Haven's Point where I grew up, although it's just an empty lot now. My brother, Ryder, doesn't even own a house, but that's a whole other story.

There are very few houses by the lake. Supposedly, there's some city ordinance about how many houses can be placed there to protect the wildlife or something, or that's the story they always told us as kids.

Wildflower Lake was named for all the flowers that bloom there. You'd think they could come up with something more original, but they simply named it Wildflower Lake. Local legend says there was some debate about whether to name it Lake Wildflower or Wildflower Lake, but that's as interesting as it gets.

As teenagers, we used to come out here and have bonfires. Mae and I spent many nights out under the stars talking about what we wanted out of life, dreaming. We spent just as much time kissing and making out, but I never got past first base out here. All of that came later, in college.

Because there's just a few houses, it shouldn't take me too long to figure out which one is Mae's. Most of the houses here are big log cabins. I figure anything with a swing set or an ATV parked out front probably doesn't belong to Mae.

I round the curve of the lake, and I see a little cottage in the distance. I remember the house that used to be there. It was pretty rundown. I can't believe this is the same one. It looks totally different now. Slowing down, a peace settles over me. This is where Mae lives.

It must be. It just feels like her—warm.

As I get a little closer, I slow the car to a crawl, seeing Mae sitting in an Adirondack chair next to the edge of the water, the chair's wood worn by the sun. She doesn't have an umbrella. She's not wearing a raincoat. She's just sitting there, staring, the soft rain falling on her.

Her brown hair looks even darker. She's got her knees pulled up, holding them in a little hug. I can't see her face, but I know she's crying. She's using the rain as a cover, but she can't fool me.

Even from a distance, I know.

When things end with someone you love, you go through stages of sadness and anger. When things went south with Mae, it hurt. It pissed me off. At the same time, my career was just taking off. Everyone around me said it's better to be single, relationships can't handle the stress of a new career in Hollywood. Other actors told me there were too many hot women, and I should explore that—I certainly took that advice.

But in the quiet moments, I always thought about Mae. I thought about her a lot, more than I should've, but I believed her when she told me she never wanted to see me again. Mae wasn't an option. God knows I explored other "options." Then when I heard her voice coming through the radio, everything came rushing back—all those years listening to her on cassette, all the feelings. I had to see her again.

Now I'm not sure whether I can leave again.

Her smile at the coffee shop was fake, I knew that much, but this is real. Me being back here is making her cry. I thought she might be angry, and maybe she is. I thought she might yell at me, throw her drink at me, knee me in the balls. None of that would've surprised me, but I didn't expect tears. Mae didn't cry often. I heard her cry over me once before, and I promised myself I wouldn't let that happen again. I broke that promise. I knew I did, but knowing it and *watching* it are vastly different.

I can leave her alone, or I can do something about it.

I've always been more of a doer.

CHAPTER SEVEN

Cassette

Mae to Knox

Age Sixteen

I'm coming to Haven's Point. Don't ask me how, after last summer's debacle, but I've convinced my parents to let me spend the summer with Gigi. They wanted me to spend the summer doing college tours before senior year starts, but I convinced them otherwise. If all goes well, I have plans to convince them to let me do my senior year in Haven's Point with you! Well, I didn't tell them you're the reason, but I'm sure they suspect. I've been dropping hints about how it would be nice to experience American high school traditions like prom, but one battle at a time. And I won the first one. Summer with you.

And this time when you see me, you better not act like an asshole. You hear me, Knox? This is your second chance. Don't blow it.

Mae

Goosebumps cover my skin as the rain slowly falls from the gray sky. I was soaked from riding my bike home in the rain, so I figured it didn't matter if I sat outside in it now. I couldn't be inside, my thoughts too big, too all over the place. They need space to roam.

Unfortunately, my thoughts are all leading to one place, to one man.

Raindrops patter across the lake, creating a rhythm. Looking up at the gray sky, the mountains in the distance, it seems like Mother Earth herself is crying, a curtain of rain flowing down. When the rain stops, the wildflowers will look brighter, but right now they droop, the heaviness of the storm weighing them down.

Knox Merrick just casually strolled back into my life, like it was nothing. Why would he *do* that? Show up after all this time? Why does my heart care so damn much?

This is probably the wrong place to be right now. Knox and I have a lot of memories at this lake. Truthfully, we have a lot of memories all over Haven's Point, but they usually don't attack me like they are right now. I'm usually better at stuffing things, feelings, thoughts, that aren't convenient for me at that moment. I get that from my dad. Military man—he can't exactly freak out while holding a loaded weapon. The freak out happens later. I think that's why so many of our finest suffer from PTSD. A person can only stuff everything down for so long, before it eventually has to come out.

Mine is choosing this moment to rear its ugly head.

It wasn't far from here that Knox and I had our second kiss. Our first kiss took place when we were six, and it took us ten years to have our second. And for me, the second kiss is the one that counts. First kisses get all the attention in movies, books, talks with girl-friends. No one ever talks about their second kiss, but I think the second kiss is the litmus test. The first one, you're nervous, not quite sure of the other person, but the second kiss, you can really sink into it.

I remember that night so well. It was my first night back for the summer. The previous summer had been such a bust, I was nervous to see him. Everly is the granddaughter of one of Gigi's friends, so Gigi thought it would be a good idea if we got to know each other. I think she was trying to get me to focus my attention on someone other than a boy, namely Knox. So my first night back, Gigi insisted I go to some bonfire with Everly. That was the last thing I wanted to do, but I couldn't make a fuss, so I left a note for Knox telling him what happened and promising I'd see him after.

I'll never forget sitting around the fire. There was a crispness to the air even for late May, and the stars blanketed the sky. It seemed like every local kid was there, and I felt like everyone was sizing me up—the boys trying to decide if I was make-out material, the girls trying to decide if I was friend material.

I felt his arm land lazily around my shoulder as he sat down beside me. Effortless, but there was meaning behind it. He was telling the world that I was his without saying a word. My heart fluttered, and the heat from the fire suddenly seemed hotter. I looked up at Knox, and he turned his head. His blue eyes searched mine, and I realized he wasn't concerned with the world, but asking me if it was okay. I reached up and intertwined our fingers, giving him my answer.

He kissed me that night. We walked home together, and I remember wondering if he was going to kiss me when we got to my front door, but instead, he stopped a good twenty feet from my house, pulled me close and kissed me, whispering he couldn't wait a second longer.

"You're going to catch a cold," Knox says from behind me, stirring me from my teenage memories.

Normally, when someone surprises you, you jump, but I think I'm too emotionally spent to be surprised he found me—again!

"Go away," I say, resting my head on my knees, abandoning my plan to act unfazed by him, which clearly hadn't worked. "Don't you have some movie to star in? Some red carpet to walk?"

He kneels down beside me, not caring that it's raining. "I'm in-between projects right now. I have a premiere next month, but until then . . ."

I get to my feet. "What are you doing here?"

"I heard you on the radio," he says, like that's some sort of explanation.

"And what? You thought you'd just pop in to see me? Call my

show? Put my identity at risk? You even used your own name," I say, heading back toward my house.

"I didn't mean to do that," he says, following me. "What name should I have used?"

"I don't know. It doesn't matter. Don't celebrities use aliases all the time, like Scooby Doo?"

"You wanted me to say I was Scooby Doo?"

"You're missing the point!" I say, throwing my hands up.

His eyes soften. "I heard your voice and wanted to get in touch."

I turn around to face him, and his steps falter slightly. He's over six feet, and I'm five-five on a good day, so I cock my chin up to be extra intimating. "Did you think about me at all when you made that decision? Or was it just about what *you* wanted?" I don't give him time to respond. "Of course you didn't think about me, what I wanted, whether I wanted to see you. Nope! As usual, it's all about Knox Merrick," I say, continuing to walk through the grass to the safety of my back porch.

His hand lands on my waist. No, it doesn't land there, he grabs me, not hard or rough, but with just enough tension to let me know he's not going anywhere. "Don't call me that."

I push his hands off me. "Your name?"

"My full name. It makes me sound like I'm not a real person."

"How did you imagine this would go?" I ask. "Honestly? What did you think my response would be to seeing you again after all this time?"

"I guess, I hoped you'd be as happy to see me as I am to see you."

That sounds like one of those perfect movie lines that are designed to make a woman's heart melt. Let's just say it's not achieving the desired goal.

He reaches for my hand, touching my fingers just briefly. My goosebumps triple in size with that one small gesture. A slideshow of memories flash through my mind, like one of those classic red View-Masters you have as a kid. Each click of the button shows you a new image.

Snap! His hand brushing my hair back.

Snap! His fingers sliding down my thigh.

Snap! His hands holding my hips.

"You're cold," he says. "Let's go inside."

Shaking my head, I say, "You're not coming inside."

He raises an eyebrow at me, and I know exactly what his dirty mind is thinking. He's remembering the time we were having sex from behind, and he pulled out and released on my butt because he didn't have a condom. I was on the pill, but we usually doubled up on protection.

"I seem to recall you not liking it when I come . . ."

Yep, that's it. I do my best not to smile, but a little one sneaks out. "Be quiet."

"That's better," he says.

"You're still not coming in."

His dirty mind is working overtime today, his grin growing. "Not yet."

"Goodbye, Knox," I say, opening the door, slamming it for good measure, and disappearing inside.

～

Gently, I pull back the curtain on my front porch window to make sure he's gone. What the hell? The rain has stopped, and I see him leaning against his car, his cell phone to his ear. He's the complete picture of a movie star, sexy and cute, with a devilish little grin.

Does he plan on staying here all night? Should I just talk to him and get it over with? Maybe he just wants to talk about old times.

A stroll down memory lane can be dangerous.

If you only go down the paths with good memories, it's too easy to get lost there, to want to take a trip back there. I can't let myself fall into that trap. I have to remember the bad roads. That's the problem with Knox and me. There really weren't any bad roads until the major detour that derailed us. Mostly, things were great between us. I would never tell him this, but I often wonder if I overreacted, if that's what led to our breakup. If I'd been a little older, a little more mature, but I guess the same is true for him, too. Truthfully, we both could've handled things better, but that was a long time ago.

Then why is he hanging out in my front yard?

And why are my panties wet, even though I changed clothes after sitting in the rain hours ago?

❧

It was another night where I barely slept. Sleepless nights with Knox used to be more fun than this. Last night, when I wasn't tossing and turning, I was checking to see if he was gone or still waiting for me outside. I'm not sure when he finally gave up and left, but I wouldn't put it past him to show up again.

This morning, I opened my front door with more caution than I've ever exercised in my whole life. I've had snakes in my driveway, lizards on the railings. I even saw a bear once, but none of that scared me more than the thought that I'd find Knox waiting on my front porch.

Lucky for me, the coast is clear. I still don't know why he's back in Haven's Point, or what he could possibly want. Everly and Gigi have been calling and texting me nonstop. I answered the first few times, but ultimately turned off my phone. If I know Gigi, she's about ready to call in the National Guard, so I'm headed to her house this morning to assure her that my chastity belt is locked up tight.

Reaching for the handle on my car door, I hear a horn. The car is inconspicuous enough, but the driver is not. Knox pulls in right behind me, blocking my car. He hops out, holding a large Styrofoam cup. His hair is slightly messy, and the stubble on his face makes my heart pound a little harder. I love a man with stubble. "Brought you your favorite."

"I don't drink coffee," I say with sass. He doesn't even remember the simplest things about me.

"I know," he says. "It's just the whipped cream."

Okay, so he remembers that. That's a pretty memorable detail about a person. Reaching for the cup, I say, "I was just leaving."

"I'll give you a lift."

"You don't know where I'm going. I could be going all the way into Denver or . . ."

He grins. "Okay, where are you going?"

Thinking fast, I say, "Boyfriend."

His eyes slowly scan up and down my body. My jean skirt and vintage Van Halen t-shirt could be casual date attire.

"It's a little early for a date," he says.

"Mornings are my favorite," I say taunting him, wondering if he remembers that little detail about me—morning sex is my favorite.

His jaw tenses. "I know you don't have a boyfriend."

"How do you know that?"

"Timothy told me yesterday," he says, opening his passenger door for me.

"Timothy doesn't know everything about me," I say, taking a seat. He simply smiles at me, slamming the door shut, and for the first time, I realize I've gotten in the car with him. I literally argued my way into his car. Crap!

He hops in, starting the car. "Where to?" he asks. "Since we know it's not a boyfriend's place."

Damn him! Of all the times to be single! I've actually been single for awhile. I don't see the point in dating someone if I don't see the possibility of a future. It took me a long time to date after Knox, and for a while, I just dated guys for fun, to have a good time. I didn't want anything serious. Eventually things changed, and there were a few guys I dated for a while, but there was always something missing. On paper, we'd look like a good match. One guy even told me he loved me, but I couldn't say it back. Things ended pretty quickly after that.

"Fine, I'm going to Gigi's house," I say, as he pulls away. "And why do you care whether I have a boyfriend or not?"

"Mae, why do you think I'm here?"

"To give me a ride to Gigi's house?" I tease. "Honestly, I have no idea."

He glances over at me. "It's not obvious?"

"Not to me."

"I miss you," he says.

My heart stings at his honesty. "Five years will do that to a person, I guess."

"Mae," he says, a bite to his voice, then he takes a deep breath.

We drive in silence for a few minutes. We never used to lack for conversation, and in the quiet moments, it was never like this—stressed and uncomfortable.

"Can we just catch up?" he asks. "How are your parents? Where are they stationed . . ."

"Dad's in France," I say, looking out to the water. "Mom died last year."

"Oh, Mae. I'm sorry. I didn't know."

"No reason you would," I say with attitude.

"Mae, you helped me through losing both my parents. I . . ."

This is the last thing I want to talk about, so I quickly change the topic.

"Where'd you stay last night?" I ask, unsure why I care.

"Crashed at a hotel," he says. "Tipped the manager to not let anyone know I was there."

"It worked?"

"Yeah, I went in through a back entrance, so none of the other staff or guests saw me. Pretty simple." We turn onto my grandmother's street, and he says, "I have to fly back to L.A. today. Something went wrong with a poster I shot, and they have to redo it before the movie comes out, but . . ."

"Okay," I say, cutting him off.

"I'd like to call you," he says.

"That's not a good idea."

"You going to make me go back to sending you cassette tapes in the mail?" he asks with a smirk.

He stops the car in front of Gigi's house. Her house is *home*. She always has a wreath on her door. Her garden is always impeccable. The wraparound porch is white with beautiful wooden moldings that accent the pink color of the two-story Victorian house. The winters can be harsh in Colorado, but Gigi always keeps her house freshly painted, her landscape freshly maintained. It's beautiful. My bedroom was on the second floor, overlooking the side yard of the house. I used to stick my head out and wave to Knox, whose bedroom window was in the front of his house.

I look out the windshield, at the empty lot across the street where his house used to be. "I was here, you know," I say. "The day it burned down."

Lightning struck a pole, and the current just followed the path into the house. The whole thing went up in flames. Luckily, it was empty at the time.

"It was just a house," he says.

"You grew up there."

"I grew up with you," he says, his hand landing on top of mine.

I look down at him touching me. God, it feels the same, like his skin belongs on mine. "Knox . . ."

"You want to know why I'm here?" he asks, and I nod. "All I know is, I've run into ex-girlfriends before, talked to them, and I never felt a damn thing—nothing. But when I heard you on the radio, it wasn't like that." His blue eyes hold mine. He doesn't move closer, just stares at me like I'm a puzzle to figure out. "There's something, even after all this time. There's something."

CHAPTER EIGHT

Knox

It's almost sixteen hours by car from Los Angeles to Haven's Point. It's about two and a half hours by plane from L.A. to Denver, then the forty-five-minute drive to Haven's Point. But no matter which way you slice it, I'm over one thousand miles away from Mae.

And the way this week is going, I'm not sure when I'll be able to make a dent in that distance. The reshoot for the poster took two days. Then there was some mix up with my schedule, so I ended up having to do some interviews for print magazines. It's been nonstop for days and days. Now my brother is in town for a concert and is crashing at my house in Malibu for the night. We don't see each other much, so I couldn't bail and go back to Haven's Point.

I didn't spend more than twenty minutes in Mae's presence the entire time I was back in Colorado, but those twenty minutes told me everything I need to know. I want her in my life.

See, that's the whole problem with falling for your best friend. When the love ends, so does the friendship.

But there's something still between us. I know for sure we could be friends again. I know for sure I'd like more than that, but convincing Mae of that isn't going to be easy. She wouldn't even give me her phone number. Before I left, I wrote mine down on a sheet of paper and slipped it under her door. She hasn't used it.

I haven't had to work for a woman's attention in years. Before the fame, there was only Mae. I wouldn't have considered myself a player, far from it. I was a one-woman guy all the way. Mae and I were easy, most of the time. Maybe it's because we were young. We were together from the summer before our senior year in high school until we were both about twenty-one. Of course, we'd been friends since we were six.

The past five years without her have been the loneliest of my life. I'm surrounded by people most of the time. Movie sets are busy places, and paparazzi follow me. I can have any woman I want. It would seem I'm never really alone, but I am.

And I hate the fact that Mae went through losing her mother without me by her side. I should have been there for her, like she was there for me.

"Why were you back in Haven's Point?" Ryder asks, plopping down on my sofa.

It's late, or should I say early? I'm tired from his concert. I stayed backstage in his dressing room and watched on the monitor then waited for him in the car. He's a country music star. I'm an actor. We can't be seen together in public without causing total chaos. People think of us as the American Hemsworth brothers—only slightly less wholesome.

This is probably my favorite house of the ones I own. It sits on a little cliff overlooking the Pacific Ocean. Hedges on both sides provide privacy, and the front is guarded by a gate. You have to go down stairs to get to the beach, but being elevated maximizes the view. The entire back part of the house is lined with floor to ceiling windows. I live alone, so the six bedrooms and seven bathrooms are a bit excessive, but I didn't buy it for the space. I bought it for the view, the privacy, and its proximity to L.A. without having to actually live in L.A.

"How'd you know I was in Haven's Point?" I ask.

I managed to sneak in and out of Colorado without causing too much of a ruckus. I flew on a private plane, so there wasn't much fuss at the airport. I don't think it made any of the tabloid sites, so how my big brother knew is beyond me.

"Maggie," he says simply.

Maggie is his . . . Well, I'm not sure what she is. Technically, I guess you'd call her his publicist, but she's more than that to him. She used to teach music at the high school in Haven's Point. She's the one who got Ryder into guitar and singing.

"She got an email from a friend who still lives there. Said it was all over town that you were there," he says, looking at me like only a big brother can. With both our parents gone, we're all each other has in terms of family, and Ryder is a loner. "So either you were there dealing with something about the land, or you were there dealing with something about a woman?"

"Speaking of women," I say, dodging, "thanks for taking the night off. Really didn't feel like stumbling upon an orgy in my living room."

He chuckles. "I don't do orgies."

"Multiple women at the same time," I say, raising an eyebrow.

I'm not a Boy Scout, so I'm not passing judgment, but a younger brother has to rag his big brother. It's in the rules.

He just shrugs. That's Ryder. Nothing fazes him. I guess when you've had the past he has, you figure you've lived through the worst. "So work or woman?" he asks again.

"Woman," I admit, placing my feet up on my coffee table to stretch out.

He shakes his head. It's not that he disapproves of Mae, or even that he doesn't like her. He disapproves of love in general. "Mae?"

"Don't start, Ryder."

"Didn't say a word," he says, then tosses a pillow, hitting me right in the face. God, are we eight years old again? "How'd she look?" he asks. A simple grin from me lets him know. "That good, huh? Better than that model you dated last year?"

Affectionately, I flip him the bird. "Better!"

He shakes his head. "What's she up to these days? Can't believe she still lives in Haven's Point. What's the town like?"

"Bigger than when we lived there," I say. "Saw where the house used to be."

"Did you go to the cemetery?" he asks.

"No."

Ryder looks up at the ceiling, soaring above us. Being older, he has more memories of Mom than I do. He and our dad had a very strained relationship. Ryder and Haven's Point, well, that relationship is even more complicated. Some bad shit went down there for Ryder. We don't ever discuss it.

"So Mae?" he asks. "How is she besides hotter than a model?"

I shoot him a warning glance. We both live our lives in the lime-light, but we don't ever go for the same women. That's sick as fuck to even think about. We are brothers, so we're naturally competi-tive—not for money or anything like that. More like, who has the better *Madden* game. Who has the better dunk shot, that sort of thing. But we never go after the same woman, ever. Still, I don't like him referring to Mae as hot or sexy, or any of that.

"I didn't spend that much time with her," I say, wondering if I should tell him what she does for a living.

"Douche," he calls me. For brothers: douchebag, asshole, moron, jackass, and twat are all terms of endearment.

"She wasn't exactly thrilled to see me, okay?"

He sits up slightly. "You plan on trying to see her again, or was that a one-time visit?" One look at my face, and he knows what a dumb question that was. "Want some advice from your big brother?"

"On women?" I ask. "No, thanks. I know how you feel about love and relationships."

"You know how I feel about love and relationships for *me*," he says. "You're not me."

"Okay," I say, "but this advice best be better than the sex advice you gave me."

He busts out laughing. He doesn't laugh often. It's good to see my brother like this. "Hey, that was solid advice."

"Virgin ass is the best ass was not solid advice!" I laugh at him. "And the bulk size box of condoms you sent to my dorm room? Mae didn't appreciate that."

"Mae loves me," he says with confidence.

He's right. She does.

He gets to his feet. "I'm going to bed. Thanks for letting me crash here."

"Wait," I say, stopping him. "What's the big advice about Mae?"

"Don't fuck it up."

~

The clock beside my bed reads four in the morning. Between being amped up after my brother's concert, and his "advice," I haven't slept at all. I wish I could say I was up thinking about something profound, but I'm not. Normally when people can't sleep, they are worried about something. Not me. The cause of my insomnia—being horny as hell.

This usually isn't a problem. Women have been plentiful in my life. I could send one text and have a woman here within a few minutes, but the only woman I want now isn't even in the state.

Thinking about Ryder sending me those condoms brings back memories of my first time with Mae. We were a couple for almost two years before I got in her pants. Two fucking years, and we'd known each other forever. It didn't happen until the end of our freshman year in college. Of course, I started *trying* almost as soon as she got to Haven's Point the summer before our senior year of high school. Looking back, it was probably too soon. Not by my standards today, but for seventeen-year-olds. Mae was the smart one. I was thinking with another organ.

It was stupid to think I'd get lucky after only a month of dating, but, again, I was seventeen. My dad was working late, and we were on my bed, making out. I started to inch my hand up her thigh, and she stopped me. "I know you're a virgin, but . . ." I said.

She sat up so fast, I thought she'd hurt herself.

"Why do you say it like that?" she asked.

"Like what?"

"Like it's an affliction, and you're the cure?"

That was our first fight, one of the only ones we ever had. She stormed out of my room, and I found a cassette in my mailbox the next day. There were only a few times that we sent cassettes after she returned to Haven's Point, and this was one of them.

∽

Cassette

Mae to Knox

Age Seventeen

Knox, I can't have this conversation looking you in the eye. That's one reason why I know I'm not ready to take the next step. If I can't even talk to you in person about it, then we shouldn't be doing it.

I didn't like what I saw in your eyes yesterday. Suddenly, it looked like I was a challenge. I don't want taking my virginity to become some sort of mission. I'm more than my hymen!

Seriously, do boys keep track of how many girls they deflower? Do they get bonus notches on their headboards or something?

I'm only seventeen, it's not like I'm the oldest living virgin or anything. Take Lisa Kudrow, she reportedly waited until she was married to have sex, and she was in her thirties. If Phoebe can wait, why can't I?

It's like I'm an endangered species. One of the last virgins left on the planet.

I'm not a mythical creature. And I don't appreciate guys looking at me like they're ready to snatch my v-card.

And just because I haven't slept with anyone doesn't make me a religious zealot, either.

I know I got off on a tangent there. Sorry about that. I just don't want this to be an issue between us. I'm not ready. I'm really hoping you can understand.

Cassette

Knox to Mae

Age Seventeen

Mae,

I don't have a lot to say. I know you know I'm a virgin, too. But here's the thing. For me, being a virgin is an affliction, and you are the cure.

But you're the cure I'm willing to wait for.

CHAPTER NINE

Mae

"Mommy, look at the crown of wildflowers Auntie Mae made for me," Gracie yells as Everly gets out of her car in front of my house. Gracie is a love, and since it's summer, school is out, and Gracie is in between summer camps, I sometimes watch her for Timothy and Everly.

Gracie hangs out at the coffee shop a lot. She loves it there. She's such a friendly little girl, all the customers love her. Around four thirty or so every day, right before The Tune Up becomes more bar than a java shop, they close down for about thirty minutes, and Gracie leaves. And sometimes that means I watch her. I love the time we spend together. I don't know the circumstances of why Gracie was put up for adoption. I don't know if it had anything to do with her Down's Syndrome, but I sure as heck hope not. Either way, we are all blessed to have her in our lives.

I'm able to watch her a good bit because my job is so flexible. It's really only one day a week that I work. Of course, there's preparation for the show, but that can be done on my own timeframe. I also do a few radio commercials here and there, which boosts the income. I make enough to afford my simple life by the lake. I'm truly blessed.

It wasn't always that way. Before the show was syndicated, when I was just a little, local Sunday evening show, it barely paid enough to cover the gas it took to drive back and forth to Denver. Back then, I worked several jobs. I even worked at the coffee shop for Everly and Timothy, but I was terrible. Since I don't like coffee, I couldn't tell the difference between an espresso and a cappuccino, but they kept me on just the same.

When I finished college, I had degrees in both psychology and communications. Back then, I could've found an eight to five job, something steady, but I always believed in my show, in what I was doing at the station. I had faith that one day the radio gig would turn into something, and it has.

"That's pretty," Everly says to Gracie. "Can you make me a flow-er crown?"

Beaming, Gracie sits down in the grass and gets to work. Everly gives me a look, reaching in her bag and pulling out a brown paper bag, which can only be hiding one thing—wine! You know you have a good friend when she smuggles you alcohol.

We meet at the back steps of my porch, taking a seat where we can still keep an eye on Gracie. The sun is shining, my best friend is here. Life is good.

"What else you have in that purse of yours?" I ask, teasing her.

She opens it up wide. "I've got chocolate and condoms, which do you need?"

"Dang," I say. "I really was hoping for a chocolate condom."

She giggles a little, popping open the bottle of wine. "Only one sip for me, I'm driving." She doesn't even bother with glasses, simply taking a sip from the bottle. We're classy chicks like that. Then she passes it to me. "I haven't slept with Timothy in four days," she says quietly so Gracie doesn't hear. "Punishment for telling Knox where you live."

"Don't do that," I say. "That's just punishing yourself, too."

She laughs again. "I'm lying. I totally fucked him before coming over here."

I laugh so hard wine comes out of my nose. Everly is the best. We just get each other. In all the years we've been friends, we've never had a big fight. It's hard to be mad at someone who carries alcohol and condoms in her purse. If the zombie apocalypse ever comes, Everly is screwed without any suitable supplies, but if a spontaneous swingers' party erupts, she's ready.

"It's fine. Something tells me Knox would've found a way to find me, anyway."

"He did look good," she says, nudging me a little.

"I know," I say, rolling my eyes. "Dangerously so."

"So?"

"He left me his number," I say. "I haven't called."

"Did you keep it?" she asks.

"Yeah. Why?"

She takes the bottle from me, putting it aside. This must be serious. "You didn't burn it or rip it in a million pieces. You kept it."

"I didn't use it," I say.

"But you kept the option open *to* use it."

"No. I'm not calling him."

"Let me see your phone," she says.

"Why?"

"I want to see if you saved his number in your contacts." She can tell by my face that I did. "Oh my God, you saved it in your phone!"

"You act like I accepted a marriage proposal. I saved his number, so what?"

"You didn't keep it on a piece of paper that could get lost. You kept it on your phone, where it will be safe."

"None of this means anything."

"Oh, I think it means something," she says.

There's that word again, the same one Knox used. What is this elusive *something* everyone seems to be referring to these days? I look out on the water, a slow ripple on the surface. If the wind blew, the ripple would grow bigger. Right now, it's just a little small—something.

"For someone who gives relationship advice, you sure are clueless," Everly says.

Of course, she's right, but I still push back. "I give *breakup* advice," I say.

"Okay, what if a caller phoned in and said that their ex came back to town after five years to see them. What would you tell your caller?"

"Depends on the situation."

"Same as you and Knox. Both single. Both successful. Everything the same."

"I'd say that if they were calling me for advice, it would mean they were still attached to this person."

"See!" Everly cries out.

"See what?" I ask. "I didn't ask you for advice about Knox. I didn't even bring him up. You did!"

"But you kept his number," she says.

"Everly," I say, my voice soft, revealing how vulnerable I feel about this whole situation. "I will always have a soft spot for Knox. He's my first love. That's special. You don't ever forget that person."

She wraps one arm around me, forcing me to lay my head on her small shoulder. She knows I've reached my limit. "How about I set you up with . . ."

"God, no!" I laugh out. "The last guy you set me up with had a criminal record."

"I didn't know!" We both laugh. "You could just have a sex thing with Knox. No attachments."

"A sex thing?" I ask.

"That's something," she says with a smile.

❦

"My boyfriend of two years gave me something interesting for my birthday," a female caller says. "I'm not sure what to make of it."

It's been a particularly crazy Sunday night at the radio station. It started with my first caller, whose boyfriend dumped her for her *mom*! It all went downhill from there. No telling what delights this caller has in store for me, and her use of the word "something" brings me back to my conversation with Knox a few days ago. He said there was "something." And then Everly did, too. What the hell does that mean? What am I supposed to make of that? He left a few days ago, and I don't know whether he plans on coming back soon, or if whatever "something" he was talking about is going to rear its head in another five years.

"Tease," I say into the microphone. "What was this something?"

She clears her throat. "A . . . a vibrator."

"Well, this is a first," I say. "I've heard about sex toys for Valentine's Day, but never on one's birthday."

"It's weird, right?" she asks.

"Was there an engagement ring on the end of it?" I joke. "Because *that* would be really weird."

She laughs. "No, but we are talking about getting married, so this just seemed . . . I don't know. Do you think he's just trying to spice things up?"

"Perhaps," I say. "Let me say this. I think you need to talk to him."

"But what do you think?"

"I have a theory about men who don't mind their wives or girlfriends using vibrators," I say. "They don't want to put in the work. And the last thing you want is a man who's lazy in the bedroom."

Seemingly satisfied with my advice, she promptly thanks me and hangs up. Amy sends me follow-up questions she thinks I should've asked. She does that sometimes, telling me she likes to play devil's advocate. I appreciate her enthusiasm for the show. She hasn't been here that long, but she's totally invested. Which I like.

The switchboard is lighting up with callers left and right. Sometimes, like tonight, the show takes on a life of its own. I'm always prepared with topics, but a lot of what happens on-air is organic. It just flows from the audience.

Tonight, there is a specific topic I want to discuss. My show works because I'm honest. I talk about myself, my bad dates, my good ones, the whole messy dating thing. When it comes to dating, I've done it all. Blind dates, speed dating, online—if there's an app, I've tried it. I considered it research for my job, and if I met a nice guy, that was just a bonus, but mostly I just got a lot of funny stories to tell. I share all of this on-air, but I never use names or any identifying information.

"I want to bring up something we've talked a lot about before. I'm bringing this up because it happened to me this past week. What do you do when your ex shows up? Let's discuss. And to be perfectly clear, I'm not talking about the casual one-night stand that you bump into at the coffee shop. I'm talking about the one who broke your heart. Lines are open."

I get caller after caller with horror stories of running into their ex-boyfriends with their new boyfriends, or vice versa. One poor man calls in relaying the time he ran into his ex at a strip club. She was on the pole!

"I can always count on my listeners to make me feel better," I laugh then see my call screener Amy jump up from her seat outside the booth, waving to me. "I've always thought the Harry Potter reference to 'he who shall not be named' sounded like every girl's slogan about her ex."

I push the button to take a quick commercial break to allow Amy to stick her head in. "There's some guy on the line," she says. "He gave some silly name, but he sounds like the same guy who called last week. You know, Knox from California."

"What name did he give?" I ask, knowing we sometimes get a few crazies.

"Scooby-Doo," she says, rolling her eyes.

Even though I don't want to, I smile. It has to be Knox. That man is ridiculous. "What line is he on?"

She tells me then asks, "You don't think it's the actor?"

The cat is out of the bag. It's kind of obvious to Amy, at least. I simply hold my finger up to my lips in the "shh" motion, indicating that's a secret. She wiggles a little before shutting the door. The commercial ends, and I answer his line.

"I understand we have a famous caller on the line with us tonight. Tell us, Scooby-Doo, did Shaggy eat all your Scooby snacks?"

"This is much more serious than that," he says.

It's Knox. Stubborn man is not going to go away. "Do tell."

"I'm being accused of breaking this woman's heart."

I don't need to ask for more details. I know them all—how long we were together, how old we were when it ended. It's my story, our story.

"You saying you didn't break her heart?" I ask, glancing up to see Amy outside the booth, her eyes wide. I'm doing my best to control my emotions, but the way my voice is shaking should make it obvious to anyone listening that this is a personal call.

"I'm saying she broke mine, too," he says quietly.

"How did she break your heart?" I ask, trying to steady myself.

"She wouldn't give me a chance to fix it," he says.

"You wanted to fix it?" I snap back, my show taking a profoundly serious turn.

"Every day for the past five years," he says.

"Maybe she was too hurt," I say.

"I want her to know how sorry I am."

On-air silence is never a good thing, but I can't speak.

"How long do you think it'll take for the hurt to go away enough for me to try again?" he asks.

He's killing me here. A tear falls down my cheek, and I quickly wipe it away. "Depends."

"Is five years enough?" he asks.

"Maybe."

CHAPTER TEN

Knox

I love the ocean at night, the way the moon reflects in the waves. You can't see the water clearly, but you can hear the crashing sound of the waves against the cliffs. I lean against the clear glass railing on my balcony, looking out into the darkness. It's the same sky Mae and I used to stare up at when we were kids. I have everything I ever dreamed of back then. I always talked about being an actor, being rich, famous, having big houses, and living in the big city. I'm only twenty-six, and everything on that list is checked off.

Mae used to talk about having a house, settling in one same place, not moving around. She'd seen the world already, traveling all over with her parents. *I just want to be in the same place for more than a couple years*, I remember her saying. She also wanted a dog—a St. Bernard, to be exact. I didn't see a dog when I was at her place, so I guess she hasn't gotten that part of her dream yet.

It's twenty minutes since her show ended. I was her last caller of the night. Maybe it's risky to call into her show, someone could recognize my voice, but I think the risk is small, and it's worth it just to talk to her. Suddenly, time seems to be moving at a snail's pace. My life is usually fast paced, jetting from one side of the world to the other—making movies, going to parties, doing interviews—but this past week has been so damn slow.

Time is supposed to heal all wounds, but not Mae. She's timeless.

The kind of love we had isn't the kind that disappears. They say time makes you forget. But not what we had. That kind of love can be put on a shelf, buried deep in our heart—like our cassette tapes—

but it's always there, always waiting for you to open it, set it free.

When it comes to Mae and me, time is a failure.

Time hasn't worked. It hasn't made my heart forget. It hasn't made the memories fade. Time hasn't done its job.

Time is a failure because nothing can heal my heart from Mae. She owns it.

I don't want it back.

Why didn't I reach out to her sooner? I could've fought for her. I wish I knew the answer. Some of it was pride. I wasn't going to grovel or beg. I was Hollywood's hottest up and coming actor, the world was my oyster. I told myself I was better off. I did one hell of an acting job on 'myself. And when you believe a woman wants nothing more to do with you, what choice do you really have?

My cell phone vibrates in my pocket, and I pull it out, not recognizing the number, but I definitely know that area code. I don't have the same number I had in college. That's long gone. Can't have random people knowing my phone number. Next thing you know, your college roommate is selling it to the highest bidder—then you've got some crazy person trying to high jump the fence to your house.

I guess she doesn't have the same number, either. I can't believe she called, but it has to be her.

"I'd like to speak to Scooby-Doo," Mae says.

"You picked the alias," I say, starting to pace back and forth on my balcony, unable to believe she actually called.

There are turning points in relationships. Times when you know things are shifting.

Like a breakup. There's a moment in the relationship—a moment when you know it's over. You might not break up right then, but it's when your heart recognizes what's coming. It's the moment when you realize the other person doesn't feel the way about you that you thought they did. It can come in the form of a look or an accusation, but your heart knows that person doesn't love you anymore. You can ignore it, try to hang on, fight, but when you look back on things, that moment was the beginning of the end.

How long that ending takes is up to you.

Then there's the opposite moment, the moment I'm having with Mae right now. The moment when you know there's hope. When you know this could lead to something. I think of Ryder's advice: *Don't fuck it up.*

"You can't keep calling my show," she says.

So that's how she wants to play this—like she's calling to scold me. "Well, now that I have your cell phone number, I won't have to." I think I hear her exhale, but there's a lot of background noise. "Are you driving?" I ask.

"Yeah, I usually drive home after the show."

That means she has forty-five uninterrupted minutes. Plus, I don't like the idea of her driving so late by herself. The roads between Denver and Haven's Point are poorly lit and curvy. I have to stay on the phone with her to make sure she gets home safely. That's as good an excuse as any to keep talking to her.

"Knox," she says. "I need you to stop whatever this is."

I stop mid-stride, that not at all what I expected to hear. I must be off my game. I thought this was going well. "Can't do that."

"You broke up with me," she says.

"No, *you* broke up with *me*," I say.

"What are you talking about?" she snaps. "You went on national television and said you were single! We'd been together for four years!"

Of course, I know what she's talking about, but that wasn't me breaking up with her.

After my dad died, I tried to stay in college, but I was restless. I'd drive back and forth to California for auditions, casting calls, any meetings I could get, hoping to get a break. I had a few bit parts, one-liners here and there, but I finally got lucky and landed a role in a major movie. It wasn't a huge part, but it was opposite a big-name actress. The film got a ton of buzz, so my agent had me making the rounds at the award shows, walking the red carpet, rubbing elbows with the right people. By that time, I'd decided to quit school. I was barely going, anyway. I wasn't going to miss my big break.

"Do you know what that was like?" she asks. "I had all my girl-friends in my dorm room, watching you on the red carpet. I was so proud of you. My boyfriend was *finally* living his dream. They stopped you on the carpet and asked you all these questions about the movie, about rumors that you were dating your co-star, rumors I never knew anything about. Then you announced you were very much single. I remember it so clearly. *Very much single.*"

I remember it, too. I'd been directed to say it by my agent. The rumors swirling around me and my co-star had helped build hype about the movie, and having a girlfriend back home wasn't in the script. So I went along with it. I was young and new, and in no position to question what my agent was telling me. I didn't think it was a big deal. I thought Mae would understand it was part of the job, just another role I was playing.

I was wrong.

"Mae, I told you before. I wasn't breaking up with you when I said that. It was . . ."

"Do you have any idea how embarrassing that was? All my friends, my family, all of Haven's Point seeing that? I was mortified!"

"It was to create publicity for the film. I never meant it. I flew home to see you the very next day. Remember that? That's when you told me you didn't want to see me again. You're the one who ended it."

"So you think I broke up with you?"

"I know I didn't break up with you," I say. There's a moment of silence. I hate rehashing all this old shit, but Mae needs to feel heard. "Maybe we never broke up?" I joke.

"The pictures in the tabloids of you and your co-star making out on some yacht *two weeks later* were clear that we did!"

I collapse into a lounge chair on my balcony, knowing she's probably seen a lot of pictures like that over the years. I'd hate to see a single picture of her even standing next to another guy, much less compromising photos.

"I guess those rumors from the red carpet were true. How long were you cheating on me with her?" she asks.

How the fuck could she think that? "I didn't," I say. "Mae, I would *never.*"

"Right," she cries. "She's beautiful and sexy."

"So are you."

"Don't do that!"

"Mae, please find a place to pull over. I don't want you driving when you're upset."

"Be quiet!" she yells.

"I had no idea you thought I cheated on you. I swear to you that I never did. I loved you, Mae." I listen to her sniffle a few times. "I'm sorry about the whole red carpet thing. Truly, I am. I was young and new to the business. I did what I was told. It was stupid, and I'm sorry. But I never cheated on you. I promise." I hear her crying softly on the other end of the phone. I've never wanted to hop on a plane so much in my life, to get to her, to hold her, to look into her eyes, and make sure she knows I'm telling her the truth. "You have to believe me. I never lied to you. Remember all those cassettes, all the embarrassing things I said? I never lied then, and I wouldn't lie now."

"No, you just lied to the whole world about my very existence!" she snaps.

That's like a knee to the balls. "If I could take that back, I would."

"You weren't sleeping with her while you were making the movie? While we were together?"

"I would never do that to you. To any woman, but especially to you."

"Let's say for the sake of argument you didn't actually cheat. How long after we broke up did you end up in her bed?"

Fuck! This is where men and women handle breakups differently. A woman will yell, cry, bitch to her girlfriends—whatever she needs to do to find closure. That process can take days or weeks or months. But women tend to do that before moving on. They don't want to take baggage into their next relationship. It's probably a lot healthier than the way the male species handles things. Men don't *want* to process their feelings. They just want them to go way, so burying them in a bottle of liquor or the nearest pussy tends to be the course of action we choose instead.

"It wasn't long," I say, but she already knows that. It was in the tabloids within weeks, just as she saw. "All I can say is that I was hurt. She'd made it very clear while shooting the movie how she felt. It was easy . . ."

"Easy?" she chokes out.

"That's not what I . . ."

"It wasn't easy for me to go fuck someone else. I didn't sleep with another man for . . ."

"Don't!" I bark. "I can't hear that. As far as I'm concerned, I'm the only man you've been with. I can't think about it any other way."

"Hypocrite," she bites out.

"I know," I say. A long stretch of silence fills the minutes. Looking up into the night sky, I'm hoping for some wisdom. I need something bigger than an apology. A simple *I'm sorry* isn't going to work, but I'm used to people writing these epic lines for me.

"I wish I knew what to say."

"There's nothing," she says. "I must've meant so little to you."

"You know better than that," I say.

"I *know* the man I love told the world he was single, we broke up, and he couldn't wait to fuck someone else. That's what I *know*."

"Then you've forgotten a lot. A whole hell of a lot. And I'm going to remind you," I say.

CHAPTER ELEVEN

Mae

It feels like a Monday—like the Mondayest of Mondays. Normally, I'd have been at The Tune Up hours ago to meet Gigi and catch up, but normally, I don't spend the night awake, crying, reliving my breakup with Knox. The way my dorm room fell silent when he said he was single—the phone calls and texts that followed from everyone in Haven's Point—the feeling of being dumped on national television. Being hurt and embarrassed was not a good combination.

It was a publicity stunt. He'd told me as much five years ago. It didn't make it any easier then, and it doesn't now. It made me feel like I wasn't enough. The girlfriend from back home who wouldn't fit in with the beautiful people of Hollywood. I just never thought Knox felt that way. He showed up at my door the next day, assuming everything was great. That what he did was totally fine. He didn't warn me he'd been coached to say he was single. He didn't call me right after to explain. He just showed up at my door, thinking I'd be happy to see him.

It's over! I never want to see you again!

Those were some of the last words I screamed at Knox. Lies! Even as I said them, I didn't believe them. I hoped saying them out loud would make them true, but it didn't.

For me, it's not over. It could never be over.

Those were some of the last words he said to me. Five years later, I guess they're still true. He's back.

Our fight that day was awful, but it paled in comparison to seeing those photos of him with another woman so soon after. There aren't words to describe it. Outwardly, to everyone else, I acted like I didn't care. If he was going to be unfazed, then so was I.

Only to Everly and Gigi did I let on how much it hurt, and even they don't know I cried every night for three solid months after. In my heart, he'd cheated on me. I have to wonder if it wasn't for those photos, if it wouldn't have taken five years for us to talk again. But those photos sealed the deal. It looked to me like those red carpet rumors were true. It looked like he cheated. Maybe it was easier to believe that. It made it easier to hate him, but deep inside, I always knew better.

After talking to him on the phone last night, I believe him when he said he didn't cheat. He's a terrible man whore, jumping from one bed to the next, but he's not a cheat. I may not understand how he can go from woman to woman so quickly. I may be incapable of doing that myself, but I'm glad to know he didn't actually cheat in our relationship.

I'm a firm believer that every relationship, every breakup, teaches us something. There are lessons we can take away. The biggest lesson I learned from my breakup with Knox is that crying burns a lot of calories. I lost ten solid pounds the month after we broke up. Of course, they found me again, but for a year I was at my goal weight!

I pull open the door to The Tune Up around 4:30, when it's about to go from coffee shop to bar. I doubt Gigi is still here waiting for me, as she usually does on Mondays. I texted her hours ago to let her know I wasn't going to make it, and to just go home, but my grandmother isn't the best at following orders. Still, I could use a shot of whipped cream right about now.

I see Gracie's little drawing that reads "No Autograph Zone" hanging in the window. I guess Knox has a new fan. As soon as I step inside, it's obvious he has more than one new fan. Knox is at the counter, a huge smile on his face. Timothy is laughing, and Everly is trying to grab something out of Knox's hand.

Knox is back in town again! He sure does like to make an entrance. I should be surprised, but I'm not. At least I have on cute jeans today, and no bike hair this time.

"What's mine is yours, and yours is mine," Timothy says, playful-ly holding his wife back.

"Mae!" Everly cries, spotting me and ending her struggle.

All three of them turn to me, but it's Knox's blue eyes that I lock on. I was on the phone with him a little over twelve hours ago, yet here he is. It's a new day after a long overdue talk, and the combina-tion of those two things has eased my anger, my pain. The sight of him doesn't make my heart hurt as badly.

Knox gets to his feet, shuffling a pile of stuff into a large enve-lope. "Thanks, man," he says to Timothy.

"What did I miss?" I ask.

"Nothing," Knox says, taking a step toward me.

"What are you doing here?" I ask, trying not to be distracted at how low his jeans hang from his hips, how his white t-shirt hugs the muscles of his arms and chest.

"I'm leaving," he replies.

"You're not here for me?" I ask.

His smile covers his whole face, and he leans in closer to me. I feel my muscles tighten at his close proximity, my heart rate speeding up. "I'm most definitely here for you."

"But . . ."

"I flew in this morning," he says. "I'm staying in town for a few days."

"But . . ." I can't seem to form a sentence.

He smiles his best Hollywood smile. "Tomorrow. Noon. I'll pick you up."

"Tomorrow?"

Lightly, his lips land on my cheek. In that brief second, my heart misses a beat. "I'm reminding you of who we are. Tomorrow. Noon."

He glances back over his shoulder at Timothy and Everly then waltzes right out the door. I have to admit his ass looks amazing, but what the hell just happened? My eyes fly to Timothy and Everly.

"What's going on?"

"I swear, I don't know what's going on," Everly says. "All I know is that . . ."

Timothy's hand lands on hers, and he shakes his head. "Let this play out."

"Let what play out?" I ask. "What's going on?"

"She's my best friend!" Everly says to her husband. "You can't expect me not to tell her what I know."

"I'm asking you as your husband not to."

"That's not fair!" Everly says, her voice rising.

"You weren't supposed to know anything about this," Timothy says.

"Why are you helping Knox?" she barks, louder than she perhaps intended. "Mae is our friend!"

"He asked, and I think . . ."

I look around the shop, customers starting to notice their fight—staring, conversations ceasing. It's not good for business, and it's not good for their relationship. Whatever's going on, I don't want them fighting over anything that has to do with me. "Forget I asked," I say, motioning with my hands for them to lower their voices.

"Mae," Everly says, her hand landing on mine.

"It's okay," I say. "Whatever it is, I know it's not worth you guys fighting about." They glance at each other. I know their fight isn't over, but I'm doing my part to defuse it. "Just tell me if it's bad or not."

Everly looks at Timothy. "I'm not privy to whatever the plan is."

"There's a plan?" I ask.

Timothy's little grin tells me there is. "It's good, Mae," he says. "I would never do anything that I thought would hurt you. Not even for Knox Merrick."

∽

Haven's Point has changed a lot over the years. The changes used to be more noticeable in between my visits as a child—a new restaurant, boutique, dry cleaners—but one thing remained the same—Gigi. No matter where I was in the world, I knew she was here, waiting for me to come back.

She knows me better than I know myself. I'm her only grand-child, so we are extra close, which is why I'm surprised as hell when I pull up in front of her house and see Knox occupying the seat next to her on the front porch swing, looking like some sort of ad for quaint, small town living. The picture is completed by the fresh squeezed glass of lemonade they each are holding.

I hop out of my car, slamming the door for good measure. It's one thing to involve Timothy in his scheme, it's quite another to involve Gigi. I reach the porch steps, and Knox leans his arm across the back of the swing. That used to be my spot, on that swing, next to him, his arm around my shoulder.

"You following me, Mae?" he asks, trying to hide his smile.

"Um, *my* grandmother," I say, pointing to Gigi.

"Thank you, Ms. Imogen," he says, getting to his feet and grab-bing a bag. "I'll see you tomorrow."

"Remember what I said," she says. "Veto power."

"Yes, ma'am," he says.

"So Gigi is coming on our date tomorrow?" I ask.

"Date?" he says with a smirk.

"You're driving me crazy!" I say.

"Tomorrow, noon," he says, giving me a little wink, then he nods at Gigi and starts toward the steps.

"Hold on a minute," I say, following him.

"I'm kind of on a deadline here," he teases.

"You have to tell me what's going on."

He holds the bag up in the air, looking behind me. I turn around, seeing a van parked on the street that I hadn't noticed before. A young, scruffy looking guy with a beard hops out, walking over to where we're standing. Knox hands him the bag. "Here's the stuff."

I'm totally in the dark at this point, having no idea what's going on, and I get the feeling that Knox likes having me off balance. "Who are you?" I ask the bearded guy.

"Do you mean, like, what's my name, or who I am on an existential level?" he asks.

Oh boy, this dude has to be from California. "Are you kidding me?" I ask, throwing a look to Knox.

"Ben is helping me with something," Knox says, motioning for him to go.

"Nice to meet you, Mae," he says, taking the bag and walking back toward the van.

"How do you know my name?" I call out. When he doesn't answer, I turn to Knox. "How does he know who I am?"

"Me."

"This cryptic shit is really getting old," I say, my hands flying around in the air.

Knox takes my hands, pulling me a little closer to him. How his touch can still be so familiar is beyond me. Everything feels exactly the same, the way he looks at me, the way my body lights up. It feels completely natural to be this close to him. "Ben is helping me with something for our date tomorrow. It's a surprise."

"And Everly and Gigi are helping?" I ask, unable to believe that.

"Timothy, not Everly," he says. "Gigi is helping, but she's laid some conditions on me."

I look over at her, sitting on the porch, pretending not to be watching us. "It's not a date," I say, releasing his hands.

"It is for me," he says, taking hold of one of my hands again.

"What if I'm busy tomorrow at noon?" I ask, but my curiosity is piqued. What is he up to?

"You are," he says. "With me. I thought we covered this earlier at The Tune Up."

I'm doing my best not to smile at him, but his relentlessness is charming. "Gigi has veto power over whatever this is?" I ask, knowing I can trust her.

"She does," he says, swallowing hard.

I can tell whatever deal he struck with her, she has him by the balls.

"Then pick me up at noon," I say, raising an eyebrow at him and turning toward the house. I know his eyes are on my butt as I walk away, so I make sure to walk slowly, so he can see what he's been missing!

Gigi pats the spot beside her for me to sit down, and I see Knox hopping in the van and driving away. "Care to fill me on what that was all about?" I ask.

"That boy is still in love with you," she says.

My hand flies to my chest, checking to see if my heart is still beating. I've been wondering what's going on all day, but that wasn't at all what I was expecting her to say. No way is that true!

"He said that?"

"No," she says. "I don't think he quite knows himself yet."

I start laughing. "You scared the crap out of me. I thought he told you that!"

"You still love him, too," she says.

"It's over," I protest. "It's been over a long time."

"You know it's true, and it scares the crap out of you."

It's no use. I can't lie to her. She can see right through me. "I will always love him. He was my . . ."

"Oh," she says, waving her hands at me. "Don't give me the party line that he was your first love, and you always love your first. Garbage."

"Why are you helping him?" I ask, unable to hide the pain in my voice. "You know how badly he hurt me. You know more than anyone."

She smiles slightly. "He came over here trying to prey on my sympathies, saying how he lost everything in the fire. All his childhood memories. Begging me to help him." She shakes her head. "He's a good actor, but you can't make shit smell like roses, you know?"

"So you didn't fall for his shit?"

"No," she says, "but then he started really talking to me. I mean, really talking. Come to think of it, I'm not even sure he was really talking *to* me. It was more like he was just talking from his heart, and something he said kept me from kicking his butt off the porch."

"What did he say?"

"He apologized to me," Gigi says.

"For what?" I ask.

"For hurting you. He said even if he could get you to forgive him, that he wanted me to forgive him, too. He said it's easier to forgive those who hurt us than it is to forgive those who hurt someone we love, and he wanted me to know how sorry he was for hurting the person I love most in this world." We smile at each other, and she places both her hands on mine. "He told me that all I have to do is say the word, and he'll leave."

"I can't believe he'd do that. He's so stubborn."

"He said that's how confident he is that he'll never hurt you again."

CHAPTER TWELVE

Mae

What do you wear for a date/non-date on a Tuesday at noon in Colorado in the summer? Heck if I know! And having no idea where we are going, what we are doing, whether it's indoor or outdoor doesn't help matters.

On my show, I've learned that surprise dates have a reputation of either being fantastic or going horribly wrong. There's no middle ground. Many engagements have started off as surprises dates. I've even had a couple callers who had surprise weddings which were phenomenal, but I've also heard horror stories. One poor guy was surprising his girlfriend with a fancy dinner on the beach, and they both got food poisoning. Another woman wanted to surprise her man with a midday date, and when she showed up to pick him up, he was with another woman. The track record is about fifty-fifty, so today could go either way.

I swear, I've tried on everything in my closet. I don't want to look overeager. I don't want to look like I don't care. I can't be too sexy. I can't be too asexual. It's an impossible scenario.

I've always had a more eclectic style. I think it's because I've lived all over. I love hats, crazy socks, and vintage t-shirts are my kryptonite. In the summer, I do my best to go without a bra. My boobs aren't huge, and nothing is worse than a sweaty bra, so I prefer to just go natural. But showing up braless seems like it would send the wrong message to Knox.

My undergarments are about the only clothing choice I am confident about. I'm wearing the oldest, ugliest bra and panties I can find.

The bra is flesh color and unhooks in the front, sure to confuse most men, and is nothing lacy or special. The panties are white cotton and have a small hole at the waistband.

These are what you call safety underwear. No way would I take these off in front of anyone, much less a man. So while I take the pill religiously, I consider these undergarments my backup birth control!

I shouldn't be thinking about birth control at all. I'm not sleeping with Knox. Not going to happen. Of course, he is the reason I went on birth control in the first place. One broken condom will do that to a girl! I'll never forget the look on Knox's face when he discovered it broke.

We were barely twenty, in college. I'm not sure what was worse for him, seeing that it broke or knowing he had to tell me it did. We sweat it out for ten whole days, wondering what if. I have to say, after the initial shock wore off, Knox was actually really great about it, assuring me that things would be fine. That no matter what, he was there for me. He let me cry, worry, yell at him. He was a good boyfriend like that. Thank God I didn't get pregnant, but I went on the pill after that.

The first time Knox and I had sex was sweet, slow, gentle. If he was nervous, it didn't show. I think we waited so long, he was too horny to be nervous. It was everything I wanted my first time to be. It wasn't the horror stories I heard from girlfriends. It wasn't so planned out that it was awkward.

One night our freshman year in college, he was in my room. My roommate had dropped out of school and gone back home, which meant I had a single room. Which also meant, Knox practically lived with me. He routinely slept over at my place, not in his own dorm.

I woke up in the middle of the night, and his arm was thrown over me. I looked over at him in the moonlight, and I knew I was finally ready. He'd been the most patient boyfriend in the history of the universe. I kissed him softly on the lips, waking him, and that was it.

Knox has a way about him that just makes you feel so loved, and that night especially, I felt he completely loved me, every part of me.

Things didn't stay so sweet and gentle for long. We soon discovered we both liked to push the envelope in the bedroom. But no matter how kinky things got, that feeling of being totally loved never changed.

No man has ever gotten me the way Knox did. Yes, I've had sex since him. Yes, some of those men gave me orgasms, but it's never been like it was with Knox. Even though I was just a teenager when we lost our virginity together, sex has never been like it was with him. Maybe that's because no man ever knew me like Knox did.

There are things he did to me that no man has since. He loved to slip his hand under my skirt in public to get me off. He knew how hot it made me when he spanked me, smacked my pussy. No other man has ever done that to me. He knows how much that turns me on.

He knows I like it a little rough, a little dirty. Nothing crazy, we aren't talking rim jobs, but I like the naughtier side of things. He just *gets* that. Most men these days are too polite in bed. I'm all for polite, but not between the sheets.

Even though we were in college, he understood my needs, my cravings. No other man has, and honestly, I don't want to have to make that request. *Excuse me, babe, would you mind tightening the nipple clamp, it's too loose.* No, thank you. Other men have given me orgasms, but never with the same level of satisfaction, never leaving me spent like Knox. The world might think there's no one like him on the big screen, but I know there's no one like him in the bedroom.

I feel my body heat just thinking about it. It's been a long time since I've been with a man. I'm not one who sleeps with guys easily. That's cost me a few relationships, but who cares? If you can't wait for me, then I don't need you. I glance at the clock, finding it's thirty minutes until noon. I've heard of many a man doing a preventative jerk off before a date. Women don't work the same way, but I certainly don't want to open the door thinking about sex.

Reaching into my nightstand, I grab my vibrating boyfriend. A girl's got to do what a girl's got to do. And the best thing about my battery-operated friend is that I can make it last as long or be over as quickly as I'd like. I'm on a bit of time crunch today, so better make it a quickie.

I hop in bed. I'm extremely weird about the whole masturbation thing. I have to do it under the covers. I'm not typically shy when I'm in bed with a man, but something about doing this alone brings out the shy girl in me.

A vibration echoes through the room, but unfortunately, it's not from my toy, but my phone. Choosing to ignore it, I nestle down deep in my bed, but find I am too distracted to turn it on. What if the text was important?

Here's the thing about me and sex—I think this is true for most women. It's hard for us to get off if something else is on our mind, and it's not easy for us to clear our minds. Men tend to be singularly focused. I think that's why they are better at orgasms than most women. We are raised to multi-task, and multi-tasking and sex don't go well together.

Reaching for my phone, I see the interrupter of my playtime is Knox. Of course, it is. Crap, he's letting me know he's on his way, and will be early.

Flying out of bed, I toss my vibrator back in the drawer and rush to my closet. I don't have time to be frustrated from lack of orgasm. I have to act fast. There's no more time for indecision over what I'm wearing, so I quickly choose a floral sundress that stops right above my knee. It's not tight fitting, but moves when I do.

I barely have time to throw my hair up in a ponytail before Knox is knocking at my door. Taking one last glance at myself in the mirror, I throw on some warpaint, as Gigi calls it—known as lip gloss to the rest of the world. Flip-flops complete my look.

Taking a deep breath, I peek out the window before I open the door, seeing Knox waiting. He's wearing a white button down with the sleeves rolled up and the top few buttons undone and jeans. Good, our outfits go together. There's nothing worse than being underdressed compared to your date.

Wait! This isn't a date.

His hands go through his dark blonde hair, messing it up enough that it looks sexy and lived in. He's still sporting slight stubble on his face, and everything about him looks perfectly sexy. He knocks again, blowing out a deep breath.

Is Knox Merrick nervous?

Surely, I don't make him nervous. But the thought that I might makes me smile a little. He looks up, like he's saying a little prayer. I wonder how long he'd wait for me. He pulls out his phone. I think he might be checking to see if I've texted him back, but he starts to type something, looking aggravated. I know it's not for me when my phone doesn't ding with a message.

Unsure if I should be excited or scared of what he has planned, I open the front door. Timothy and Gigi are going to get a piece of my mind if this crashes and burns. I want to apologize for making him wait, but *sorry I was on the verge of masturbating* doesn't seem like an appropriate way to start a conversation, let alone to greet one's ex.

His eyes start at my legs, slowly sliding up until he reaches my eyes. Knox has a way of looking at me that makes me have very dirty thoughts. "You look beautiful," he says, holding my gaze.

There was a time when I would've discarded his compliment, dismissed it with a "this old thing" reply, but over the years, I've learned when someone pays you a compliment, take it. "Thank you." And while he looks sexy as all get out, I won't tell him. He probably hears it all the time, anyway. Hell, he has online polls naming him the sexiest man on the planet.

His phone dings, and it doesn't take a rocket scientist to see he's not happy about it. "Sorry," he says, pulling it out of his pocket. "I'm turning the damn thing off."

"Who is it?"

"My agent, my publicist, the director—take your pick," he says.

"You were early. It's not quite noon yet," I say. "Finish what you need to."

"Not a chance," he says, powering down his phone. "Our date begins now."

❧

Every town has one—a majestic old theater that used to show the classic films of days gone by before big cineplex and streaming services ruled the world. Haven's Point is no different. *The Royal* is home to one screen. It looks like something from an old movie with its huge marquee out front and single man box office. These days, it's mostly used for charity events, special screenings of classic movies, or corporate rentals.

Knox pulls the car right up to the curb. "You're taking me to the movies?"

"Classic first date," he says.

"Only this isn't a date, and certainly not our first."

Getting out of the car, he hurries to my side to get my door for me. I'm not sure what I thought he was planning for today, but this wasn't it. "Let me guess, you're the star of the movie?"

"One of them," he says, placing his hand at the small of my back, leading me toward the entrance.

"I'm not in the mood for a Knox Merrick movie marathon," I say. "I've managed to avoid seeing any of your films this long."

"You've never watched my movies?" he asks, his voice quiet and low, more sadness than surprise.

I look up at him, and he's unable to hide the pain in his blue eyes. I can tell my lack of interest in his career hurts him.

"Not one?" he asks.

I shake my head.

"I've made eleven movies in five years," he says. "You never watched one?"

"It hurt, Knox," I admit. "I didn't want to spend two hours watching the person I lost. It's not that I'm not proud of you. I am, more than you know. I just couldn't put my heart through that."

Gently, he takes my hand. "You were with me in all of those movies. I'd read a script and wonder if you'd like it. If you'd tell me to take it or not. I'd need to deliver a line about love or loss, and you were always my inspiration."

My heart starts to flutter in my chest just like it used to, so I make a joke to break the attraction. "Next you're going to try to convince me that you thought of me during sex scenes."

He leans in to my neck. "Sex scenes are much too boring to think of you during."

I turn my head slightly, our eyes meet, his lips inches from mine. It would be so easy to kiss him right now. It would be the easiest mistake I'd ever make.

~

Cassette

Knox to Mae

Age Sixteen

I love you, Mae.

I know we've said that to each other before. But this time I mean it in the more than friends way. Next time I see you, I don't know that I'll have the balls to say that to your face right away.

I mean, I guess I should kiss you first, for real, but the thing is, I don't need to kiss you to know that I love you. Guys are always talking about how far they got with some girl. My friends are losing their virginity left and right. I've never even kissed you, except that one when we were six, and that doesn't count.

This cassette is going all wrong. I should've just told you about the horror that is Honors Chemistry. My teacher asked my dad out on a date! Can you believe that shit? My dad turned her down cold. I think my grade is suffering because of it. He hasn't been on one date since my mom died. Ten years. Not one.

I told him he could. That I wouldn't be upset. As long as it wasn't my teacher. He laughed at that. He told me he promised my mother forever, and he intended to keep that promise.

So that's my promise to you, too. Forever.

I don't need to kiss you first, or get to second base, or anything else. Although I definitely want those things. I lay awake thinking about those things. But I don't need them to know I love you.

CHAPTER THIRTEEN

Knox

Middle row, middle seats, we sit in the theater. Normally, I prefer an aisle seat, but since we're the only ones in here, it really doesn't matter. I rented out the whole theater for this special showing. I don't have popcorn, sodas, or snacks. This movie isn't long enough for all that. Movies are sometimes made solely for entertainment purposes. Other times, movies are meant to make you think.

This time?

This movie is made to help her remember.

That's what the best movies do. They help us remember what it's like to be a kid, or fall in love, or lose someone. Sure, some movies are purely for fun. I've made all kinds of movies—action flicks, drama. Comedy and straight up romances aren't in my wheelhouse, but my favorite movies to watch and to star in are the ones that make people feel something.

I turn around slightly, raising my hand in the air for them to start the show. The title, *Unfinished Love*, rolls across the screen with a picture of Mae and I when we were six, the summer we met.

Her head whips around. "What did you do?"

"What I do best," I say. "Make a movie."

"Of us?" she asks.

"Us," I whisper.

Her face is priceless as she turns back to the screen. I don't need to watch the film. I've seen it at least a hundred times in the past two days, editing it, making sure it was perfect. I didn't want it to come off like a cheesy home movie. I wanted it to read like a classic love story.

So far, I think I succeeded in that mission. Imogen watched it this morning and left with tears in her eyes. That was one of the conditions she set for helping me. She had to see the movie first, and she had veto power. Without passing Imogen's inspection, Mae wouldn't be in the seat next to me.

Once I collected pictures and keepsakes from Everly and Imogen, and all our cassettes from my place, I had Ben piece it all together with my help. Ben is a wannabe director who's interned on a few movies I've worked on. He jumped at the chance to help me, knowing I'd put in a good word for him for future projects. That's how Hollywood is—you scratch my back, and I'll scratch yours.

Mae grabs my hand when some drawings we made as kids flash on the screen. One touch from her only makes me want more. More time, more memories, more of her hands on me, and mine on her.

Our teenage voices from our cassettes fill the theater. "Oh my God," she whispers, covering her mouth. "I forgot about that."

The song we danced to at prom, pictures from the yearbook, snapshots from our life together float over the screen, our voices giving them life. She leans forward, captivated by our story. It's a journey of love and friendship, and it's not over.

Not even close.

I've sat in many premieres wondering whether my performance would resonate with the audience, whether they'd enjoy the movie, but I've never been more nervous in my whole life than I am right now. Movie critics can be hard, and audiences can, too. I can pour my heart and soul into something for months and months, live and breathe a character, and have it ripped to shreds, or classified as a flop because it doesn't bring in enough money. It hasn't happened often, but as disheartening as it may be, it's easy compared to this.

Mae can't just *like* this movie. She has to feel it in her heart. It has to make her forgive me. This movie has to give me a second chance.

That's what I want. When I first heard her voice on the radio, first called her show, I told myself it was just to get in touch, see how she was, hopefully be friends again. I'm man enough to admit that was me hedging my bets, not wanting to scare her off, or get my heart stepped on. But it's so much more than that. I want *her*. It's that simple.

She watches the movie, and I watch her. I know her by heart. I know when she cocks her head to the side slightly, she's smiling. I know when she bites her bottom lip, she's trying not to cry. I know how she tastes, how she moves, how she moans when I'm buried deep inside her.

And I know I have to have her in my life. All my dreams of getting away from this small town, becoming famous, rich—those were the dreams of my childhood. And they were wrong.

Mae is my dream.

There is no *The End* at the credits; instead, the last frame of the movie reads *The Beginning*.

When the movie is over, she sits, staring at the now blank screen. I place my hand on her thigh, hoping this little reminder worked, hoping she remembers who we are, everything we had.

"We are so much more than how we ended," I whisper.

She looks back at me, a single tear rolling down her cheek. "We are," she says softly.

"Can you forgive me?" I ask.

She takes my hand from her leg, moving it to the back of her seat, before leaning back into my arm, her head landing on my shoulder.

"I can," she whispers. "Play it again."

∽

She hasn't stopped smiling since we left. She insisted we watch the movie four times. I told her I had a copy made for her, but she said it was better on the big screen.

We need more people like her; the movie business is quickly becoming something we do in our homes, by ourselves, separated from others. *Going to the movies* now means going to the sofa just as often as it does going to a theater. Movies should be experienced with other people.

I stop in front of her house then hop out to open her door. Taking her hand, she looks up at me. If this was a movie, I'd kiss her, but this is real life, and you can't rush everything into a two-hour window.

"Now what?" she whispers.

She wants to know where we go from here. After you forgive someone, what's the next step? We can't go back to how things were, just pick up where we left off.

"How about a walk by the lake?" I ask.

She nods, a coy smile on her face. She looks relieved that I'm not initiating some big, serious conversation. We start walking toward the lake, the sun still high in the afternoon sky, making the colors of the wildflowers look more vibrant. Or maybe it's the woman beside me making everything brighter.

"I guess I need to watch your movies now," she says, bumping me with her shoulder.

"You can skip . . ."

"Nope. I'm going to watch them all."

"Be kind," I say. Criticism is hard from anyone, but having someone you care about judge your work is even harder, and Mae's opinion is important to me.

In my career, I've never gotten hung up on reviews, or what critics thought of me. I work hard, do my best, and let the chips fall where they may. I think that attitude comes from losing my mom so early in my life. A negative review isn't the end of the world when you color everything through that lens. Still, I want Mae to be proud of me.

She turns to me, grabbing my shoulders. "I have the best idea. Let's stay up all night like we used to. We can watch all your movies. It's binge watching Knox Merrick *with* Knox Merrick!" she says with a giggle.

I never watch my movies once the premiere is over, but I'm not about to turn down her offer. Eleven movies is about twenty-four hours, give or take. I can't think of a better place to be than with Mae.

She takes both my hands, walking backwards toward her house, her eyes on mine, a sweet smile on her face. I know that look. She's got more than watching movies on her mind. Or at least I hope so.

"What's your new movie about?" she asks. "The one coming out next month."

"Period war drama," I say flatly.

"You don't sound too happy about it," she says, releasing my hands and walking toward her house.

I pull out my phone, knowing it's going to blow up with notifications when I finally power it back on. "Lots of problems post-production. I'm learning a lot about what not to do in my own company."

"You have your own production company?" she asks, opening her front door.

"Just started it," I say. "I wanted some say in what goes in front of an audience."

She turns to me, pausing in the doorway. "Like what?"

"I want to specialize in book to film adaptations," I say. "I'm hoping to tap into the indie author market. There are some really great writers out there that people need to know about."

"I kinda love that," she says. "But you better be careful. The book is always better than the movie!"

"I'm going to change that," I say, following her inside.

She kicks off her shoes, drops her purse on a side table, and walks into the kitchen talking about books she's read that I ought to consider.

I see an alarm panel on the wall, but it obviously wasn't set. Her place is relatively small. The den and kitchen are combined. The only eating area I see is at the kitchen island, which holds a vase of wildflowers. There's a fireplace made from this old grey stone that matches the floors. There are two sets of French doors that lead outside with great views of the lake. I have to smile at the fact we both have water views.

The decor is a mix of colors and fabrics. And I know immediately that, unlike my houses, no designer has touched this place. It's completely Mae, and I love it. There's a framed poster and a coffee mug touting her radio show. We've got that in common. Branding is everything.

My eyes land on her bookshelf, an old, battered cassette player resting there. That has to be the one she used to record all our tapes. She kept it. She kept that little piece of us. Like me, she never totally let go. I wish I'd known that sooner.

"Hungry?" she asks, looking at me from behind the refrigerator door. She's got a baby blue refrigerator. Of course, she does!

"Yeah."

She holds out two bags. "Frozen fries or pizza rolls?"

You know you've gone Hollywood when the first thing you think is that your trainer and nutritionist are going to kill you. This is a far cry from the women I'm used to, who wouldn't eat processed food to save their life. "Both," I say.

"Good man," she says, starting the oven.

She pours both the fries and pizza rolls on the same baking sheet, sticking them in the oven before it's even preheated. Who knows if they are even supposed to be cooked at the same temperature! Silly little things like that about Mae make her so fucking adorable, and she has no clue. She never has.

"Bathroom's through there," she says, pointing out some doors. "That's the spare bedroom, which I use for an office, and my bedroom's through that door. That's the grand tour. I'm sure you're used to bigger places, but it's the perfect size for me."

"I like it," I say. "You said earlier you were proud of me, but I don't think I told you how proud I am of you. How great your show is. I can't believe my Mae has her own radio show. I mean, I always knew you'd be great at whatever you did. You never talked about radio, but you're a natural."

"Thanks," she says, walking over and handing me a bottle of water. We both sit down on her oversized sofa. "I haven't been to the store. This is all I've got."

I know she doesn't like beer, and it makes me happy she doesn't have any. Beer often indicates a man has been around. From my brief glimpses, I don't see any photos of old boyfriends. That's a good sign.

"I just kind of fell into the whole radio thing," she says.

She places her bottle down, staring out the window toward the water. Suddenly, she looks like she's a million miles away. I follow her lead, putting my drink down, and inch closer to her on the sofa. "Everything okay?"

"I was interning at the radio station after we broke up. One Sunday night, the host didn't show up, and they threw me on the air. I didn't know what to do, and they just told me to talk about me. Even though it had been a while, our breakup was still fresh in my mind. That's how *The Breakup Bible* was born." She looks over at me. "I wouldn't have my career if we hadn't broken up."

"I probably wouldn't have mine, either," I say.

"Yes, you would," she says. "You were on your way when we ended."

It might be forward and fast, but fuck it. Five lost years is enough. I don't want to play games. Looking into her blue eyes, I whisper, "I'd give it all up to have never lost you. To have those five years back."

Her breath catches, and she looks down. "But then who would save the world from all those alien attacks?" she teases, making fun of the worst career choice I've ever made.

Her little joke lets me know she's not ready to talk about what this is between us. Not yet. "I'm glad you didn't see that one."

She smiles a little, reaching for the ends of her hair, twirling them. "Today? What you did with the movie, that was really something."

"Something," I repeat, scooting closer, feeling the something between us growing, expanding, filling up the whole room. One of us better do something soon before we combust.

"Definitely something," she says, her eyes falling to my mouth.

That's it. Those two little words are enough to reassure me that she finally admits there is still something between us. That's the only go ahead I need.

There's no director here yelling where to place our hands, how to angle our bodies. There's no lighting crew making sure the mood is right. There's no wardrobe person or makeup artist to make sure we look our best. It's just me and Mae, the way it's meant to be.

Placing my hand on her cheek, I urge her to me, drawing her closer with each beat of our hearts. There's so much I want to tell her, say to her, promise her, but no one is handing me a script to read from. I have to figure it out myself.

Fuck it! Actions speak louder than words, anyway.

Impatience takes over, and I yank her to me, seeing her smile, but before my lips land on hers, a knock comes from her front door.

"You've got to be fucking kidding me!"

She laughs a little, getting to her feet. "I'm not expecting anyone."

"Amazon Prime order?" I joke.

"Nope. Although, I do love that two-day shipping," she says, opening the door.

A camera immediately flies in her face. From my position on the sofa, they can't see me, but I sure as hell know what's going on.

"*Denver Daily News!*" the man says, practically yelling at her. "Reports are all over town of Knox Merrick sightings last week and this week. Rumors are swirling that you and he . . ."

Jumping to my feet, I slam the door, looking down to find Mae standing frozen. Shit! I should've predicted this. I can only hide out for so long. Eventually, word spreads, and the media want their story. Why am I in town? How long am I staying? Who am I screwing? They think they're entitled to all that.

I place my hands on her waist. "Mae?"

She doesn't look at me. She doesn't say a word. I'm so fucked here. If she's not ready for us to talk about whatever's going on here, she's certainly not ready for it to be splashed on the front page. It was only a Denver paper, but it won't be long before it hits national entertainment news outlets. This is why people who live their life in the limelight tend to date each other; you don't want to drag someone else into the chaos. It's hard for others to understand if they don't live it. As much as I hate it, I did choose this career and all that comes along with it. Mae did not.

"Mae," I say again.

Her eyes shift to mine. "That pile of shit!" she curses, so loud I'm sure he heard it. She opens the door again, ready for a fight.

The guy is still standing there. His eyes shift from me to Mae then back to me again. Clearly, he has no idea what to do at this point.

"How much will it take to make this story disappear?" I ask. "Leave her name out of it?"

The son of a bitch cocks his chin up, like he can't be bought. Like freedom of the press is incorruptible. Dealing with the press is a double-edged sword. On the one hand, I need them to promote my movies, but times like these, they are intrusive and overstep. Sometimes I wish someone would shove a camera in their girlfriends' face and see how they'd like it.

"No," Mae says, holding her hand up to stop me. "You won't pay him a dime."

I look down at her, taking her hand. Normally, I find it best to keep the press happy, to smile. Fake politeness can go a long way. My brother, Ryder, has the opposite approach, known for throwing them the middle finger, but I've found it easier to just play nice. "Mae, you don't have any idea . . ."

"Mae?" the reporter repeats, a smug look on his face, like I just gave him some piece of information he didn't already know. He's standing on her front porch, for fuck's sake, I'm sure he already had her name.

"Yes," Mae says. "That's M-A-E, not May like the month. Make sure you get that right. It's a pet peeve of mine when people misspell my name."

What the hell is she doing? I know she's not with me for fame. I know she's not an attention whore, looking to get her name in the paper. What game is she playing?

"And your name is?" she asks.

"Vincent Jones," he says.

"Perfect," Mae says. "You see the road back there?"

"Yes," he says, looking back over his shoulder.

"And to the left, that clearing past the wildflowers?"

"Sure."

"And on the right, all the way at the end, there's that pole."

"I see it."

"I own all that land," she says.

"So?"

"So, Mr. Jones, you are trespassing on my property, and if you don't get your ass off my porch, I'm going to call the police. And if you print anything about me or Knox, we'll both sue you, and while we may not win, we will make sure to run your paper into the ground with legal fees." She flashes him a big smile. "Now, have a good night."

His jaw on the floor, Mae waves her hand at him, shooing him away. She may have just handed him his balls, but he looks pissed about it. She just made him an enemy. He starts off her porch. Her threat might have worked this time, on a Colorado paper, but it won't when it comes to the bigger outlets.

She looks up at me, a satisfied smile on her pretty face. "He won't be the last," I say. "You can't threaten them all."

"No," she says. "But I can keep them off my property."

"Mae," I say, taking her hands and leading her back to the sofa.

"You can skip the warnings," she says. "You've spent the past two weeks working your way back into my life. You can't try to warn me off now."

She's right.

Mae's always been smart, tough. I know she can handle herself. Plus, she has me.

"I think you promised me a movie date?" I say, letting her know I'm all in. We both plop down on the sofa when a smell comes from the kitchen.

"Oh no!" she cries. "If that asshole made me burn the fries and pizza rolls, I'm going to be so mad."

～

Under the guise that movies are best watched in the dark, I closed all the curtains in Mae's living room. Really, I wanted to make sure that, if there were other reporters out there, they couldn't get a shot. I briefly turned on my phone and checked to make sure there weren't any reports online anywhere. There was nothing, so at this point, I think it was just the Denver press sniffing around.

Mae decided we should watch all my movies in the order in which they were made, which means the first one we watched was the movie that led to our breakup. The one I promoted by walking the carpet and denying being in a relationship. I didn't have a huge part, but it was still weird to sit next to her and watch it. Thank God, there weren't any intimate scenes in this one. I'm not sure how I'm going to sit next to her and watch her watch me kiss someone else. That's fucked up.

The second movie we watch is my first featured role. I remember being so nervous to act alongside two Hollywood A-listers in the film, but judging by the look on Mae's face, I held my own. Midway through, Mae leans back on the sofa, her feet across my lap, the hem of her dress inching higher every time she moves.

This was our go-to television viewing position as teenagers. My dad walked in once while we were watching a movie, found Mae's head was in my lap, and you would've thought she was giving me head right then and there. So after that, only her feet could rest in my lap. Long after we weren't living at home, we still maintained this position.

I wonder if her other favorite positions are still the same. She used to love it when I was on top or took her from behind. I really hope she hasn't lost her adventurous, dirty side. I've missed it. Casual sex with semi-strangers doesn't lend itself to the naughtier side of things. At least not for me, it hasn't. One has to be careful when you don't really know the other person. Straight up vanilla sex tends to be the name of the game in those situations. It's a bit harder to tie up someone that you just met.

With my fingers, I trace small circles around her ankles. The skin of her legs is smooth and soft. Mae is a strong woman, sassy, feisty—as the newspaper guy just found out—but in the bedroom, she likes to be taken. I love that about her. She trusts me to give her exactly what she needs. She puts her pleasure in my hands, and I make sure to deliver.

Well, I used to.

My eyes wander up her long legs. Dresses are a man's best friend. Hike it up, yank her panties down, and I'm in. Hell, I don't even have to take her panties off. I could just push them aside. Panties are the single worst item of clothing ever created. They just get in my way. Bras do, too. Mae should do away with all her undergarments completely. I can't help the small grin that comes to my face with that thought.

I really shouldn't be thinking about her naked, or what I'd like to do with her naked body. I haven't even kissed her in five years.

Actually, I don't remember the last time I kissed her, or even the last time we slept together, for that matter. Both must've been before that fateful trip to California, but I don't recall. If I'd known it was our last time together, I would've etched it into memory. I would've kissed her longer, deeper, slower. I know I took kissing her for granted, like her lips would always be mine, her body would always be in my bed.

There came a time that I never thought I'd lay eyes on her again, much less be in her house, rubbing her legs, listening to her laugh.

You don't get second chances a lot in life.

This is ours.

"What?" Mae asks, looking up at me. "You're staring at me."

"I was trying to remember the last time I kissed you," I say, looking into her blue eyes.

Without breaking eye contact, she reaches for the remote control, turning off the television. "I don't remember, either," she whispers.

"Come here," I say.

She starts to sit up, and I take her by the waist, situating her legs so that she's straddling my lap. My dick's hard, and I can feel her heat. Her hands slip through my hair. We've had a couple first kisses, the one when we were kids, then the one when we were teenagers. This will be our third and final first kiss. It has to be. I can't lose her ever again.

"I feel like I need to tell you something," she says softly.

Maybe there is a man in her life. Maybe she just wants to be friends. Perhaps she doesn't want to have a long-distance thing. Dear God, don't let it be that she's not on the pill, because I really don't want to suit up with her.

"What?" I ask.

"I have on really ugly underwear," she says, turning bright red. "I thought it would be a good deterrent, but now I don't care."

She starts laughing. She's adorably crazy. Smiling, I pull her to me, telling myself to remember this moment forever. The moment we get another chance. The moment I get to kiss her again.

Leaning closer, her breath mingles with mine, her pink lips parting slightly. My mouth lands on hers, and the past five years melt away, like no time has passed at all. The feel of her mouth on mine is still fresh, familiar. Her lips are so soft, sweet. She moans quietly as our tongues meet, our kiss deepening.

I've kissed a lot of women, some work related, others personal. But no one has ever compared to Mae, the way she tastes, how her body molds to mine. I move to her neck and whisper, "How bad are these underwear?"

"Bad," she says, breathless. "Really bad."

I want to do really bad things to her. Reaching under her dress, I grab her panties, yanking them. "Let's get rid of them, then."

She suddenly leaps off my lap, straightening her clothes and hair. "What are we doing?" she cries.

Shit! I moved too fast, but honestly, I'm not used to women turning me down, or wanting to wait. It's all been too easy for me in the past. Clearly, I misjudged this situation. As much as I'd like to, I suppose we can't just pick up where we left off.

Getting to my feet, I take hold of her waist and reply, "Anything we want."

Shaking her head, she backs away. "I don't think we want the same thing," she says.

My heart sinks. This is the last thing I wanted, for her to think I'm just here for sex. Nothing is farther from the truth. "Mae, I'm not here to use you. I want to be with you. I want us . . ."

"Sex," she says. "That's what I want. No strings. No commitments."

My jaw hits the floor. Totally wasn't expecting that!

"You're kidding?" I've certainly had those kinds of mutually beneficial non-relationships before. I'm not opposed to them. Any other time, I would welcome it, but not with Mae, not now. Not when I want more.

"No," she says, shaking her head. "We're good at being friends. It's obvious we have chemistry."

"Friends with benefits?" I ask, my voice getting sharper than I intend.

"I figured you'd . . ."

"No," I say, leaving out the fact that it would never work. Those kinds of arrangements only work when there aren't feelings involved. With Mae and me, feelings are flying all over the damn place.

"You're turning me down?" she asks, her hands flying to her hips.

"Yep," I say smugly.

I expect something to come flying at my head, but instead, she starts crying. Oh God, what have I done? I clearly made the wrong choice. Should have just had sex! I reach for her, but she pushes me away.

"I feel so stupid," she says. "You can have any woman in the world. Why would you want me?"

"Of course, I want you."

"Just go," she yells at me. "Get out."

"Mae?"

"Now, Knox! I'm not kidding. Get the hell out!"

My stomach twists like it's the morning after I've tied one on. Her tears are coming faster now. She shoves me out the door, slamming it behind me.

Outside, I stand on her front porch, staring at the closed door. What the hell just happened? I must be crazy! I just turned Mae Sheridan down for sex. I've officially lost my ever-loving mind.

One second, we're hot and heavy. The next, she's in tears. I know Mae. She's not the type to have sex casually. I realize I haven't seen her in a few years, but a leopard doesn't change her spots. It took me years to get her into bed, and we were in love. Granted, we were young and virgins, but you don't go from that to what I just heard in there.

I'm a little slow on the uptake, but I suddenly realize what this is about. She's scared. I hurt her. I hurt her bad. This is her way of testing the waters. She gives me her body while keeping a lock on her heart.

I know I can unlock it, but not from out here.

My mistake five years ago was that I got caught up in Hollywood bullshit, then I stopped fighting for her. I let her shove me out the door then, too. Not this time. I learn from my mistakes.

I'll never stop fighting for her again. I fly back through her front door, finding her on her sofa, still crying.

"I do want you," I say. "Even in whatever ugly ass underwear you have on." A smile breaks through her tears. "It's just that I want more. You just said we are great friends, we have great chemistry. You know what that equals? It's not friends with benefits. It's forever."

"Don't . . ."

"Haven't you figured out why I'm here?"

"Tell me," she says.

"I came back to fix what I broke."

"Knox," she says softly, disbelief in her whisper.

I hate the look in her eyes right now. She doesn't believe me. She doesn't believe I'm in this one hundred percent. "I know you're afraid I'm going to hurt you again."

Her eyes tell me I'm right. "You promised me forever once before. Forever is too big a word."

"Friends with or without benefits is too little," I say.

"You sure you don't just want a sex thing?" she asks with an embarrassed smile.

"This will definitely be a sex thing," I say, capturing her in my arms. "But it's more than that."

"All I can promise is right now," she whispers.

Pulling her to my lips, I kiss her. I'll work on forever later.

CHAPTER FOURTEEN

Mae

He called my bluff last night. There's no way I could ever *just* have sex with someone. It's not who I am. I should've known Knox would know that, too. For one more night with Knox, I would've tried, though.

I would've lost my heart to him again, but it would've been fun. Instead, when he took me to bed, we just talked. He caught me up on his brother, Ryder's, life. I filled him in on what the past five years have been like for me. Work, family, travel—I left out past boy-friends. He didn't need to hear about those epic fails. We could've just as easily been talking into our old cassette recorders. We were just that comfortable with one another.

I fell asleep to him twirling the curly wisps of hair framing my face, and I woke up this morning to his handsome face sharing my pillow. It should've been a romantic moment, but instead, my cell phone rang.

Apparently, the higher ups at the conglomerate that owns our station want a face-to-face with me. My station manager seems to think this is good news, that they want to test my show in new markets. Normally, I'm left to do my own thing. I produce the ratings. They leave me alone, so this meeting is a bit out of the ordinary. But if my station manager isn't worried, then I'm not going to worry, either.

I wish I could say the same for Knox. While taking my work call, he checked his messages. His mailbox was full, and he's been returning calls ever since. He's currently pacing my back porch. From the looks of things, I'm probably going to have to replace a few boards. His hair isn't doing much better; he keeps running his fingers through it over and over again.

He catches my eye through the window, mouthing *sorry* to me, that it's his agent. As far as I'm concerned, he never has to apologize for working hard. Knox is sexy in his own right. There's no denying that. Yes, I'm attracted to his body, those killer eyes, his perfect, full lips, but a man has to be more than a pretty package. He needs to have a brain, a work ethic, a sense of humor. For me, there is nothing sexier than a successful man. And I'm not talking monetary success. I don't care what his job is, as long as he works hard, and takes pride in it. I like a man who isn't afraid to get his hands dirty, who values what he does for a living.

I open the back door, and Knox lifts one arm for me to take my place beside him. I guess that's where he thinks I belong. It's certainly where I feel the most at home, but it's harder to trust someone the second time around.

It was easier to trust when we were kids. This was before he broke my heart, obviously, but kids are just more trusting than adults. Maybe that's because they haven't been hurt—yet. They aren't jaded. Anytime you begin a new relationship, sure, you're cautious, look for red flags, but when you're giving someone a second chance, the red flags are already there. You've already seen them, felt them, lived with the aftermath.

We might wish we could give someone a clean slate, but it's not that easy. That's why I'm going to take this slow with Knox. Things are different now than when we were kids. He's a bonafide movie star. How would this even work? I like my privacy. That guy on my porch last night was nothing. Do I want paparazzi following me, the media critiquing my every move? I've been avoiding the spotlight for years with my radio show. Dating Knox would be the exact opposite of that. My secluded life in my little cottage would be impossible.

So slow is the name of the game.

I'm not talking about the physical part, either. I highly doubt that part is going to go slowly. I'm not stupid, but the rest of it—the feelings portion of this scenario—that's the part where I have to put the brakes on.

A second chance in my bed is one thing. A second chance in my heart . . . that will be much harder for him to win.

I've listened to him on the phone with his agent for half an hour now. Normally, my place is peaceful, looking out on the water, the flowers, but Knox is killing that vibe. At least I got him to stop pacing. We're currently stretched out on the chaise lounge, me between his legs. One hand holds his phone, the other is holding mine. For the most part, I can't hear what's being said—though I do hear the agent saying something about threatening letters. Knox doesn't seem to mind that—he's probably used to it—and is only giving one-word answers, and that word is usually "no." When he starts to playfully ram his head against the back of the chair, I snatch his phone from him.

His blue eyes sparkle as he grins, not at all upset with me. Holding the phone to my ear, I hear some man talking about press junkets.

"I'm sorry," I say. "Knox is busy right now."

"Who the hell is this?" the man barks.

"The woman he's busy with."

"You're just one of many," he says. "Put my client back on the phone."

"No," I say, my heart dropping a little. "Oh yeah, well you're just one of many. A dime a dozen, too."

I hang up, handing the phone back to Knox. He runs his fingers through my hair, pulling me into a kiss, but I don't kiss him back. It's not like I thought Knox has been pining away for me. I know he hasn't. But it's tough to hear what that asshole said. Tough to accept that everyone is going to think of me as one in a long line of women, a passing fancy.

Knox pulls back slightly, searching my eyes. "What did Heath say to you?"

That's Agent Asshole's name! I shrug, sitting up. "Just reminded me that you're no choir boy. Nothing I didn't already know."

His phone rings again, and he turns it off. "You can't hold the past five years against me," he says.

"I know," I say. "It's just the average man has about seven sexual partners in his lifetime, and . . ."

"How do you know that fact right off the top of your head?"

"I do research for my show." Grinning, he motions for me to continue. "I don't need to know your body count or anything like that. It's just, I liked being your first. *Not* your hundred and first."

He takes my hand. I'm not sure if he regrets the way he's conducted his personal life, and I'm not going to ask. God knows, there are men I wish I never dated. Don't think I slept with any of them, though. "You're the first, the best, and how about I make you the last?"

He flashes me that grin that always makes me smile. He's such a smooth talker. "Please tell me I won't be number one hundred on the long list of chicks Knox Merrick has banged?"

"That would mean over the past five years, I'd slept with a new woman . . ." He looks up, doing some quick math in his head. "Every two and a half weeks."

I raise a questioning eyebrow at him. "That's doable."

"Christ, Mae," he says. "I *have* had some long-term relationships."

"Have you at least been a responsible man whore?"

"Of course," he says, releasing a deep breath. "I'm not an idiot."

"Okay," I whisper, slightly relieved he at least has used protection. I'd think most men would avoid this topic at all costs, but his openness brings me some comfort.

"I'm not gonna lie. I want you back in my bed," he says with a devilish grin. The heat in his eyes makes my toes curl. "But I'll wait. I'll wait as long as you need to."

I knew that already, but it's still sweet of him to say it. "It's just . . ."

"You know for someone who makes her living talking, sometimes it's like pulling teeth to get you to open up," he teases.

"I know," I say.

"And I know I hurt you," he says. "We weren't together, but me being with those other women hurt you. If I ever thought I'd have you back in my life, I'd have been celibate!"

I can't help but laugh. "Liar."

He pulls me close. "I'm not. Truth is, I'll wait. We can use condoms. Whatever you want, but you should know that before I do any movie, I have a complete physical. The production companies insist on it. I'm healthy."

"This conversation is about as sexy as a root canal," I tease, but I know it's necessary and responsible, and I appreciate that he's willing to have it.

He tickles me a little. "I can have Heath fax you a copy of my clean bill of health if that will help ease your mind—and, of course, expedite things."

Giggling, I take a few steps off the porch and quietly ask, "Do you have to go back to California?"

"Afraid so," he says, walking with me. "Tomorrow. Lots of press stuff coming up. I'll be going to New York, too, but in between, I'll be here."

I'd be lying if I said that didn't make my heart race with happiness. We're really doing this. Whatever *this* is. And this time, he's a legitimate movie star. God help me!

"I want you to think about coming to the movie premiere with me," he says. "I'll do my best to keep things between us out of the press between now and then, but if you come with me to the opening, that will be announcing to the world that we're together."

"I . . ."

"Think about it," he says, kissing me sweetly. "As soon as the world finds out we're together, your life will change. I need to know you understand that."

"The guy on my porch last night was a dead giveaway."

"It gets crazier than that," he says. "I just want you to know what you get when you sign up to date me. It worries me, bringing you into this."

"Why? You don't think I'll fit in, or are you worried about whether I can handle it?"

"Neither" he says, leaning his head onto mine. "This life, what you've built here. This is so much better than anything waiting for me in L.A."

"You couldn't wait to leave Haven's Point when we were kids."

"Now I don't want to leave," he says, looking into my eyes.

Every cell in my body yells "stay," but my heart overrules everything else. I'm still finding it hard to believe that this is real, and nervous about what the future holds. There are a lot of unknowns here, a lot I could worry about—the press, his past women, our own past—but no amount of worry is going to win with him staring at me like that.

A car horn breaks our connection. Turning, I see Timothy's old blue pickup truck pulling in front of my house. He hops out, sporting his usual beanie, and is followed by Gracie, who starts running toward us, carrying a huge container.

"I tried to call," Timothy says as he walks over to meet us.

"I had a work call this morning," I say, hoping I didn't forget I was supposed to watch Gracie for them. "What are you doing . . ."

"Auntie Mae, I bought bait. Can we go fishing?" Gracie asks.

Timothy gives Knox and me an apologetic smile, running his hand over his daughter's head. "Remember, baby, I told you we weren't staying long."

"But Auntie Mae is the only one who fishes right," Gracie says, her lip in a little pout.

"Honey, I told you I need to talk to Mae then we're leaving."

"I'll take her," Knox says.

"Yay!" Gracie screams.

Timothy starts shaking his head back and forth at a rapid pace. Knox has no idea what he just volunteered for. "Where are your fishing poles?" he asks.

Timothy and I both bust out laughing, knowing what's coming. "No poles," Gracie says, taking his hand. "I'll teach you."

Knox looks back at me as Gracie leads him toward the dock. Smiling, I call out to him, "Good luck."

"We should stay close," Timothy says, taking a few steps in their direction. "Everly sent me over."

"Checking on me," I say.

"She was upset I gave Knox that stuff from when you were younger."

"It's fine," I say.

"No, like *this*," we hear Gracie telling Knox, who is down on one knee, so he's more at her level. Timothy and I continue to observe as Gracie reaches into her container, pulling out one cheese ball, and throwing it into the lake water. "So we don't use poles?" he asks her. "And our bait is a cheese ball?"

He's getting a kick out of her, clearly amused. Gracie doesn't want to hurt the "fishies," as she calls them, so she simply throws the "bait"—in this case, cheese balls—into the water, and waits until she sees a fish come to the surface and starts nibbling on it.

"Well, Everly wanted me to come over and apologize to you."

"Not necessary," I say, bumping his shoulder slightly. Timothy's a good guy. "We're all good."

He gives me a smile, and then we continue to observe the fishermen.

"So what do we do when we see a fish?" Knox asks Gracie. "How do we catch it?"

"Like this," Gracie yells, getting a running start.

"No!" Timothy and I both cry at the same time, but Gracie is already mid-air, cannonballing into the lake.

The first time I took her fishing, she did the same thing. After that, Everly and Timothy made sure she had swimming lessons. She's actually a really good swimmer for her age, but Knox doesn't know that.

Without hesitating at all, he jumps right in after her. The water splashes up on the dock, and Gracie pops up from the water, giggling. "Did you catch the fish?" she asks Knox.

"The fish?" Knox laughs, pulling her into the safety of his arms in the water. "I caught you!"

CHAPTER FIFTEEN

Knox

There's a window at the top of Mae's shower that gives a clear view of the mountains. After fishing with Gracie, I needed to shower off. I like kids. I always have, but that little girl is something else. I doubt you could have a bad day with her around. She's so damn cute, always happy.

I feel the same way around Mae.

Happy.

She makes me so damn happy.

I think the worst shit could be happening around me, and Mae could still make me feel better. Like this morning, with all that work crap, she walked out on the porch, and I instantly felt better. Of course, I'd feel a whole lot better if she was in the shower with me right now. She declined my invitation when I asked her to join me.

Apparently, she needed to get ready to go see her grandmother's performance group. I was advised that I'm expected to attend, as well, which is fine. I'll follow Mae anywhere, but a senior citizen dance crew? This should be interesting.

This is really about Imogen checking up on her granddaughter. I couldn't have produced the movie without her. That woman hangs on to everything—literally. She had a whole lifetime of our memories in an old cedar chest. She threatened me within an inch of my life if I hurt Mae again. Promising her I wouldn't was the easy part, getting her to help me took a little convincing.

Stepping out of the shower, I grab a big white towel Mae laid out for me and start to dry off. The towel reminds me of the ones you get in luxury hotels, thick and full. Something else in this room is thick and full, and the towel isn't doing a damn thing to hide it. Idiot! I could've had her flat on her back last night, but I blew it. I know I did the right thing, though. I want more, but my dick doesn't appreciate my chivalry. The cock is not a noble organ. Selfish, yes. Noble, not so much.

I had my bag with clothes and toiletries in my car, hoping I wouldn't have to stay in a hotel again. It's a pain to have to bribe the managers to keep quiet, sneak around. Plus, I don't usually stay in the same place for more than a night, unless I've made plans in advance. In my mission to get Mae back, I'm flying by the seat of my pants.

Throwing on some clothes and brushing my teeth, I make sure to leave her bathroom as clean as when I entered. This isn't a hotel. She's not my maid. I open the door that leads to her bedroom. She may not be the maid, but I've definitely found maids like this in my hotel rooms before.

She's in her bra and panties. "Oh my God," she cries, reaching for a shirt to cover up, not putting it on, but holding it to her chest, trying to stretch it to conceal more of herself. "Knox, I'm naked!"

Of course, the maids I've found in their underwear didn't protest, and sounded happier to see me. They were always sent on their way.

"Hardly," I say, stalking toward her. "This underwear certainly isn't ugly." And I really hope that means something. She doesn't say a word. I reach out, grabbing the shirt she's using to try to cover herself and toss it aside.

Christ, why did I ever let her get away? She's perfect. Her body is the stuff men go to war over, her curves so dangerous you could easily lose yourself in them for hours. Her pale skin is silky, without a tan line, and she has on the sexiest light blue and white lace panties and bra.

I run my finger under the strap of her bra. "You don't like bras, especially in the summer." Her eyes hold mine, looking surprised I remember that. "Take it off," I say.

She doesn't even pause before reaching around the back and

unhooking it, letting it drop to the floor. I'm much more of an ass man than a tit man, but Mae could convert me. She's not big, but what she does have are round and full and fucking gorgeous. She's completely natural, which I haven't seen in a while, but it's her nipples that fucking slay me. They're hard and erect and begging to be sucked and nibbled on. I know how much she likes that, likes to have them tugged and bitten, how wet that makes her.

"Panties, too," I order. "Off."

Something flashes through her eyes. It's brief, but enough for me to know that, despite what she said last night, she's not completely sure about this.

Leaning into her, I whisper, "I want to be able to slip my finger . . ." I let my finger slide up her inner thigh, just barely toying with the edge of her panties. She grabs my shoulders for support, her legs wobbling. ". . . inside you whenever I want, wherever I want."

Slowly, she bends down, sliding her panties down the smooth skin of her legs. I've barely touched her, but her body's ready. It's her heart I'm worried about.

My dick cursing at me, I say, "Put a dress on. We're going to be late."

Mae squirms in the seat next to mine as we drive through town, crossing and uncrossing her legs over and over again, no doubt trying to quench the desire between them. I'd forgotten how much fun it is to play with her. I place my hand on her thigh, pulling her dress up, so my hand is on her warm skin.

I have the air conditioning on in the car. It is summer, but what Mae hasn't realized is I also have the button pushed that heats her seat. The setting is on low, but enough to do its job. I want heat between her legs. I don't want her desire to die down at all. I want to keep her open and poised, waiting for me.

She spreads her legs apart, letting me know she wants me. I've finger fucked her many times—while driving, in elevators, at the dinner table, in restaurants, but not today. I squeeze her thigh, letting her know I'm not going any higher. She leans her head back on the seat, taking a deep breath. This is what I want—to make her want me so badly she gets out of her own head, forgets any reasons she may think this is a bad idea.

"Why are you teasing me?" she moans.

"Because you like it."

She turns her head to me, smiling, and says, "Payback is a bitch."

Trying not to laugh, I stop in front of the hall where the rehearsal is taking place. I love her. I haven't admitted that to myself since all this started. I haven't let myself think those words, but I know I do. It may seem fast, but the truth is, I never really *stopped* loving her. I just told myself she was someone that I'd forever lost and couldn't have. That didn't make the love go away, it just made it possible to live with.

Sliding my hand up her body to her neck, I pull her to my lips. She's not ready to hear those words from me. If I told her I loved her, I half expect she'd bolt out of the car. So I hope my kiss tells her what I'm feeling.

Her hand on my cheek, she studies my face. "I still can't believe you're really here. That we're . . ." She shakes her head. "Do you feel like that?"

Women always want to talk about feelings. How they feel, how you feel, how they *think* you feel. And the feelings can't ever be simple. Happy, sad, scared, angry? No, they have all these complex emotions, like confused-happy or happy-sad. How are you sad and happy at the same time? Fuck if I know, but apparently, women can feel both simultaneously.

"We never felt over to me," I say. "I always believed someday you'd be back in my life."

"You did not!" she says playfully.

See! I tell her how I feel, and she says I'm wrong. Confusing female! "All those cassette tapes," I say softly. "Those didn't come from Everly or Imogen."

Her blue eyes widen. That little piece of the movie hadn't dawned on her. "You kept them?"

"Every single one," I say.

Her head shakes a little as she looks at me. "Did you ever . . ."

I know what she's asking—if I ever listened to them. "Sometimes," I admit.

Right after our breakup, I packed them away, not listening to them, but then something would remind me of Mae or her birthday would roll around, and I'd find myself longing to hear her voice, and I'd pull one out. You'd think listening to her would make me sad, but it didn't. It was comforting to have that little part of her, of us.

"I never really let you go, Mae. If I did, those tapes would've been tossed off a cliff or burned, but instead, I kept them with me."

She smiles as a tear rolls down her cheek. I catch it with my finger. I guess this is what happy-sad looks like.

~

"He better move his hand!" Mae says under her breath.

I wrap my arms around her from behind to keep her from storming the stage. The Silver Sirens rehearse in a local veterans' hall. There is a stage, dance floor, plenty of room for them to move around. This is just a rehearsal, no audience, so I wasn't expecting the energy to be so high. After all, we are talking about the much older generation. I guess seventy really is the new forty.

We happened to walk in while Mae's grandmother and her partner were practicing a ballroom number. Let's just say, Mae was hoping for a fun Foxtrot, not a sexy Rumba.

"I can tell he has his eyes set on my Gigi," she says, her entire body tense in my arms.

"More like she has her eyes set on him," I say, doing my best to look anywhere else in the room. Two senior citizens grinding against each other is not something I want etched in my brain.

"Gigi loved my granddad," Mae hisses at me. "She would never!"

Apparently, Mae has forgotten her grandfather has been gone for some time now. "Look at them," she whisper-shouts. "They're practically having sex up there." Her eyes grow wide. "You don't think they've actually . . ."

No safe way to answer that question.

"A man his age," I say, trying to shrug it off as not a possibility.

Mae releases a deep breath, the invention of Viagra apparently slipping her mind. Those two are definitely bumping uglies.

"And that costume," Mae says. "She looks naked!"

"I think she looks very elegant," I say. The costume does have a pretty high slit and is low cut, but Imogen can totally pull it off, even at her age. She has the attitude for it.

"Elegant? She might as well be wearing pasties!"

The music ends and a few of the other members clap for them. Mae simply crosses her arms in front of her chest, glaring at the stage. Imogen catches her look, whispering something to her dance partner, who looks our way. Something about him seems familiar, but I can't place it.

"I want proof he's a widower," Mae says to me. "He could be a poser!"

"You think that old dude is pretending his wife died?" I ask, trying not to roll my eyes at the absurdity. Mae flashes me a look like I'm in big trouble.

"What? Gigi has money. Grandad saw to that. She's attractive."

"Please don't ask the poor man to produce a death certificate," I say.

They walk toward us. They're not holding hands. He doesn't even have his hand at the small of her back, but Mae still doesn't offer a smile.

"I'm calling Daddy," Mae whispers as they reach us.

For fuck's sake, she's planning on telling her father that his mother is dating! That should be an interesting phone call.

"How are things here?" Imogen asks as they approach us, her

eyes going back and forth between Mae and me.

I wrap my arm around Mae's waist. "Good. Thanks to your help," I say, since Mae is too busy shooting the death stare at Imogen's partner. Mae's protective side is just as adorable as the rest of her.

"Knox, Mae," Imogen says. "I'd like you to meet Thomas. He's pretty new to the group."

I reach to shake his hand. "You look so familiar," I say.

"I was just thinking the same thing about you, young man," Thomas says.

Imogen laughs. "Thomas used to play football for the Broncos and . . ."

"You did some commentary too, right?" I ask. "I grew up watching you on Monday Night Football." He smiles, shaking my hand. I flash Mae a look. This guy is hardly a gold digger. "Knox Merrick."

"Of course," Thomas says. "The screen actor. Nice to meet you."

His eyes turn to Mae, and I elbow her a little. "I'm Mae," she says. "Gigi is my grandmother."

"Oh, I know," he says. "She never stops talking about you."

"How'd you hear about the group?" Mae asks, digging for information like she's on a recon mission.

"His wife reached out to me," Imogen says, looking up at him.

There is definitely something there. You'd have to be blind not to see it.

"She knew she didn't have long, and she'd seen our group perform somewhere. She reached out and asked me if I'd contact Thomas after she passed. One year after she passed, to be exact."

"Your grandmother kept her promise," Thomas says, lightly touching her arm. "Stuck a brochure in my mailbox."

"That didn't work," Imogen laughs, her whole face lighting up.

"So she stalked me!" he teases.

"Gigi!" Mae cries.

"Not really," Imogen says. "I just happened to show up at his church."

"Sat next to me in the pew," he says. "And practically followed me to my car after until I agreed to come to one practice."

"Gigi always gets what she wants," Mae says, catching her grandmother's eye.

"Well, it was very nice to meet you both," Thomas says. "I should get back to rehearsing. Hopefully, I'll see you again."

"I'm sure you will," Mae says, making them both smile.

Thomas gives Imogen a small wink before walking off. "You could've warned me," Mae says, lightly pinching Imogen's arm.

"And missed your little temper tantrum?" Imogen deadpans. "That was quite exciting."

"She almost demanded a death certificate and proof of his net worth," I laugh.

"Hey, you're supposed to be on my side," Mae says.

"I can kick his butt back to California," Imogen says. "Knox's on *my* side."

Mae takes her grandmother's hand. "You're happy, Gigi? He treats you nice?"

"Very happy," she says. "It almost feels like his wife knew this would happen. And I think your grandfather would like him."

"Okay, then," Mae says, with a nod of approval.

Imogen kisses us both on the cheek before heading over to start practicing again. Then she turns back to Mae. "And don't worry, we're being careful."

"Gigi!" Mae laughs. "I wasn't exactly worried about you showing up pregnant."

"STD's are on the rise in older people. My God, girl, educate yourself," she says with a smile. "That might be a good topic for your show!"

CHAPTER SIXTEEN

Mae

Knox is back on the phone. I get the feeling his "people" aren't happy he's spending so much time in Colorado, but Knox assures me that they all work for him—and that they will just have to deal with it.

It's evening, after what has been a wonderful day together. After visiting Gigi, we just hung out here at my house, ate dinner, talked, kissed. There was nothing glamorous about it. No visits from the press. It was just me and Knox, and it felt perfect. But reality is seeping back in. I can see him through my bedroom door, making sure he has everything in his bag. He's leaving really early tomorrow morning to drive back to Denver to catch a flight back to Los Angeles. It's been a crazy twenty-four hours.

I hate that now he's already making plans to leave.

He'll be back. We aren't sure when, exactly—but just a few days from now. He's hoping Sunday or Monday at the latest. For the next few weeks, this will be our life together, him jetting back and forth. I haven't offered to go with him, and he hasn't asked, other than urging me to think about going to the movie premiere.

I think he wants us to have a few weeks of "normal" before the press gets wind of our relationship, and things get crazy. Which is fine by me. I gave him a key to my place. I'm not sure why, other than it made it feel more real, like some sort of guarantee that he'll be back. I shouldn't have to give him a key to feel that way. His word should be enough, but I've done my radio show long enough to know that long distance is never easy, and second chance romances are even harder.

Gigi looked so happy today. I don't want to think about her having sex with Thomas, but I do like the idea of her not being alone, having a companion. She's got too much life in her to spend it alone. She and I have always been close, but I know it's not the same as sharing your life with someone.

I wonder if I look as happy as she does. Nothing about her or Thomas looked scared or doubtful. They looked content. Do they know something I don't?

They've both lost the loves of their lives, yet here they are, trying again.

It's not the same as Knox and me, but in a way it is. We're trying again, too.

I see him hang up the phone, a deep sigh leaving his chest. He stares down into his duffle bag, like he hates the damn thing, like it's the bag's fault he has to leave. That warms my heart.

"Everything okay?" I ask.

"Nothing for you to worry about," he says. "Some of my fan mail has been strange. It's got my agent worked up."

"Strange how?"

"I haven't seen it," he says, kissing me on the forehead. "Really, don't worry. This has happened before. My agent tends to overreact."

Walking to him, I say, "I wish I could drive you to the airport in the morning or something."

"I have the rental. Plus, I don't want you to have to get up," he says, taking my hand. "I don't like to think about you driving those winding roads all alone."

"I do it all the time," I say, then tease, "you might be a leading man, but I don't need you to rescue me."

"Still, I'm hiring you a driver," he laughs, taking me down to the bed. "I don't want to think about leaving you right now."

His lips land on mine. This kiss is a journey, like our relationship. It starts off slow, like when we were little, building up over time. The years we spent apart, growing up. Then it erupts into when we fell in love. Without warning, he breaks apart from me—abruptly, like we ended—and looks deep into my eyes. Then it begins all over again—where we are now—starting over.

A popular topic on my show is how to know, be sure it's the right time to begin an intimate relationship with a new partner. That's always a hard one to answer, mostly because it's so personal. Some advice is just universal, like don't cheat. Duh, that's a no brainer. But when to take the leap into a sexual relationship isn't so straight forward, probably because there's more than just the brain involved. You could make a pro/con list until the cows come home, but at the end of the day, it's a feeling. Now, that could mean something you feel in your heart, or it could be something you feel with an organ a little lower—but either way, when you know, you know.

I place my hand on his face, feeling his stubble beneath my fingers. "If we do this now," I say softly, "I'll wake up to an empty bed in the morning."

"In that case," he says with a million-dollar smile, "I'll wake you up before I leave."

"Or you could just keep me up all night," I say, my voice flirty.

"I like the way you think," he says, pinning me to the bed with his hips.

The fabric of my dress is thin. The fabric of his jeans is rough, giving me the perfect amount of friction. I feel my muscles clench, begging for him. But I know Knox. Unless we're in public, he likes my pleasure to be long, intense.

My mother used to tell me that you shouldn't have sex with someone unless you're prepared to be bound to them for life. An unwanted pregnancy could certainly tie you to someone else, but she said there was more to it than that. She used to tell me that when you have sex with someone, they become part of your story. Whenever you have to share your sexual history with a new partner or your doctor, that person is present in your story. She would warn that, even if you don't remember their name, they become a part of you, your life's history.

Knox is already a part of my history—a huge part of it. Now he's also my present. Will he be my future?

When you sleep with someone for the first time, there's excitement and usually a few nerves. How will things go? Will it be good? Will I satisfy my partner? Will they like how I look naked? Did I shave? Those kinds of things.

I know the answer to those questions with Knox, but I still feel the same butterflies, a mixture of nerves and excitement. And I'm glad we had a truthful conversation about his past relationships. Honestly, I wouldn't be on my back right now if we hadn't. That talk needed to happen.

Knox sits back on his heels and takes my hand, encouraging me to sit up. His eyes lock on mine as he slowly lifts my dress over my head. Per his request, I don't have anything on under my dress. Tossing it to the floor, he lightly kisses my lips until I'm flat on my back again.

His fingers lightly go through my hair as he whispers, "Do you want me to use a . . ."

Shaking my head, I pull him into a kiss and whisper, "You, just you."

He leans back slightly, his eyes roaming my body. I love the way he looks at me, like I'm the most beautiful woman in the world. That look is why he's a box office phenomenon.

"I don't know where to start," he says, his voice low. I reach for the button on his jeans, knowing exactly where I want him to start and finish. He smiles down at me, liking my impatience. "We'll get there, I promise. But first . . ."

His fingers trace my collarbone lightly, making my body quiver. Five minutes naked with Knox is already better than any sex I've had in the past five years, and he's barely touched me. "Knox," I beg.

"Yes, baby," he whispers against my neck.

All I can do is moan softly in response, my body a tight ball of need that only he can unwind. His hand slides down my torso to the small tuft of hair between my legs. I haven't dated in a while, which means I haven't waxed in a while. Things are still in good shape, mind you, but I'll admit that I was better groomed when Knox and I were dating.

He gives it a gentle tug, making me whimper a little. "This stays," he orders.

"Yes," I groan as he tugs again. On instinct, my legs fall open, inviting him. Heck, they're practically begging for him. I can feel my wetness, how open I am. It hurts in the best possible way, and I know I'm with a man who can take it away.

Without warning, he gives me a little smack right between my legs. I cry out, the base of his hand hitting my clit, his fingers tapping my opening. "More!" I cry breathlessly.

For a second, he's stunned, pulling back slightly. I never asked for anything in bed before, I simply waited for him to give it to me. And he always did. I was never left unsatisfied, but the past five years without him changed me. I learned to ask for what I wanted, knowing I wouldn't get it otherwise.

My eyes fly to his, and I find him grinning down at me. He doesn't mind my request at all. His finger outlines my folds, opening me wider, but his finger doesn't invade me. "Don't worry," he whispers. "More is coming."

He starts to kiss my neck, the whole time his finger toying with me. I've never wanted something inside me so much. I start to move, to try to position myself to push his finger inside, but he simply chuckles at me.

"Do I need to tie you up to get you to behave?"

"Knox!"

He raises his head, a sexy smirk on his face. I'd almost forgotten how fun he is in bed. We laugh as much as we fool around. I like a little rough play as much as the next girl, but that's all it ever is—play. He might spank me, tie me up, but it's never as punishment. It's always for pleasure, both mine and his.

"It's been five years," he says. "Let me take my time."

God, he's sweet. I toss my hands up over my head, like I'm submitting to him. "I'm yours."

"Yes, you are," he growls, gently biting my nipple.

The pleasure shoots right between my legs. A woman's breasts are the most under-utilized sexual organ on her body. Men are so obsessed with them, but put a pair in front of their faces and most of them are struck dumb, like boobs are hypnotic or something.

Knox, however, knows exactly what he's doing. I let him suck, bite, and lick one while his hand works the other. The muscles between my legs clench hard, over and over. The only thing I can think about is how badly I want to come. He hooks his finger around my nipple, giving it a little tug. My back arches, wanting it harder. He knows exactly what I need, sucking down on me, pulling my nipple between his teeth.

Just when I think I can't wait one more second, he gives me another little smack between my legs. "Ahh!" I cry out, my orgasm so close.

My body starts trembling. "Shh, baby!" he whispers, his kisses lighter now, trailing down my body. When he reaches my belly button, he stops, pulling his shirt over his head and tossing it aside.

His tan, broad shoulders over me, I watch his head slip lower and lower. I like sex. A man's hands, his penis—I like it all, but oral sex is my favorite. When you have a man that knows what he's doing, it's almost addictive. And Knox knows what he's doing.

I used to tease him that I taught him everything he knows. Basically, we taught each other, but make no mistake, the man has innate talent with his tongue.

I feel his warm breath. My eyes close, waiting for the first feel of his mouth. He starts with a light kiss.

One.

Two.

Three.

His tongue slips deep inside me on the count of four. "God!" I groan, tightening around him, relief flooding my body at finally having a part of him inside me.

He hikes my thigh up on his shoulder, deepening his kiss, his hand reaching up and finding my breast, teasing my nipple.

"I love your pussy," he whispers, continuing his assault on me.

When some men try to talk dirty in bed, it feels wrong, like it's unnatural for them, but dirty talk is Knox's second language, and it only makes me hotter.

"I'm going to eat until you come," he growls.

I spread my legs wider, letting him know that's exactly what I want. He sucks hard on me while his tongue does this circle thing. Forget the alphabet technique, whatever the hell he's doing is next level.

The tension in my body builds, my hands gripping the bedsheets. The only thought I can hold in my head is how much I need this. At this point, it's a need, not a want. I need him to finish me like I need air in my lungs.

He starts moving faster, never losing suction, his tongue continuing to stroke me. I feel myself building, more and more, and then my vision goes totally white as I explode around his expert mouth.

Still trembling from my orgasm, he quickly undoes the button of his jeans, flips me over, giving my ass a hard smack before he unapologetically rams inside me.

He pounds into me, taking me, claiming me as his. And I quickly come again—hard and long—but he doesn't slow down. He's getting five missed years of fucking out in this one session.

He spanks my ass again. "More," he demands, reaching under me and stroking my clit. "Come again."

I'm not sure how, but my body responds to his call. That familiar sensation of need rolls through me.

"That's my girl," he says. He slows down a bit, slipping himself in and out of me. His fingers trace my spine, and I arch my back.

On my knees and elbows, I rock back on him. "Fuck," he groans. "Pull my cock." I do as he asks, tightening all around him, giving him what he wants. "Christ, baby, you feel good," he says.

Suddenly, I don't care about finishing again. I could, but I don't care. I only care about his pleasure. Reaching under us, I give his balls a gentle tug. I feel him tense up, but he doesn't let go, refusing to leave me with anything left. His hand starts to move faster across my clit, circling me.

I continue to stroke him, hearing him cursing under his breath. It's now a race to the finish. It's only when I fly over the line that he follows along behind me.

We're naked in bed, smiling, staring at each other. Neither of us ever thought we'd be like this again. Every other woman in the world would probably be calling her girlfriends right now, bragging that she banged a movie star, but that's not who Knox is to me. He's my childhood friend, my college sweetheart, the man who taught me what real love feels like.

I have no idea what time it is, and I don't want to know. I don't want the morning to come, for him to leave. I'm just going to enjoy him, in these hours while they last.

"I need that ass," he says, running his hand across my bare bottom.

This is one point of contention in our sexual history. He wanted to claim all of me, but I'm an exit-only kind of girl. Laughing, I buck my hips a little, my version of *no way in hell.* I'm on my belly, so I lean up on one elbow to look at him resting alongside me. "Still haven't changed my mind about that."

He rolls me to my side, his dick finding his home buried deep inside me.

"Again?" I playfully protest.

"We don't have to do anything," he says. "Just let me feel you."

There's a lot of sides to Knox, but his sweet one is the one I first fell in love with. His hand strokes my face, brushing my hair behind my ear, playing with the few curls. He follows the path of my body, down my breasts to my waist, hips, and thighs. I feel his dick twitch inside of me, coming alive.

I run my fingers through his dark blonde hair, down to the stubble on his handsome face. He's finally naked, too impatient the first time to fully undress. His body is even better than before—broader, stronger. He's one hundred percent muscle, with that perfect v-cut that leads to the promised land.

He hikes my leg up to his hip, cupping my booty in his hand. His blue eyes sparkle, and I wonder what he's thinking. Even though I've known him most of my life, he still surprises me.

"It feels the same," I whisper. "Like we haven't spent a day apart."

His dick pulses again, making me moan a little. "It does."

Our hips grind against each other, slowly. He wants to make sure I feel every single long inch of him. I grab his shoulder, feeling the desire in the pit of my belly. He runs his fingers through my hair, gazing at me, then moves his finger to my lips, parting them.

I slip his finger between my teeth, teasing him, sucking him. He spent considerable time on me, but I haven't returned the favor yet. This is a promise that I will. He flashes me a naughty look, and I think it's because he knows what I'm thinking.

But when he moves his hand to my ass, I realize he had something else in mind. As avid listeners of my show know, I've had guys try to slip their fingers in my ass before. That was always a buzz kill. I even had one poor guy tell me he missed my hole. If his sense of direction was that bad, he needed to go, and if he was lying, then he's a jerk.

Knox clearly knows what he's doing. He watches my eyes. He'll stop as soon as I ask, or show any signs of discomfort.

"I need to know you're all mine," he whispers.

What the hell? Why not? It's just a finger. And if anyone could make this enjoyable, I know it's Knox. I give him a little nod.

He holds my eyes, not allowing me to look away. His hips move slowly, his dick hitting just the right spot. "Focus on my cock," he whispers. "How good it feels."

I try, but as soon as I feel his finger poised at my entrance, I tense, and he senses it.

He kisses me softly, keeping his finger still, just barely applying pressure. "My cock, your pussy," he says softly. "Me fucking you."

"Mmm," I say, repeating his words in my head.

"I've fantasized about you over the years," he says, slipping his dick in and out of me.

"Me, too," I say.

"When you touch yourself?" he asks.

"Yes," I whisper, my breath growing ragged.

"Will you let me watch you?" he asks. "When I'm away, will you fuck yourself and let me watch?"

"Yes," I say.

"Fuck, that makes me hard," he says, and I feel proof of what he is saying, his dick growing firmer and longer inside of me. He leans over, giving my breast a lick. "Touch yourself now."

I follow his command and reach up, playing with my nipple, feeling the wetness between my legs growing.

"I'm going to have to eat that pussy one more time before I go," he says through gritted teeth. "Will you let me?"

"Yes," I moan loudly, as he pushes his finger in. My eyes flash wide. Have I just lost my last virginity? Does this mean I'm not an anal virgin anymore? Do fingers count? His hips keep rolling into mine. "Oh!" I bite down on my bottom lip, grabbing his shoulder.

With his finger in my ass and his dick inside me, everything is that much tighter, that much more intense. My muscles convulse, over and over again. I can't control it.

"Fuck, baby," he growls.

I start moving faster. It feels good, like nothing I've ever felt before. Forbidden and dirty, and I'm dripping. He pushes with his finger, and I swear it's like he's pushing right on my G-spot. The words that come out of my mouth aren't even English—a series of moans, half curse words. I can't control myself. I come so hard that I pull his orgasm right out of him.

I nuzzle into his chest, listening to his pounding heart settle. With each beat of his heart, I make a wish. One beat—for time to stop. Another beat—that it will always be like this. Another beat—for this to last forever.

"I guess you liked that," he teases. Feeling my face heat, I look up at him. He rests his forehead on mine, saying, "I can't leave in a few hours."

"My ass is that good," I tease.

He grins. "Your ass is that good."

"You have to go?" I ask in a whisper.

He only nods. "In the contract."

"We have our own contract," I flirt. "Involving you having me for breakfast and phone sex."

CHAPTER SEVENTEEN

Knox

Getting off the plane in L.A. is like walking into the gates of hell. The paparazzi are always camped out, waiting to catch a glimpse of some unsuspecting "celebrity."

Celebrity—what a bullshit word.

Fame—another bullshit word.

V.I.P.—even bigger bullshit.

I'm an actor, an entertainer. I'm not saving the fucking planet. There's nothing noble in what I do. I try to use the money I make for good, to fund various charities, that kind of thing. I support a lot of cancer charities because of my mom, and set up a few scholarships for kids who have lost a parent to cancer. Special needs causes are also important to me, things that would benefit kids like Gracie. But I avoid giving to any political causes. For the life of me, I've never figured out why anyone would care who an actor is voting for. It's not like we're political experts, for fuck's sake.

"Celebrity" is fleeting. I know that. Very few people can hold their A-list status for life. And frankly, I'm not sure why you'd want to. There are far more important things than being recognized on the street.

Like love.

Like family.

Mae.

There's an hour time difference between Haven's Point and Los Angeles. I left really early, and she was cuddled under the covers when I kissed her goodbye. I'm hoping she finally went to sleep after

I kept her up all night. It was fun.

Mae and I have had some epic nights together, but last night is definitely up there. It wasn't just the sex, although she's still the hottest woman I've ever had the pleasure of sharing a bed with. It was more than that. She makes me smile and laugh like I haven't in a long time.

I always have a smile for the cameras. It's my actor smile. The one that says I don't have a care in the world. The fake one—the one I have on my face right now as I step off the plane. It doesn't matter how much money or fame I have, that doesn't equal happiness. Mae equals happy.

Carrying my duffle bag, I put on my sunglasses. It's usually sunny in California, but it's not the brightness of the morning sun I'm worried about. It's the blinding flash of cameras being shoved in my face.

I flew on a private plane to avoid the chaos at LAX, but that won't shield me completely. They've caught on to that trick, now staking out the smaller landing strips, as well, armed with cameras and recorders and ready to strike as soon as they catch a glimpse of some celebrity—or you drive by them in your car.

The pilot, flight attendant, and crew all know not to ask for pictures or autographs. They've all signed non-disclosure agreements. Otherwise, everyone in the free world would know I've been back to my hometown several times. It helps that Haven's Point isn't a hotbed of the entertainment world, either.

I'm not sure how long I can keep my relationship with Mae under wraps. So far, it's been pretty easy to sneak in and out of Colorado. Reporters may see me take off in L.A., but they don't know my destination. And the Denver airport isn't exactly covered with reporters. Flying on private planes helps keep my comings and goings hidden. I don't know how long that will last, but for now, it's working.

I've had a lot of practice sneaking around in the past, but I don't want to stifle Mae like that. I don't want to tell her that I can't go to

The Tune Up with her, or see her crazy grandmother dance because we'll be followed and harassed.

But there is a price I pay to have this life, to do what I do. I'm not complaining. I made my choice, but I'm not sure Mae fully understands just how different a life with me would be. There is an ugly side to fame, to celebrity. Being recognized in public, hounded for pictures, and the total lack of privacy are just the tip of the iceberg. Then there are the stalkers and crazy letters from deranged people. None of that has forced me to travel around with security, though—I don't want that. Still, most days, it's worth it. I have a great life, but other days, it sucks. It's a tradeoff, but it's not one I'm totally sure Mae wants to make, and I'd be lying if I said that doesn't concern me.

Staring down at my phone, I ignore all the emails, the dozens of texts from co-stars, producers, and the like. I'm only checking to see whether Mae has reached out.

Nothing. Maybe that means she's sleeping.

I walk to the car outside waiting for me, seeing a few scumbag reporters snapping pics. It's normal for me to have a car service from the airport to my house, but today, my agent, Heath, is picking me up. I think it's his way of making sure I actually made the flight and came back home.

Heath sometimes forgets I'm *his* boss.

It's a private fucking plane. I'm the only passenger. I doubt they would've taken off without me.

I take a deep breath, knowing as soon as I open the car door, it's going to begin—the rush, the stress, the demands on my time. I like acting, making movies, but I hate the rest of it—all the marketing and bullshit that comes along with it. As I see it, my job is to produce a good product. I want no part of the movie world after production wraps. It doesn't always work that way, though. There are teams of marketing executives, publicists, research analysts, test audiences. None of that is my focus. At least, I don't want it to be. I want my focus on perfecting my craft.

But I've become a commercial product—a mechanism to sell tickets, put asses in seats.

What people fail to realize is, I'm one person. Yes, I'm often the face on the movie poster, the star of the show, but there are literally hundreds of people that bring that character to life—costumers, lighting crew, directors, prop makers, craft service, sound crew, producers, directors. It's a team effort. I couldn't do what I do without them.

If you've ever been on a movie set, you'd know. That chase scene where I ran up the stairs took two hours to get right—two hours to get *ten seconds* of film. I spend the ten seconds running, but there are a team of people setting up that shot, making sure it's just right.

Making a movie can actually be kind of boring at times. There's a lot of sitting around and waiting. The editors are really the ones that pull the movie together, make you laugh, cry, or scream. All these people make me look good. I'm grateful for that.

A rush of cool air hits me as I open the car door, the air conditioning on full blast. Central California doesn't get that hot, so I'm assuming the air is to compensate for Heath's stress level.

The driver pulls away, and some paparazzi give chase. There are always one or two at minimum. That's just another reason why being in Haven's Point has been so nice. It's a break from the chaos.

"Ryder's been at it again," Heath says, tossing me the most recent photos of my big brother. These show him shoving a reporter who got in his face.

"It's not like they haven't been warned," I say. "They know how Ryder is. They do it on purpose to get a response."

"Talk to him," Heath says. "This kind of shit hurts your reputation, too."

I just nod. Ryder doesn't take advice from me. I can talk until I'm blue in the face. Besides, I agree with him. Most of those guys are scum. I just choose to handle them differently.

Heath launches into my schedule—interviews, topics to avoid, clothes fittings—but it's nothing I actually need to know. The car will shuttle me from one event to the next. I'm literally just along for the ride today. Heath will tell me what to do, where to be. A trained monkey could do it.

My phone dings. Heath continues to talk, and I open a text from Mae. It's a picture of her with the covers pulled all the way up covering everything but her beautiful blue eyes.

Mae: *My spot for the day. I'm too sore.*

She ends it with a little wink face emoji. A big fucking grin on my face, I type a response.

Me: *I did my job well then.*

Mae: *Oscar worthy.*

"Who's the woman?" Heath asks.

Damn it! I can't have any privacy. Quickly, I turn my phone over.

"Just wondering if I need to get the ball rolling on you two going public, security for her. That kind of thing."

"I'll let you know," I say.

"Where's your security?" he asks.

That doesn't deserve a response. We've talked about this a million times. I'm a grown man, and I'm not the President of the United States. I'm not traveling with a security detail. There are times when security is a necessary evil—red carpets, for example. My houses all have state of the art security systems, but I'm not willing to be followed around. I can take care of myself.

"We've gotten a few more letters," Heath says, showing me the latest.

I get a shit ton of fan mail. There's a team of people that sort through it and pass the letters on to me, if they find something particularly special. Most of the time, they send a stock letter with a copy of my signature. Most of the letters I receive are harmless, but there is the occasional nutjob that requires my team to get the authorities involved. They also track letters by zip code to try to identify potential stalker tendencies. It happens, I know it happens. I know fellow actors who've had their houses broken into, been held up, received death threats. I've been pretty fortunate where my fans are concerned, but that doesn't stop my team from freaking the fuck out every time a woman sends me a lock of her hair. Yep, that's happened. And panties are a regular offering, too.

Heath lives in fear that my luck in these matters will one day run out. I can't live like that. I keep my life pretty low key, not partying at the latest hot spot or doing reality television. That's never been my scene. Hunting for attention and fame isn't why I do what I do.

"Colorado," he says, pointing to the postmark. "All of those are from Colorado. Which has raised some red flags, since you've been spending so much time there."

I shrug. "That's probably why."

"How much do you know about this woman you're seeing?" Heath asks.

"Trust me, it's not her," I say with a laugh.

He throws a Ziplock in my lap, a typed letter inside. "You should read this one."

I look down at it, seeing the heading. "A thank you note?"

"Just read it," Heath says.

My eyes roam over the words. I read lots of scripts. I've gotten good at knowing good writing, what will move people. A few lines into this "thank you note," and my blood runs cold, the hair on the back of my neck standing up. No threat was made. But it sure as hell is implied.

Still, it's not enough for me to turn my life upside down. It's one letter.

"Heath, we've been through this before. It always turns out to be nothing."

"I'm telling you this feels different."

"How?"

"For one, it's typed."

"You're telling me I've never gotten a typed fan letter?"

He rolls his eyes at me. "Most stuff that comes in the mail is handwritten. You know, cards and stuff. But it's not just that. There's no request for pictures or an autograph. The strangest thing is, there's no return address, no signature. Nothing. Most fans want an acknowledgement, even if it's the stock letter we usually provide, so they include their return address, at a minimum."

I clench my fists then let out a deep breath. I'm coming off a great visit with Mae. This is the last thing I want to deal with, to talk about. But I know Heath isn't going to be brushed aside this time. He can be like a dog with a bone.

"Just keep an eye out," I say. "Let me know if I get any other letters like this one."

He nods then gives me a nosy smile. "So do I know her? This woman who has you flying back and forth to Colorado every other day. Is she an actress or. . .?"

"No," I say. "She's not in the business."

"Normal, average woman? That's not your usual type."

"There's nothing average about her," I quickly say.

"Can I at least know her name?"

"Her name is Mae Sheridan," I say. "We've known each other since we were kids."

"Okay," he says. "First up today is an interview, then wardrobe fittings for the rest of the press junket."

~

The only good thing about wardrobe fittings is not having to step foot inside a store. Having someone bring racks of clothes to your home is certainly not one of the downsides to fame. I hate shopping for clothes or shoes or . . . come to think of it, I don't remember the last time I even went shopping. I've got a stylist that brings me clothes. I have an assistant that does the grocery shopping. My cars were purchased over the phone. I guess the last thing I shopped for was this house, which is hardly the same thing. I haven't been inside a mall in I don't know how long.

Not that I want to go to the mall, but it's just not feasible. I've seen fans get pushed and shoved to the ground when a crowd gets too large. That's the last thing I want, so this kind of thing is a necessity. I would, however, prefer to select my own clothing. Of course, then I'd never wear anything other than jeans and t-shirts.

"Leather jacket or blazer?" the stylist, Brynn, asks. Only she's not asking me. She's asking everyone's opinion but mine. There's a virtual army standing by to decide which jacket will look better on camera, which will photograph better, what kind of lighting there will be in the interview room. My opinion on the subject doesn't matter. And it's not her fault. Brynn has worked with me a long time. She's knows I'd rather be left out of these discussions. And she knows what I like, what I'm comfortable in, so normally it's a pretty easy process.

Press junkets work like this—I'll be in a room, usually at a hotel or some neutral location, and every entertainment source under the sun will come in and ask me the same questions over and over again. Some of the bigger magazines or entertainment shows will get exclusives, insider information, maybe even come to my house, or I'll appear on their morning or late-night television shows. I need wardrobe for all that. Why I can't wear the same thing all day makes no sense to me. It's exhausting, but through it all, I'm expected to be charming and energetic, excited about the movie even if I didn't like how it turned out, not letting on about the post-production prob-lems, the infighting among the actors, the blowjob the director got from the craft service guy, and whatever else.

I pull out my phone and text Mae.

Me: *Big debate at the moment. Leather jacket or blazer?*

I see the little bubbles pop up to indicate that she's responding. I'm anxious to end this circus and talk to her, find out about her day, see if she is still in bed. Of course, her promise to let me watch her get herself off is also a motivating factor—and I'd like to see that sooner rather than later. But it's more than that.

Mae: *Shirtless!*

"Knox?" Heath says, his voice louder than normal, letting me know he's repeating himself.

"It's summer. Why do I need a jacket?" I ask.

My comment starts a flurry of discussion. Will I look too relaxed without one or the other? Does a jacket indicate I'm trying to hide something? Is a blazer too formal? How cold will the hotel room be?

For fuck's sake!

With the debate raging on, Heath steps closer to me, leaning in. "I need to know about the premiere. Are you bringing a date? Who? Do I need to arrange a dress for her? Is your brother making an appearance? The usual."

"I'm working on it," I say, turning back to my phone.

I'm not going to bring it up to Mae again so soon. I told her to think about it, and I want her to. I don't want to rush her. Sure, I might have pressed fast forward on the sex thing, but she didn't seem to mind. I'm not going to rush the rest of it.

Love can't be rushed. You can fall fast, or you can fall slow, but you can't force it.

What is love?

Is love *swinging from the chandelier* sex?

I hope so.

But is it more than that?

Is love up all night talking?

Is it someone who makes you laugh?

Is it someone who you can cry with?

Does it need a happily ever after?

Or is happy right now good enough?

Is it all of these things, or just some of them?

Is love different for every person?

Are the ingredients that one person needs to fall in love different from those of another person?

Three parts sex, one part talking, with a dash of laughter and boom, you're in love?

Movies would have us believe that love is about happiness, joy, all the good moments in life. But I think love is about the negative shit, too—anger and grief and sadness. Love is about those things. That's when love is its most powerful.

Maybe it's not about what love is, but about what it *isn't*.

Love isn't quitting.

Maybe that's all there is to it. Love is sticking it out no matter what. Love is never walking away. I learned that the hard way five years ago.

"Suit! Navy!" Brynn says, with a clap of her hand. "Yes, classic. You can never go wrong with a suit."

I pull up Mae's text. No doubt, she is the love of my life.

Me: *I'm in clothing hell!*

Mae: *Sinning can be fun!*

CHAPTER EIGHTEEN

Knox

"Put the phone between your legs," I say.

"I'm not doing that!" Mae laughs.

"You promised you'd let me watch you."

"I just did," she says, her head resting on her pillow.

Through my phone, I see she's laying on her side, her brown hair falling all around. When I suggested she let me watch her girl's night in, I was expecting a little less face time and a lot more body. She barely gave me a glimpse of her tits. Sitting on my balcony, I feel so far away from her. Sexy calls are fun, but it's not the same thing as being there. I didn't even join in the fun. I watched her, talked dirty to her, but if I can't have *her*, I certainly don't want my damn hand.

"You know you like my head between your . . ."

"Oh my God! Shut up!" she laughs out.

"At least put on some of that ugly underwear of yours and send me a pic," I tease.

"Maybe," she says, smiling.

"Did you finish the movie we started the other night?" I ask.

"Yeeeeeeeah, about that," she says, drawing out the first word.

"That doesn't sound good," I say, pacing my balcony. "I guess you didn't like it."

"Am I allowed to say I didn't?"

This is sensitive terrain we are entering. No one likes to have their work criticized. Unfortunately, having a career in the arts is setting yourself up for it. You can't please everyone, but Mae's opinion is important to me. I want her approval and support more than anyone's, so it's going to be damn hard to hear her criticism.

"You can say whatever you want," I say, taking a deep breath and bracing for impact.

"You won't get mad?" she asks.

"I can't promise that," I say. "But I'll try."

"I couldn't finish it," she whispers.

It's not my favorite film of the ones I've made, but to DNF it? Damn! The back of my neck suddenly feels hot, a sure sign I'm getting really pissed. "Maybe we shouldn't talk about this."

"Every time you kissed her . . ." Mae looks away, her eyes no longer staring into the phone. "I was holding it together until the sex scene. I just couldn't watch anymore."

A part of me is relieved her issue wasn't with my performance, but another part of me is concerned. Romance hasn't factored a great deal into my movies. I've never done a romantic comedy, and I don't care to. It's just not where my interest lies. But there are times when I do intimate scenes. And usually, my co-star is hot, but filming those parts of a movie is anything but. It's weird to have people watching, yelling directions at you, telling you where to place your leg. And sometimes, these scenes can be shot early on in a movie, before you even get comfortable with your co-star. I've literally met my co-star and done a sex scene the same day. Nothing hot about that.

"How about the movie where I got beat to hell? Could you watch that one?" I ask, trying to lighten things up.

"I had no problem with that," she says, smiling shyly.

"You know it's just acting, right?"

"I couldn't do that," she says. "I couldn't just kiss someone I felt nothing for. Lay naked with someone I wasn't attracted to, so I don't understand, I guess."

"Mae," I say, looking up at the night sky. "When we were together, you saw me do plenty of plays with kissing scenes. It never bothered you then."

"We don't need to talk about this," she says. "I shouldn't have brought it up."

"Yes, we do," I say. "Where is this all coming from?"

I see her take a deep breath. "Five years of you fucking anything that moves. Those pictures after we broke up. It's like a slap in the face."

And hearing that's like a punch to my stomach. I didn't have sex with those women to hurt her. Mae wasn't in my life then, but I'm still paying for it.

"We talked about this. I thought we moved past it."

"What are we doing, Knox?" she asks.

"Things were fine when I left," I say. "Hell, they were fine five minutes ago. Where is this coming from?"

"I guess it's easier to think straight when you aren't here," Mae says. "And there are reasons . . ."

"You mean it's easier for you to talk yourself out of this when I'm not there," I say, staring down at my phone screen, determined.

"We don't even live in the same state," she says.

"I'm only a few hours away by plane."

"But you work all over the globe. I'm happy here in my little corner of the world."

"I control what projects I take. How long I have to be gone. It's not like it was when I started out. I can be picky. Do what I want. You'll see."

"We spent so much time apart when we were kids. It seems like our lives always take us in different directions. I like my privacy. You live your life under a microscope. No one really even knows what I do for a living. We live totally different lives."

"You're thinking about this way too much," I say.

"There are more reasons for us not to work this time than there were last time, and we crashed and burned."

"I don't get where all this is coming from. We said we'd take things slow. Day by day. You watch one of my movies that happens to have a sex scene, and suddenly you're backtracking."

"I know what I said," she says.

"Just tell me what's bugging you," I say gently.

"I know you're busy, and I'm not going to make demands on your time, but . . ."

"You don't need to demand my time," I say. "I want to be with you *all the time.*"

"Knox," she says in a sweet whisper.

"What is it you want?" I ask, taking a seat on a lounge chair. "Make your demands."

"I only have one," she says.

"Okay."

"No other women. Just don't humiliate me like that."

The fact that she thinks she even has to ask that of me is bullshit. She should know better. Anger burns in my chest. It's all I can do not to rip her a new one for saying that to me, but then I look into my phone, at her blue eyes staring back at me, like she honestly believes I might deny her. I knew I hurt her, but it's not until this moment that I realize just how bad, just how humiliated she was when I jumped into another woman's bed so quickly. And it's not just that. I kept jumping from woman to woman for the next five years. This is why the sex scene bothered her. It reminded her of seeing those pictures of me with someone else just weeks after we broke up.

I release the breath I'd been holding and my anger along with it. "That's not a demand," I tease. "That's a given."

"Okay," she whispers.

"My turn," I say, relieved.

"Your turn for what?"

"I have some demands for you," I tease.

Smiling, she rolls her eyes. "Of course you do."

"First, I demand that sexy pic you promised."

CHAPTER NINETEEN

Mae

The radio station is like a second home to me. It's comfortable, relaxed, casual—even more so when I come in late on Sunday nights, when there's usually not so many people around. It's often just me, Amy, a few randoms, but that's it.

Not today, though.

I'm not used to being here in the middle of the day on a weekday. There's a lot of hustle and bustle, much more of a corporate culture. I don't know any of these people, and they don't know me. Because I work nights and it's important my identity doesn't get out, I'm not part of the "in" crowd here at the station.

It's a radio station, not an office building, so there aren't fancy boardrooms to house meetings. There is one conference room, if you can even call it that. It's got a long table, a coffee pot, telephone, and a smart board, but that's it. There aren't even any windows. It's pretty sad as far as meeting rooms go, and I'm sure it's a far cry from what the big wigs coming to see me are accustomed to.

Our little radio station is owned by a corporation which owns lots of smaller radio stations. Together, we form a force to be reckoned with on the airways. We are just a small slice of a huge pie, but I know my show makes up a big percentage of our market share. I may not care to know the number of people tuning in to my show each week, but I sure as hell know what my advertisers pay between the hours of ten and midnight on Sundays. It's not Super Bowl numbers, but advertising during my show will cost you big time. That tells me all I need to know.

I swirl my chair around, my legs sticking to the fake leather on the seat. I might be a little nervous. I wore my best *don't mess with me* outfit. A black pencil skirt and a vintage Chanel shirt that was my mother's. She found it in a flea market just outside Paris. Supposedly, it was discarded by Coco herself, or so the merchant told my mother. That would make the shirt at least fifty years old, but I don't care. I need the power of Coco and my mother today. I don't have a good feeling about this, or maybe that's just the nerves talking.

The door opens. One look at my station manager's face as he walks past the open door, and I know my gut is right. But I don't know what the problem could be. My shows have been great lately. I know when I'm off, when I have a bad show, but I haven't had that feeling lately.

Two suits walk in. Both women.

I hate to judge, but I know women like this. I've seen their kind before. I'm not sure they are women. More like trained assassins, ready to strike you down. They smile in their designer shoes and handbags, but behind your back, you know they've been talking about you.

I get to my feet, peeling my legs from the fake leather, and reach out to shake each of their hands. One has her hair in a tight bun, and the other is well over six feet in stilettos. They each tell me their names, but I forget as soon as we sit down. I'm terrible at names, and that only gets worse when I'm nervous.

I shouldn't be nervous, but I'm outnumbered, and I'm better one on one. Always have been. Maybe that's because I spent so much time alone as a child. I think that's why I like doing radio so much, it's just me and my caller. Or at least, I can pretend it is.

Tight Bun starts. "Your contract with the station is expiring at the end of the year."

I hadn't even thought about that. Renewal seemed a foregone conclusion, but maybe I was wrong.

"So we thought this might be a good time to remind you of a key point in your contract. Anonymity."

"I'm the one who put that in the contract," I tell her, "so I don't need to be reminded of it."

"Apparently, during a broadcast a few weeks ago, a caller used your first name. You covered, but it still happened."

I bet if they knew the identity of that caller, they'd change their tune. Knox Merrick calling *The Breakup Bible* would crash the airwaves, but I'd never use my relationship to further my career. Never!

Stiletto Amazon takes over. "Part of the appeal of your show is that people don't know who you are. It adds mystery. You know, there are people that really think you're a nun! Maintaining that intrigue is part of the marketing magic behind the show. We're willing to overlook that one indiscretion. We just thought a little face-to-face might be necessary."

I know a threat when I hear one, even if it's dressed up and smiling. "Since we're passing along friendly little reminders, I have one to share," I say. "Let me remind you that I own the creative on the show. My title. My voice. My concept. My contract goes, and I take all that with me."

Friendly went to feisty in two seconds flat. I think I see a bobby pin or two fly out of Tight Bun's hair. "You have a non-compete clause."

"One year," I say. "And I don't believe it includes podcasts or writing a book or . . ."

Stiletto Amazon holds up her hand. "Mae, we are on your side. We've had a very productive relationship for several years."

"And if you'd like that to continue," I say, getting to my feet, "I suggest you don't threaten me again."

My heart pounds as I walk out of the room and towards the parking lot. I can't get out of here fast enough. I'm sure my sweat is ruining my mom's fake Coco shirt. What the hell just happened? Mentally, I'm tallying my savings in my head. Do I have enough saved that I could go a year without being on the radio? Could I even find another station in the Denver area to hire me? One that's *not* owned by my present employer?

Radio is a fickle business. One day you're hot, and the next you're not. I'm lucky I've had such a long run already. Of course, I've worried about what I'll do when it comes to an end, but I never thought the reason for that would be Knox. Maybe I'm getting ahead of myself. Don't panic.

Still, I doubt there is any way I'll be able to keep my identity a secret once my relationship with Knox goes public. I suppose he and I could try to keep things private, but I don't know how realistic that is. And the media is going to want to know about the woman he's dating. The public is going to want to know, too. And what I do for a living is part of that. I'm going to have to tell my bosses that I'm dating Hollywood's hottest leading man at some point, but not today. Not without talking to Knox first. Of course, he's the reason I'm in this mess, calling my show and using my name.

"Mae!" Amy calls out, catching me as I step out into the parking lot. She's wearing a cute dress, her strawberry blonde hair up in a relaxed bun.

I knew she worked other shifts at the station, but I'm still surprised to see her. It's odd seeing someone out of context, like when you run into your old yoga partner at a dinner party. You're used to seeing them one place, and then they're at another.

"Everything okay?" she asks. "I heard about the meeting."

"Fine. You didn't mention anything to them about that caller?" I ask with a wink. "Scooby-Doo?"

"Your secret's safe with me." Amy smiles broadly then squeals, "I can't believe you know Knox Merrick! What's he like? Is he just as cute in person? Are you dating?"

"Whoa, he's just from my hometown," I say, downplaying things. "Lots of people in Haven's Point know him."

Knox and I haven't talked about how to handle these situations. We probably should have. Everything has just been happening so fast. I'm not sure I'm prepared to come out as his . . . Well, his anything.

"I've actually been thinking of moving to Haven's Point," she says. "It's a great town, and so much cheaper than Denver. But there aren't many apartments there." She's right. Haven's Point is mostly single-family homes, the occasional townhome. "I'm planning on looking there this weekend."

I have no idea when Knox will be back, and I'm hosting Gigi's birthday party at my house, but I like Amy, and it's good to keep your co-workers happy. "Why don't you stop by my house Saturday?" I offer. "It's my grandmother's birthday. You'll meet a lot of locals. Maybe someone will know of a place."

She clearly likes that idea, and is in the process of thanking me when my cell phone rings in my purse, and I start digging to find it.

"I'll text you the details," I tell Amy, and she waves as she heads back to the building while I continue to search for my phone and walk to my car.

My purse has a nice little pocket designed to store your phone in, but in my rush to get out of my meeting, it must have slipped out into the deep, dark recesses, where old breath mints and tampons go to die. I finally find it just in time to answer. I see who's calling and am relieved I didn't miss him. The eight-hour time difference doesn't make connecting easy.

"Hi, Dad," I say.

Ours has always been a close relationship, though he doesn't call me by some cute nickname from my childhood. He never called me pumpkin or baby girl. My mom said he never once used baby talk with me. He used to tell me if I acted mature, he'd treat me that way. That's not to say he wasn't fun or silly with me. He was deployed a lot, but when he was home, he was always playing with me. No matter what I wanted to do. He was the best tea party guest a girl could have.

"So your Gigi tells me she finally told you about Thomas," he says.

"You *knew*?" I exclaim.

"I'm her only child," he says. "I've known for awhile."

"Why did no one tell me?" I ask, taking a seat in my car and pressing the auto start button.

The Bluetooth connection comes on, so I miss a little of what he says in the transfer. "Wasn't my place to say," he says.

"It wasn't Gigi's place to tell you that Knox is back in my life, but I'm sure she told you, anyway," I say.

"Knox?" he asks, like he's never heard that name before.

Oh shit, I guess Gigi didn't spill the beans. "Forget I said that."

"Not likely," he says. "How long has this been going on?"

"Not long."

"You happy?" he asks.

I stop at a stop sign, looking around before I continue my drive. "I am."

"Okay, then," he says. "What else is going on in your world?"

"Really? That's it?" I ask. "You're not going to go all hardcore, overprotective dad on me?"

"When have I ever done that?" he teases.

"Hmm, let's see. How about when Mom found my birth control pills? Or when Knox and I wanted to go on that overnight church trip our senior year? Or when . . ."

"Isolated incidents," he says with a chuckle.

It suddenly hits me that Gigi has a new beau, and I have someone in my life, but my dad is alone. To my knowledge, he hasn't dated anyone since my mom passed away. "What about you, Dad?" I ask. "Are you happy?"

"If you're happy, then I'm happy," he says with a twinge of sadness in his voice.

That's always been his motto. He used to say that if his wife and daughter were happy, then he was. With Mom gone, I guess he directed all that focus to me.

I take a deep breath, looking down at my mom's shirt. My dad is only in his fifties. He's handsome and kind and fit, and way too young to spend the rest of his life alone. My mom wouldn't want that, and I don't want that. "I know I didn't have the best reaction to

Gigi dating, and I know you don't need my permission, but I would be okay if you . . ." The words get caught in my throat, and I can't finish.

"It's a little soon," he says.

"It's been over a year," I say softly.

"I was with your mother more than half my life," he says. "A year isn't that long."

My eyes fill up. A part of me is relieved. I can't imagine what it would be like to see my father hold another woman's hand, kiss her. It would definitely take some getting used to. And God forbid, he played the field, and I'd have to see him with multiple women. Thank God, he lives in France.

"Will you tell me if you do start dating?" I ask. "I'd prefer not to be blindsided again."

"I will," he says. "And you'll tell me if Knox hurts you again. I'll make sure he doesn't get a third chance!"

"There's my overprotective Dad!"

He chuckles. "Now tell me what you have planned for Gigi's birthday. I'm so sorry I'm missing it."

CHAPTER TWENTY

Cassette

Mae to Knox

Age Sixteen

Knox,

I got your cassette. You know the one. The one where you said you loved me. I loved it.

Love . . .

Is love a choice? A decision? Or are we all victims to it?

I don't think you woke up that morning and thought, I'm going to love Mae today. You made the decision to tell me, but was loving me a decision, or was it something that just happened to you?

You happened to me, Knox. I like to think with my head. A pro/con list is my best friend, but with you, it doesn't matter how many cons there are. Honestly, there aren't many. Really, only the distance.

I know how hard it must have been to make that cassette, to send it, to wait for me to respond. To me, the most important thing about love is to appreciate it, and protect it. Not to overlook it. My dad always drops me and my mom off at the door of a store if it's raining. That's love.

My mom sends him a text when she's running late. Love.

Most love isn't big. It's not jewelry and flowers. Love is in the details. The small, everyday acts.

The cassette tapes.

That's the key to a long relationship, I think.

Notice the love.

This is me noticing.

This is me saying . . .

I love you, too.

Mae

Gigi's party is in full swing. It's a beautiful Colorado evening. The sky is painted in pinks and oranges, the wildflowers are in full bloom. The lake looks extra bright today, like Mother Nature knows it's Gigi's day. I've got tables and chairs set up outside. My place is too small for everyone to be inside. All of Gigi's friends are here, Everly and Timothy included. Amy showed up, too. I'm glad she came; it's good to see her away from the office. I've got music playing. It's been a warm day, so I'm wearing a bikini top under my tank top and shorts. Several party goers are already swimming in the lake. It's low key, but it's been a wonderful time.

Two of the three tiers of birthday cake are gone. Gigi didn't blow out any candles, but the Silver Sirens did perform a very sultry version of "Happy Birthday" in her honor. It was a hoot!

Thomas has barely left her side all day. I still can't get used to it. That was always my grandfather's job, being her sidekick. He worshipped the ground she walked on, opening every door for her, never letting her carry a single bag in his presence. Seems like Thomas has the same affliction.

There are a lot of single people here. Granted, most of them are AARP members, but for the first time in a long time, I feel like something, or rather someone, is missing.

My sidekick.

I'm in my twenties. Most of the time when I go to functions, people my age are coupled up. It's strange, but it's human nature. We are pre-programmed to seek companionship. I think it's the only explanation for blind dates and arranged marriage. We scrounge up dates to weddings, parties, class reunions. Hell, I've even had a caller or two that took a date to a funeral.

Normally, I'm okay flying solo. My own company is often better than a random guy, but today feels different. I wish Knox was here.

I catch myself. Wishing for him is bad, unbelievably bad. No matter what he says, I don't think he's here to stay. He has a big life. Haven's Point wasn't enough for him when we were kids, and it's not going to be enough now.

Maybe what I'm really wondering is whether I'm enough.

Am I enough to keep him coming back? And for how long?

I step outside, a bit away from the party, and pull out my phone to text him. We haven't talked yet today. He's doing media interviews all day, but he did send several cases of vintage champagne over to toast Gigi. That was a sweet touch. I send him a quick thank you text, not expecting him to respond, but my phone dings almost immediately.

Knox: The least I could do after that picture you sent me.

He didn't exactly get the ugly underwear picture he asked for, but I figured he'd prefer a full nude, anyway. If we're going to do the whole long-distance thing, I figured we had to find ways to keep things spicy. I just sent a body shot, though. The first rule of nude selfies is *don't ever show your face!*

Knox: Naughty girl!

Me: Don't get callouses!

"Don't tell me your phone is blowing up, too?" Everly says, walking up to me. "These GroupMe school moms are about to drive me crazy."

Startled, I hear my phone ding again, but don't look at it. "GroupMe?"

"That app is the devil," she says. "It's like a group text on steroids. The preschool parents at Gracie's school are all on it. In theory, it's a good idea. Helps everyone keep up with things."

"That doesn't sound bad."

"It is when everyone has to thank each other for responding. Then a dozen or so *you're welcomes* follow. Do they not realize that everyone is seeing this? And then there are the randoms that ask things totally unrelated to school, like where is the best dry cleaner. This is why moms go crazy, I swear."

"You're a good mom," I say. "I know it was tough right after Gracie came to you, but you guys have crossed that hump, and she's an amazing little girl."

Everly looks over at a patch of wildflowers, where Timothy is swinging Gracie in the air, her purple dress twirling around with her. She lets out a long sigh. "He wants another."

"Already?"

She nods. "He doesn't care if we adopt again, or have a biological child."

"What do you want?" I ask.

Her phone dings again, and then again. "For these damn moms to stop messaging. I don't care what Thai restaurant they ate at last night!"

I put my arm around her. Everly and I just know things about each other without having to say a word. I know she's not ready. She's got a lot on her plate, and Gracie is still little. "Does Gracie ask for a baby brother or sister?"

"A mermaid," Everly says. "She only asks for a mermaid."

We both laugh. "Me, too," I say. "By the way, do me a favor and talk to Amy. She's looking for a place in Haven's Point, and if anyone would hear of a place, it's the local coffee shop guru."

"Sure," she says, motioning to my phone and asks, "Knox?"

I nod. "Yeah."

She smiles at me. "Mae, your heart is gone already. I can see it in your face."

She's right. As much as I try to convince myself that we are taking things slow, it's a lie. My heart has a mind of its own.

"I know you don't like him, but . . ."

Everly holds up her hand to stop me. "Girlfriend code. When you hate him, I hate him. When you love him, I love him. That's the way this works."

"And when I'm confused?" I laugh out.

"You're not confused," she says. "You know exactly how you feel. You're scared. And you have every right to be. He's far away. He's famous. He hurt you before."

"How am I supposed to trust my heart? It's been wrong so many times before. I've made a career out of how wrong my heart is," I say, throwing up my hands.

"Your heart only has to be right one time," she says. "Is this that time?"

◠

The party rages on. Who knew the AARP crowd were such party animals? After playing tea party and chase with Gracie for half the afternoon, I decide to check the food and drink tables to make sure there are still plenty of refreshments.

I'm pouring chips into a bowl when my phone rings. I step inside the house when I see who my caller is, the man saved in my phone as Scooby-Doo. I didn't want to put in his real name for fear I might lose my phone, and then someone could sell his number to the highest bidder.

"How am I listed in your contacts?" I ask, answering.

"Your name," he says. "Why would I have you as anything else?"

"I don't know," I say. "People do it all the time. They'll have House CEO for their mom or dad. I have you as Scooby-Doo, and Everly as Gangsta Babe because she's always got my back."

He laughs. "Okay, I'll change you to something better."

"Like what?"

"Think I'll keep that a secret," he says.

"No fair," I pout.

"How's the party?" Knox asks.

I fill him in a little, and then he asks how I am doing. I keep it sweet and light. I don't tell him about the meeting with my bosses or any of my other fears. I don't want him to worry, and I don't want to get into anything heavy when I know he doesn't have long to talk, and I need to get back to the party.

Looking out my window, I see Amy and Everly talking. There are no signs that anyone will be leaving anytime soon. I guess that's what happens when you give a good party.

I want to know when he'll be coming back, but I don't want to ask. It seems too couple-like, too desperate, too much of a commitment, too fast for all that. My heart needs to slow down and give my head a chance to catch up.

But then he says, "As soon as I finish here, I'm catching a plane to Denver. It will be late. I have tomorrow off, but need to be in New York first thing Monday morning."

My heart swells. He misses me, too. "Tomorrow is Sunday," I say, reality hitting me. "I have to work."

"I don't care if I get to see you two hours or ten, I'm coming," Knox says. "I've got to get back to work now. I don't know how late I'll be tonight, so don't wait up."

"Wake me when you get here," I say softly.

"Sleep naked," he says before hanging up.

There's a soft knock on the back door. Seeing it's Amy, I step back outside. She leans in and whispers, "I don't want to freak you out, but there's some car parked down the road. I think the guy has a camera."

I look in the direction she's motioning. Though the car is some distance away, I recognize the guy from my porch the other day. He gives me a snarky wave. He's not on my property this time. "Piece of crap reporter. Vincent something or other."

"Want me to ask him to leave?" Amy asks.

I shake my head, not wanting to draw more attention to him, perhaps ruin what's been a great party. "He's trying to get the money shot of me and Knox, I'm sure."

I guess he needs photo confirmation before he can run his story exposing me and Knox. Sleaze! Why is it anyone's business?

"Knox isn't even here," Amy says.

"He won't be here until much later tonight, so let's just let this asshole waste his Saturday," I say with a smile. But I'd be lying if I said my stomach wasn't in a knot. "He'll have to earn his money another way."

～

I don't understand people who can sleep naked. Don't you get cold? Or worry about bugs? It's the same thing as women who don't wear panties with pants. I don't get that, either. We are women. I don't want to be gross, but there are things that come out of us that I don't want on my jeans. And seriously, put on some drawers when you work out. No one wants to see your crotch sweat.

Perhaps, I should bring this up on-air sometime. It could be an interesting topic for discussion. Ideas hit me at the oddest times. I'm always looking for fresh and fun conversation starters, but sometimes they strike you when you least expect it.

Despite my practical objections against it, I'm as naked as a jay bird when I hop into bed, pulling the covers all the way up to my neck. I must've checked the curtains in my bedroom at least three times to make sure there weren't any slits anywhere. I'm not sure why I care. I don't think the deer are peeping Toms, I have no neighbors close enough to catch a glimpse of anything, and that reporter drove off hours ago.

Turning my head, I see the clock reads eleven on the dot. It's not that late, but I'm tired from the party. Having no idea what time Knox will show up, I decide it's best to get a few hours of sleep, because God knows I won't get any once he arrives. At least, I hope not.

Taking a deep breath, I close my eyes, snuggling deeper into my mattress. It's quiet out here—a far cry from the party a few hours ago. It was a great time, but I love the quiet. It's one of the reasons I bought this place. I never hear a car drive by in the middle of the night. There's no noisy neighbors. I hear the occasional owl or bird, a ripple from the lake, but for the most part, the whole world seems asleep out here.

Creak.

My eyes flash open. That sounds like it's coming from the wood on my porch, but I didn't hear a car. It can't be Knox, and that scum reporter wouldn't have the balls to trespass again.

I wait a second to see if I hear the noise again, but I don't. I close my eyes, only this time, the bed isn't quite as comfortable, so I roll to my side, yawning a little. This is my usual bedtime ritual—say my prayers, then think of something happy for a few minutes before I roll to my back and fall into a deep sleep.

Tonight's happy thought is Knox.

His name makes me smile. The thought of him waking me up with some kinky little game makes me even happier, but it's not going to help me sleep, so I think about us as teenagers. All the times we spent out at this lake, talking, walking, kissing. My breathing slows. It's hard to keep the thoughts clear. I feel myself drifting to sleep.

My eyes flash open. The clock says eleven thirty now. I just barely fell asleep.

Creak.

My pulse rate jumps through the roof, and I shoot up in bed before remembering I'm naked, then quickly lift the covers over my chest to cover myself.

Creak.

Reaching for the lamp next to my bed, I flick on the light. "Knox?" I call out.

Nothing but silence fills the air.

I reach for my phone, seeing I missed a text from Knox a few minutes ago. He got delayed. He's just now on his way to the airport. He won't be here for a few more hours.

I've never been scared out here by myself. Never! But my current heart rate is higher than it should be. Maybe being naked has me paranoid. That has to be it. I'm just feeling vulnerable.

Glancing to the alarm panel on my bedroom wall, the light is still green. I didn't set it before I went to bed, and I seldom do. It was Gigi's housewarming present to me. I'd have preferred a Smeg refrigerator. I love their whole line of stuff, all the fun colors, but I had to spring for that myself.

Right now, though, I'm thankful that Gigi sprung for the alarm. She even pays for the monitoring service because she knows I wouldn't have kept up with that. I get up, keeping the blanket wrapped around me, and activate it. When it's fully armed, I get back in bed and shut off the light.

I feel a bit better, but this time, it'll take more than one deep breath for me to fully relax. My happy place seems a bit farther away. I finally seem to be making some progress when I hear another noise, only this is more like a rustling than a creaking sound.

Shit! I feel myself starting to sweat. At this point, I'd pee my pants if I was wearing any.

Trying to convince myself it's just a wild animal who's gotten too close, I get out of bed, throwing on a sweatshirt and sweatpants. If I'm going to be mauled to death or murdered, I want to be covered up and warm. I don't want to be found dead naked—how embarrassing.

I don't turn on any lights in my bedroom, but make my way into the main part of the house. For a fraction of a second, I wonder if Knox is playing games with me. We never really did any role playing in our sex life before, but maybe this is some new thing that gets him off. I just don't think he'd scare me, though, not on purpose.

I make my way to the front door, flicking the switch for the outside lights to come on. I'm not about to open the door to a bear or a burglar. Peering through the windows, I scan my porch. I can't see much beyond that. It's pitch black. That's one of the things I usually like about it out here. It gets so dark without lights from buildings or street posts, but right now, I'm reconsidering my position.

I don't see anything, not even the shadow of anything moving. Some people enjoy being scared, watching horror movies, riding thrill rides, jumping out of planes. I'm not one of those people. I don't scare easily, but it's not a feeling I particularly enjoy or crave.

Making my way to the back door, I do the same check, feeling pretty stupid when all I see is a tiny squirrel running across my porch. He's cute, and my heart settles. Shaking my head at myself, I turn off the lights, but just to be careful, I flip on the motion detector lights.

They've been installed forever, but I leave them off because there are so many animals out here. Odds are that critters like my squirrel friend would trip them all the time. Right now, I have the sensitivity set to the lowest level, so hopefully, they won't be activated by a passing animal. Saying a prayer that the bulbs still work, I make my way back to bed.

I'm okay. Knox will be here soon. Everything is fine. Just need to close my eyes and fall asleep.

It's exactly midnight when the motion lights flash on, lighting up the house like the Fourth of July. No squirrel is going to do that.

CHAPTER TWENTY-ONE

Knox

All the rental car places were closed when I arrived at the Denver airport, so I had to take a taxi to Haven's Point. It's dark, I wore a baseball cap, and it's the wee hours of the morning, so I don't think the driver recognized me. He barely makes eye contact with me as I unload my bag. That's a good sign.

Grabbing my suitcase, I head toward Mae's house. I had the driver stop pretty far down the driveway because I didn't want the car to wake her. I have a more pleasant way in mind to wake her up.

Despite the fact that I haven't slept all night, my cock still twitches at the thought. It's only been a few days since I've seen her, but it's been way too long already. Each absence feels like an eternity, like it did when we were younger, and I was waiting for one of her cassettes to arrive in the mail. I'm not a patient person. And my dick is certainly not a patient organ.

So even though I'll have less than twenty-four hours with Mae, I still made the trip. The naughty little photos she sent are incredible, but they can only go so far. I need the real her.

Rocks and leaves gently crunch under my feet as I make my way through the darkness. I'm closing in on her porch when I'm suddenly blinded by lights. I'm used to having lights flashed in my face, even when I'm not expecting it. Normally I smile, try to play nice—but not at this fucking hour, and not with high powered motion detector lights, either.

Holding my hand up over my face, I step onto her porch. I feel it before I even smell it—the slick, squishy feel under my shoe. Crap!

Yes, literally crap.

I just stepped right in a pile of shit. Happens to us "famous" people, too. We are not immune to sticking our foot in it. But if any woman is worth stepping in shit, it's Mae. That still doesn't stop me from mumbling a string of F-bombs. I know she likes living at the lake, close to nature, but this is a little too close.

Back in the day, my brother Ryder and I used to do a lot of camping and hiking with our dad. He routinely showed us animal droppings. If you spend any time outdoors, it's good knowledge to have. Deer shit looks a lot different from bear shit, and you do not want to pitch your tent next to bear droppings.

It's all mushed under my shoe, so I can't tell what animal left this lovely gift for Mae. I'm certainly hoping it was an animal of the less lethal variety.

If I wasn't living this at the moment, I'd think it was a movie comedy sketch. Guy shows up late at night for a booty call and ends up stepping in shit. That could be pretty funny. I wonder how that story would play out.

I slip off my shoes and place them on the porch. I'll clean it all up for her tomorrow. I have other—better—things on my mind now.

Using the key she gave me, I unlock the door, and a head splitting siren hammers my ears. Fuck!

If the security lights or my outburst after stepping in crap didn't wake her, this is sure to do it. Mae didn't warn me she'd have the alarm set or give me a code to shut it off!

"Knox!" I hear her call.

"Yeah! What's the code?" I yell back, dropping my suitcase.

She yells it back to me, and I quickly turn the damn thing off. I'm about to apologize when I turn around, and Mae comes flying into my arms. She's not naked like I requested, but I don't know that I've ever seen someone so happy to see me, and that's saying something. I try to pull back to kiss her, but she clings tighter to me.

This isn't a romantic embrace. I feel her trembling.

"Baby, what's wrong?" I say, trying to get a look at her face.

"Nothing," she says. "It's nothing."

"Then why are you dressed?" I tease, tickling her a little.

She lets out the tiniest giggle, relaxing a bit, then I pick her up, her legs wrapping around my waist. She rests her head on my shoulder as I carry her into the bedroom. But I don't make it past the doorway before I freeze at the sight of the shining silver blade of a huge kitchen knife resting on her nightstand.

Mae places her feet on the ground, knowing what stopped me in my tracks. "It's nothing. I got a little scared," she says, going to get the knife.

I take it from her. "A *little* scared?" I ask, guessing the blade on this thing is at least eight inches long.

"It's stupid," she says. "Earlier, I thought I heard something on my porch. The motion lights came on. I just freaked myself out."

Mae is beautiful no matter what state she is in. But I can see the worry on her face. She's more than a little scared. "Whatever it was," I say, showing her my bare feet, "I stepped in its shit on my way in."

She covers her mouth with her hand to try to hide her laugh. Apparently, my stepping in animal feces is a riot.

"So that's what it was! I'm so sorry," she says, still laughing. "God, now I feel really stupid."

"Why didn't you call me?"

"You were in California getting on a plane," she says.

"Still," I say, combing my fingers through her hair, "if you were afraid, you should've called me."

"I wasn't sure if we were doing that."

"Doing what?"

"I don't know," she deflects. "I'm tired."

"So am I."

"Then let's not get into it now."

"I want to know why you didn't call me, and don't tell me it was because I was in California and flying. Tell me the real reason."

"Because it felt like something a girlfriend would do. Call her boyfriend when she's scared."

My eyes narrow because I don't like hearing that. The crap on her porch didn't piss me off, but this shit certainly is. But perhaps she's right, and we shouldn't talk about this now. She's tired, I'm tired, it's late. That's the recipe for a fight if ever there was one.

"And a man flying overnight to see his girl for just a few hours feels more like . . . what?" I ask. "A long-distance booty call?"

"You trying to say you didn't come here for sex?" she asks, her hand finding her hip.

"Of course I did," I say. Her cute little mouth falls open slightly, but before she can say anything, I cup her cheek in my hand. "I'd really like to have sex with my *girlfriend* now."

She's clearly been hesitant to label this, us, to go all in. And I haven't been able to pin her down. It hasn't bothered me too much. I know she's worried about getting hurt, but I don't like the fact that she wouldn't call me when she was scared.

She flashes me a smile and says, "I'll call you next time."

Damn right, she will! That was the only answer I was going to accept this time. I move closer to her, lifting her shirt over her head, her gorgeous tits coming into view. I love that she doesn't reach to turn out the lights, allowing me to see her, enjoy all of her. Her nipples are hard and erect, and I know her little bud must be the same way.

The plane ride was enough foreplay for me, thinking of nothing else but this moment.

The moment I get to have her.

I slip my hands under the waistband of her sweatpants, gliding them down the soft skin of her legs. She steps out of them, and I step back just a little to get a look at her. Damn, her body is perfect—curvy, her skin flushed as she stands naked before me.

Sinking to the floor, I rest my back against the footboard then pull her to me, burying my head between her legs. One long, slow suck, then I let my tongue circle her. I love eating her pussy. There's no other way to say it. I love focusing solely on her, her pleasure. During sex, I'm obviously thinking about her, but not like now. Now,

I don't miss a moan, a tremor, or a delicious taste of her. It's all mine for the taking.

Placing my hands on her ass, I pull her tighter to my mouth, slipping my tongue just inside her. Her muscles clench. She loves this as much as I do. That's just one of the many reasons we are so compatible.

Some guys see oral sex as a means to an end, a necessary evil to get to intercourse. Not me. Some of my greatest memories are of jerking myself off while eating her pussy. That was a daily occurrence back in college before we had actual sex. It's probably one of the reasons she kept her virginity for so long—she knew how satisfying she was to me.

Still, as good as this is, there is nothing like being buried deep inside her, her eyes glued on mine as her orgasm builds inside of her. I feel it now on my tongue, the slightest quivers of pleasure about to explode. She starts to thrust ever so slightly. It's the best feeling in the world to have Mae fuck my mouth. I use my fingers to spread her open wider, and she cries out, her orgasm making my dick pulse against my jeans like she's calling to him.

Lightly, I plant little kisses along her folds and down her inner thighs. When I'm sure she has total use of her legs, I work my way to my feet, wrapping my arms around her and whispering, "Bend over."

She doesn't question me. Mae's up for most anything in the bedroom, and she trusts me completely. Running my hand across the smooth skin of her ass, I'm in awe of how incredible she looks, naked and bent over the bottom of her bed.

"Stay there," I order softly.

Quickly, I retrieve my suitcase from where I dropped it in the den, taking out a couple items. When I walk back into her bedroom, she's exactly as I left her—ass in the air, waiting for me.

Kneeling again, I plant a kiss on her ass cheek as I tie one of her ankles to the bedpost with my silk necktie. Thank God, she doesn't have one of those huge California king bed frames, or this would never work. I fasten the other ankle with a different tie. She lets out a breathy moan, the anticipation making her horny as hell again.

Unzipping my jeans, I look down and watch her toes curl. Mae loves sex. It's one of the things I love about her. I never have to convince her or hope she's in the mood. When she was with me, she pretty much lived in the mood.

Making quick work of the rest of my clothes, I step up behind her, my dick poised at her entrance. She's warm and wet and so ready for me. I've missed this freedom so much. The freedom of being with someone who is your sexual equal. Some women would shy away from being tied up, but not Mae. She loves it.

Being a famous actor has hindered me in the bedroom. I used to love nothing more than slipping my finger inside Mae in public, watching her quiver and secretly orgasm under my fingers. I can't do that stuff anymore. It's too risky. If some photographer caught a picture of that, the scandal would never die, and I would never put a woman through that, especially Mae. It would kill me to see her go through something like that. So we're just going to have to keep our sexual creativity private.

Binding her ankles forces her to stay spread wide for me. Using the head of my cock, I outline her. Her slick wetness slides over me, gliding me inside, back where I belong. She releases a sensual moan, and it's the only go ahead I need to take hold of her hips and slowly slide myself in and out. It's like the best torture. So slow that I know I won't come, but it feels so damn good. Slipping my hand between her legs, my fingers circle her clit. It's like an on button, making her push back on my dick faster and harder.

The fact that she can't really move her legs is making her clench her muscles that much harder, desperate for release. I can tell she wants it, needs it—now. I don't want to torture her. So I'll give her what she wants, but I'm not ready for this to be over.

She tosses her head back as the walls of her vagina convulse around me, and she collapses onto the bed. I slip myself out of her, untying her ankles. Kissing a path up her body, I join her in bed, flipping her over, and taking my place between her legs. She groans, and I know she's sore.

Love that.

So this time, I'll be gentle. Her blue eyes flutter open as I grind my hips into hers. "Slow this time, baby," I whisper.

She reaches up, running her hands through my hair, her eyes never leaving mine. This is the other great thing about Mae in bed. While she likes being tied up, and doesn't mind the occasional spanking, she doesn't *need* it. She can just as easily come like this. Just me and her—without toys or kinky shit.

The only thing she really needs is me. And the only thing I'll ever need is her.

We're spending a lazy summer Sunday afternoon at the lake, something we used to do all the time as teenagers. Back then, it was the perfect excuse for me to see her in a bikini. Now, I wish we were skinny dipping, but sadly, we're not. Even though it's pretty private back here, no one else is around, and her house blocks anyone from spying on us from the road, I still wouldn't risk it.

We've been swimming in the lake for the past hour or so, both of us trying to ignore the fact that our little reunion soon is coming to an end.

"Sorry about your shoes," Mae says, splashing some water on my head.

"They're just shoes," I say, pulling her into a kiss.

By morning, my shoes had disappeared from her porch. I can only assume some animal, perhaps a stray dog, is having a field day gnawing on the leather.

She glances around a little. "I need to start thinking about getting cleaned up. I have work."

"Quit," I tease.

She giggles. "Why don't *you* quit? Then you can stay here with me all the time."

"I just might do that," I say, kissing her again.

"What time is your flight?"

"One in the morning," I say. "I pushed it as late as I could. That will give me just enough time to get ready for the morning show circuit."

"My show's not over until midnight," she says, her lips in a little pout.

"I could come with you?" I offer. "Watch you in action on the radio."

She doesn't say yes, but she doesn't say no. She looks like she's thinking hard about it, making a pro/con list in her head.

"That way we can spend more time together," I say.

"Maybe so! No one's really at the station at that hour, so no one will see you. It would be easy enough to sneak you in and out," she says, weighing the options. "Amy will be there. She screens calls for me. She'd love to meet you. I think she's a fan."

"Then I can come?" I ask. She nods, and I twirl her around in the water, making waves. "Any way I can convince you to fly to California for the week?"

"Aren't you in New York?"

"Only Monday," I say. "I could meet you at my place on Tuesday."

"Don't you have work things to do?"

"Yeah, but there's nights," I say, giving her butt a healthy squeeze.

"I . . ."

My heart sinks a little. Her hesitation is enough of an answer. I'm not going to get what I want, and I don't like it. I'm willing to keep flying here for her, but I need to know that she's eventually going to be a part of my life, too. This can't be a one-way street. Releasing her, I move toward the edge of the lake to get out.

"Knox," she says, taking hold of my elbow. "It's just, I like you coming here. It feels like our own secret escape. Like nothing can touch us here."

"I love your life here, Mae. But I want to share my life with you, too. I want to show you my house, the beach, my favorite places to eat. My life."

"Can we do those things without ending up on the cover of some magazine?" she asks.

"We can try," I say. "You have your life. I have mine. Both are great, but we have to figure out what *our* life is going to look like. Yours and mine, together."

"I need to talk to the station heads first," she says.

"Why?"

"Because when you and I go public, it won't take long before someone figures out what I do for a living, who I am. My contract demands my identity stay hidden. They're already upset . . ."

"About what?"

"You calling the station," she says, getting out of the lake. "Using my name."

"Did they know it was me calling?" I ask.

"No," she says.

"Perhaps me going to the station with you tonight isn't a good idea, then," I say.

"Tonight will be fine," she says, sounding confident about her decision.

"When did you find out they were upset?" I say, rushing out of the water to catch up with her. "You never told me."

"A few days ago. I had a meeting with some of the higher ups."

I take hold of her waist. There's more. I know there is. I can feel it.

"They thought it was necessary to remind me about the terms of my contract, and that I'm up for renewal at the end of the year."

"They threatened you? And you didn't think to tell me this?"

"I handled it," she says with a shrug.

"Not the point," I bark. "Christ, Mae."

"Look, as soon as they find out that it was Knox Merrick calling the show, and not some random ex-boyfriend, they will be singing a different tune."

"Then why didn't you tell me?"

"Because I figured you were busy, and I didn't want to bother you. And also, I'm not going to use our relationship to advance my career. I talk about myself on my show, my experiences."

"I've heard," I say, an edge in my voice. It wasn't easy to listen to her talk about dating other guys.

"I never used names. I always keep things vague, but I won't be able to do that with you. And I'm sure your people won't like me talking about our personal life so publicly."

"No, they won't," I admit.

"So as soon as you and I hit the newsstands, my career is going to implode."

She has a point. I'm not sure what to say. We are just standing in her yard, staring at each other. My body feels heavy, like someone just laid a ton of bricks on my shoulders, and everything around us must feel it, too. There's not a bird chirping, or a wave rippling. It's total silence. I hadn't considered any of this.

I knew I was asking her to give up her privacy to be with me, but I didn't know that included her career, everything she's worked so hard for. When I showed up in Haven's Point, Mae asked if I had considered her when I made the decision to come back, if I considered what it would mean for her, how she would feel.

The truth is, I didn't. At the time, I only thought about what I wanted. How much I wanted to see her again. My singular focus on winning her back was selfish. I just didn't realize how much so until right now.

"I'll do everything I can to protect you, your identity, your job."

"I know that," she says, but we both know there's only so much I can do. The media hounds can be ruthless. "I just don't think me flying to California on Tuesday is going to work."

"I understand," I say and lower my head.

Gently, she tilts my chin up with her fingers. "I might need until Wednesday."

My eyes dart to hers. "Mae, I won't have you put everything you worked for on the line for me."

"Not for you," she says. "For us."

~

"Looks like someone drank from the *I need a man* Kool-Aid," she says to a caller.

I watch Mae through a window that looks inside the radio booth, while listening to her show on a pair of headphones. Though she's alone in the booth, it's like she's conducting a symphony orchestra—there's a crispness to her words, a rhythm to her movements, occasionally grabbing the microphone, controlling other equipment before her, giving signals to Amy during and in-between callers. She's literally running the show.

I imagine this is the way she used to look when she recorded cassette tapes for me—smiling, eyes sparkling, in control.

This is her set, only she does it mostly on her own. I need a director, writers, costumers. She does it all on the fly. Well, I know that's not true. She does prep work and research, but her show is more like improv – you're never quite sure where it's going to go. Still, she's in total control.

"My advice is, don't worry about falling in love with a man. The person you need to fall in love with is you!"

I feel a light poke on my shoulder and look over, seeing Mae's call screener, Amy, practically floating in the air, seemingly amazed that I'm real, that she just touched me. Slipping one headphone to the side, I smile at her.

"That was good advice, don't you think?" Amy asks me.

"Mae's very good," I say, trying to position the headphone back over my ear, but she starts talking again.

"I've got some ideas for topics for the show."

"Do you aspire to be behind the mic?" I ask.

"Me?"

"Why not?" I ask, seeing her skin turn bright red.

"Amy?" Mae says, sticking her head out of the booth during a short commercial break. "That last caller wanted financial advice."

"Sorry," Amy says.

"My fault," I say. "I think I'm distracting her. Maybe I should go."

"No, don't leave," Amy cries out.

"Amy, get real callers!" Mae says then rolls her eyes at me. "And trust me, Amy, he's just a guy like any other. Bad breath in the morning and everything."

Mae gives me a little wink before returning to her place behind the microphone. "I don't believe you have bad breath," Amy says, and I chuckle, putting my headphone back on.

I listen to Mae take caller after caller. It's almost like speed therapy, if there was such a thing. She's funny and empathetic and, most importantly, what she says makes a lot of sense. I often think common sense isn't so common these days. Take the current caller, who thought it was okay to propose with the same ring he gave to his ex-fiancé. Hasn't this dude seen enough bad romances to know that's never a good idea? Mae set him straight real quick.

"The only acceptable used jewelry to give is a family heirloom," she says.

My phone vibrates in my pocket, and I reach for it, placing it down beside me. It's only my agent, Heath, giving me the schedule and itinerary for tomorrow's round of interviews. I don't want to think about any of that. Mae's driving me to the airport when her show ends, and I'm not entirely sure when I'll see her again. Hopefully, she can work things out with her bosses, and it will only be a few days. I don't even want to think about her losing this gig because of me. She belongs behind that microphone.

"Do you believe in second chances?" the caller asks.

Mae's eyes catch mine through the glass. "I never used to," she says, "until I gave one."

CHAPTER TWENTY-TWO

Mae

It's a bit of a surreal experience to watch the man you had sex with yesterday on a news show the following morning, especially when he's wearing the tie he used to bind you to the bed.

It's not an official watch party, but Timothy has the television in The Tune Up tuned to Knox's interview. Every time one interview ends, Timothy changes the channel to catch him on the next show. I've been sitting at the bar the entire morning, just watching.

I'm not sure how Knox does it. He's smiling and bright eyed, even though he couldn't have gotten more than a couple hours sleep. He must have an IV of coffee pumping into his veins. Or maybe Everly and Timothy sent him with some of their finest whiskey to get him through. If it wasn't so early, I'd be asking for a hit. But damn, he looks handsome. Most of the questions are about the movie releasing in a few weeks. A couple interviewers try to slip in questions about his brother, but Knox always deflects.

A part of me wonders how he would answer if asked about his personal life. Would he freeze up? Would he say he's single? Would he do that to me again? Would I want him to tell the world about me? Would he keep it vague, but acknowledge there's someone in his life? We haven't discussed any of that. We've simply been living in our little sex bubble.

But I get the feeling it's about to burst. He's been here a lot, and we can't keep our relationship a secret forever. Then there's the reporter that was hanging out down the street. I just know I'm going to see my face on the grocery store magazine aisle one day soon.

Before things go any further, I have to talk to the station. It's the professional thing to do. I can't afford to lose my job. If they are blindsided, my job is over.

A cup of whipped cream slides under my nose. Gigi is the one feeding my sugar craving this morning. "Looks like you've got something on your mind," Gigi says.

I swipe a biscotti stick from a container behind the counter. "Knox asked me to come to California for the week."

I look back up at the television, and Gigi does the same. "And?" she urges. I shake my head, the uncertainty weighing on me. I know I told Knox I'd talk to my bosses, but it's not going to be easy. "You talk for a living, but it's like pulling teeth to get you to open up."

"Knox literally said the same exact thing. Look at him, Gigi," I say. "I'm not sure I want that life. Cameras, people following me. Having to make announcements to the world about our marriage, or the birth of our children."

"Marriage and children, already?" she asks.

"Maybe? I don't know, but I have to think about this long term," I say. "Being with someone like Knox can't just be casual. It will change my whole life."

"You've already done it," she says. "You've already made the decision to be with him." She places her hand on top of mine. "Let me fill you in on a little secret. Sooner or later, all love involves loss. The two go hand in hand."

I have to think about that for a second. Love does inherently mean loss. You lose some of your free time, and a certain amount of freedom, in general. You lose always getting to eat what you want for dinner. Some people lose themselves in their partner—lose their identity. And like Dad and Gigi, you will eventually lose the person you love.

"The question to ask yourself isn't what you will lose, but what you will gain," she says, turning my head to the television. "Do the losses outweigh the gains?"

"I could lose my job," I say, turning my eyes to her. She knows it's a requirement that I keep my identity a secret.

"Walk away, then."

"What?" I cry, my eyes darting to hers. "How can you suggest I put my career before . . ."

"There," she says, pointing her finger at me. "Your gut reaction. Mae, honey, I hate to break it to you, but you love him."

She says it like she's not sure if she's giving me bad news or good news. I can only laugh. God help me, I'm not totally sure which it is, either.

"I wish you'd let me charter a plane for you," Knox pouts on the phone.

Late yesterday, after a brief talk with my bosses, I finalized my plans to visit Knox's turf. Since then, we've already discussed this private plane thing at least three times. I want to be a normal, economy class person as long as possible.

"I thought we agreed that you buying me the ticket to come see you was more than enough."

"You only agreed to that in hopes I'd shut up about the private plane. Otherwise, I know you would have insisted on buying it yourself." He's right, but he's being a total baby about this. "It's safer if you fly privately. I could pick you up at the private hanger then. There's no way I can show up at LAX to get you."

"That's fine. I'll take an Uber."

"The hell you will," Knox barks.

"What's wrong with Uber?"

"It's a poor man's chauffeur driven Town Car."

"Snob."

"It's not about being a snob. It's about keeping you protected. You don't know who is behind the wheel. Haven't you heard the stories about . . ."

"I happen to have a five-star passenger rating on Uber."

"Proud of that?" he asks, snidely.

"Yep, it got down to four point nine once, and I couldn't sleep. I took several more trips just to get it back up to a five."

I listen to Knox make his argument against Uber. I should give him a coronary and tell him I'll take the bus. That would really make his gorgeous head explode. Instead, I just let him ramble, while opening a suitcase on my bed. I've only got a little while before I leave for the Denver airport. Knox would be happy to know that Amy is driving me. I asked her to take care of a few things for the show while I'm gone, and she offered to drive me to the airport. It was sweet. She was going to be in the area anyway, continuing her apartment search, and would be heading back to Denver around the time I needed to head to the airport. So I figured we could knock out some work on the drive.

I'm only planning on being at Knox's place for four nights. Normally, I would pack an extra pair of socks and panties. So if I'm going for three nights, I take four. But I think I'll mostly be hanging out at Knox's house, and I doubt I'll even need panties.

This is what a long-distance relationship comes down to: panties or no panties.

I know I'm packing too much, and it's silly to check a big suitcase. I should probably just take a carry-on bag, but shoes take up a lot of room, and I'm packing five pairs. Yes, one for each day and an extra!

"Mae, are you even listening?" Knox asks.

"Stopped at least five minutes ago," I say with a smile.

"I can't wait to see you," he says sweetly.

"Me, too."

"You'll get here faster in a private car," he says.

"Knox?"

"Limo!"

He's sweet, but I get the feeling that if I start giving in this early, he'll only get worse, probably demanding private security follow me around.

"This is part of it," he says. "This all comes with being with me."

"But you know I don't want that stuff."

"I know that," he says. "I know you aren't impressed by private jets and designer clothes. But some of this stuff is necessary for privacy and safety."

I exhale and begin to consider his offer. "A limo, huh?"

"Black, stretch, fully-tinted windows."

"That's a lot of room just for me," I tease. "But if a certain man was waiting for me in the limo. . ."

"Done!"

"I'll see you in a few hours," I say.

"You never told me how it went with your bosses. How did they react when you told them about me?"

"I didn't tell them who you are," I say. "Just that I was seeing someone in the public eye, and that it is a real possibility that my identity as Mother Superior could get out."

"How did they take it?"

"They were appreciative of the heads up," I say.

"And?"

"And they didn't make any promises. Basically, we have to wait and see. If ratings tank because I refuse to talk about you, or my name gets out, or for any other reason, then the writing will be on the wall."

"I'm sorry."

"It's really no different than how things are now," I say, but that's not entirely true. "I have to perform. If my show isn't good, and ratings go down the toilet, then I lose my job. That's just the nature of the business. Anyone who does this kind of work knows you live with an axe over your head. You know that, maybe better than anyone."

"Your listeners love you," he says. "They're loyal. You'll be fine. I believe that. You need to believe it, too."

"Thanks."

"No matter what," he says, "I'll always be listening."

Baggage claim is the worst. Hundreds of people all standing around, waiting for their bags. It's hot. Everyone is ready to be out of the airport. And there are never enough bathrooms in the baggage claim area. I always seem to have to pee when I get off an airplane, no matter how short the flight or how many times I went on the plane. Maybe Knox has the right idea about flying private.

Then there's the wondering if you are at the right baggage carousel. Searching the faces of the other people waiting, hoping you recognize a fellow passenger from your flight, any indication you are in the right place. Then you have the people that position themselves right at the front where the luggage comes out, in such a hurry to get their bags.

Then there's the anxious feeling in the pit in your stomach when the belt has gone around a few times, and you haven't seen your bag. I've only got one bag today. It's bright yellow so I can find it. This is not my first rodeo. For the life of me, I can't figure out why anyone would ever purchase black or navy luggage. And I have no clue why luggage companies would continue to manufacture those colors. Let's not make it any easier for the airlines to lose our luggage by creating another anonymous-looking black suitcase.

Still waiting for my bag, I text Knox that I'll be out shortly. He's supposed to let me know where to meet the limo. LAX is huge, but how many limousines can there be at an airport? Looking up from my phone, I spot my suitcase coming out.

Suddenly, everyone around the carousel starts to snicker and laugh. When the bag gets closer, I realize why. My suitcase is vibrating, making a loud noise against the hard shell. It's obvious what all these perverts are thinking. Another reason to hate baggage claim. Hashtag, things that only happen to me.

With attitude, I pull it off the belt, laying it on the ground to unzip it. I feel the need to defend my honor. I shuffle around some items then pull out the offending object. "Facial brush!" I call out, holding my Clarisonic over my head so everyone knows I'm not traveling with my vibrator.

And so what if I was? Put the judgments aside and mind your business, people!

My phone rings, but I ignore it, trying to stuff everything back in my suitcase. I'm sure it's just Knox letting me know where to meet. I'll call him when I get outside.

I'm not one of those women who look like a supermodel when they travel. I've searched high and low for good travel clothes, but even the stuff that is recommended on websites doesn't look as comfortable as my yoga pants, t-shirt, and cardigan. Yeah, it's slouchy and makes me look like I'm shaped like a puffy cloud, but it's comfy. Who are these women traveling in heels? Hats off to you.

And I know Knox isn't going to care one bit about what I have on. Hopefully, he undresses me in the backseat of the limo, anyway. Pulling my luggage, I make my way through the airport doors and outside to the drop-off and pickup area.

"There she is!" someone screams, and I turn around, looking behind me for whoever they're talking about.

That only gives them time to get their cameras right in my face. I find myself instantly surrounded, encircled by vultures. My heart starts to pound, my legs feel weak, and I'm pretty sure I just started shaking. Bulbs start flashing, and I struggle to see past the glare and the crowd.

Click, click, click.

What the hell is happening? People are yelling questions about me and Knox. I can't hear myself think, much less think of a way out of this.

"Please," I say over and over again, trying to make my way through them, but there seems to be no end to the mob. "Let me pass."

I'm not in Haven's Point. I'm not on my front porch. I can't shoo them away. I'm trapped.

CHAPTER TWENTY-THREE

Knox

This is not a drill. This is the real deal. The shit just hit the fan. Our relationship will be front page news tomorrow.

Hopping out of the limo, I rush toward Mae. I can't see her, covered by a sea of paparazzi. As soon as they spot me, I become their prey, which is fine by me. I know how to maneuver around them, make my way through, and that's just what I do.

Mae's eyes find mine, a mix of surprise and fear. All I can say when I reach her is, "Sorry."

Wrapping my arm around her, I lower her head, trying my best to shield her. This is bad, but I know it can get much worse. How did they know she was here? Who she was? Which flight she was on?

Not answering any questions being hurdled at me, I guide Mae to the car, helping her inside. Some asshole literally places the camera right up against the glass, trying to get one last shot. At least the windows are fully tinted.

The driver hops out, taking her suitcase and placing it in the trunk. I hop inside, slamming the door shut, and the driver quickly does the same, speeding off. Thank God, the privacy shield is raised. We don't need any more spectators.

I glance over at Mae, who looks exactly like you'd expect someone to look after their whole life just changed.

Lost.

Confused.

Shocked.

I can't imagine what this is like for her. I live this every day, but for me, it didn't happen overnight. My fame grew slowly. The first time someone recognized me in public, I was thrilled. The first time someone asked me for my autograph, I thanked them and bought their coffee. I didn't wake up one morning and have a camera shoved in my face. It grew over time into the hysteria it is today, but Mae just got thrown headfirst into the batshit crazy.

This wasn't supposed to happen this way. Announcing our relationship was supposed to happen on our timeframe, under my control, not like this. This was not my plan.

Mae trembles next to me. She wouldn't admit it, but she's scared. The adrenaline coursing through her body right now is surely through the roof.

"I can't stop shaking," she says, looking at me.

Wrapping both my arms around her, I hold her tightly, hoping she'll settle, but she continues to tremble. As with most limos, this one is stocked with all kinds of drinks and snacks. I offer Mae both, but she simply shakes her head, clinging to me.

"I'm here," I say, kissing the top of her head, but my words offer no comfort. My promises are useless at the moment.

There's nothing I can do to change what just happened, but I can help her body quiet down. Fear is an enormously powerful aphrodisiac. It's part of the reason people get off on the idea of sex in public, being caught. The fear heightens the arousal. I know it's worked that way for Mae in the past. Why should now be any different?

"Let me help," I say, gently tugging on her yoga pants.

Her lips part, but I'm not going to give her a chance to think about it, to talk herself out of this. So, I kiss her sweetly, letting my tongue slowly stroke hers. I'm sure sex is the last thing on her mind right now, but she needs a release, and I'm going to give it to her.

Keeping my eyes locked on hers, I slip both her pants and panties down, then I guide her hands under her thighs, urging her legs apart. "Spread your pussy." I lean back on my heels, taking a good look. I've been all over the world, and nothing compares to Mae spread wide for me. "You're so fucking open."

She whimpers a little, wanting me to touch her. Normally, I warm her up, teasing her, but not today. Today, she needs to come, and I'm not going to make her wait. I reach over to the champagne chilling and grab an ice cube. Her eyes spark. Ever so lightly, I outline her, watching the water drip, her heat melting the ice. She cries out a little, her nails digging into her skin.

In one smooth motion, I slip the ice cube inside her, give her pussy a smack, unzip, and bury myself inside her. Her body jumps slightly, like she's about to jump out of her skin. She's biting her bottom lip so hard, I'm afraid she'll draw blood.

Neither one of us cares that the only thing separating us from the driver is a privacy window. We don't care how fast we're going down the road, or about any potholes or turns we might make. All I care about is her.

I grind my hips into hers in a few short, hard thrusts. "Oh, oh, oh," she cries, her muscles convulsing as she comes all over my dick.

It took all of two minutes, but her body relaxes in my arms. I'm not concerned with my own orgasm at the moment. This was truly all about her. I slip myself out of her, readjusting our clothes. My dick is pretty pissed at me at this point, but he'll just have to get in line. I'm pretty pissed at me, too, for not anticipating the disaster at the airport, for not having a contingency plan in place.

I pull Mae into my lap, cradling her. Her body is relaxed in my arms, the trembling gone, but I know her brain is working overtime. She rests her head on my shoulder.

"I'm sorry, Mae," I say. "It shouldn't have happened like that."

I feel her tears soaking my shirt. She's not making a sound, but there's no hiding her tears. As much as I hate her crying, and want to tell her to stop, that everything will be okay, I don't say any of those things right now. She just had her whole life turned upside down, and she's got to be freaking about her job. If all that doesn't deserve a little cry, then I don't know what does.

So, I just hold her while she cries. It's a different kind of release, but one she needs just as much. After a few moments, she lifts her head and takes a deep breath, composing herself, as ever the good little soldier. I guess she gets that from her father.

"I just wish I'd had on some lip gloss or something," she deadpans.

Pushing her hair off her face, I say, "You look beautiful."

A little smile on her lips, she says, "Well, that's over and done with. Now we don't have to hide anymore."

"I tried to call you when you got off the plane," I say. "To warn you."

"You knew they were waiting for me?"

"My agent, Heath, got a call wanting a confirmation that we are together."

"How did they know? How'd they know my name?"

"Heath suspects that Denver reporter tipped them off. Probably got paid a pretty penny. It's all a game to these fuckers."

"What happens now?"

"That depends a lot on you," I say. "We can issue some sort of statement. We can do nothing, and let them speculate all they want. I'll do whatever you'll be comfortable with."

"You must have an opinion," she says.

"Issuing a statement gives us a little control over the narrative. It gives a feeling like we are playing nice. Doing nothing is more like flipping them the bird."

She proudly holds both her middle fingers up in the air.

That's my woman.

~

There's pressure when showing a woman your house for the first time. My house in Malibu is prime California real estate. I'm not so much worried about her liking the house or its location on the beach or how it's decorated. I can always renovate or redecorate to her preferences. It's not about any of those things. It's more about her feeling at home here. I hope she'll be spending lots of time with me, and I want her to be comfortable. I want it to feel like her home, too.

There are a few paparazzi waiting at the gate as we pull in, but the most they'll get is a far away photo of us as we walk into the house. After the airport experience, that's nothing.

The limo driver takes her suitcase to the door before he leaves. I hand Mae a key—her key to my place. She smiles, and I motion for her to open the door. This is the beginning of our life here. I know it's going to be different for her, and it's not the fact that I have a maid that comes twice a week, or a trainer and private chef—although I did give them all the week off. I want to have Mae all to myself.

The Pacific Ocean greets us as we walk inside. Once you get past the foyer, the view really opens up. When you live a life like I do, you sometimes feel trapped. I have the means to go anywhere I want in the world, but what good is it if you have to stay in your hotel so you aren't mobbed, or forced to travel with security all the time? It can be stifling, so I don't want my homes to feel that way. I need them to feel open and vast, like I'm free.

"I think my whole house could fit in this one room," Mae says, looking around, mouth open.

She's exaggerating. Besides, it's not the square footage that matters. It's the feel of the house that's important. And her cottage on Wildflower Lake in Haven's Point feels exactly the same as this house—limitless.

"I might get lost."

I take her hand. "Then I'll just show you the important rooms. The kitchen and bedroom." She laughs, following me around the house. Mae's not a cook, so I'm sure she doesn't appreciate the state-of-the-art range or pasta arm, but she smiles just the same. The master bedroom is downstairs, and all the other bedrooms are upstairs, along with the workout room, theater, and library. I take her upstairs first, showing her around there, before leading her into my bedroom.

It's got floor to ceiling windows just like most of the rest of the house, so if the curtains aren't drawn, you can wake up to the ocean. There's no balcony from the bedroom like off the main part of the house, but the view is just as spectacular. The master bath has a huge shower with body jets and a deep soaker tub. It even has these lights on it that change the color of the water. Why anyone needs to make their water pink is beyond me, but I point it out to Mae, anyway.

We end the tour by stepping out onto the balcony, the crashing of the waves providing background music.

"When we talked on the phone, and you were here, I never imagined this," she says.

"How'd you imagine my house?"

Her cheeks start to blush the faintest hint of pink. "It's silly, but I always imagined you in your old teenage bedroom."

"I've upgraded since my twin bed."

"It's beautiful."

"I want you to like it," I say.

"Of course, I like it."

"No, I mean, I want this place to be like a second home."

"I remember when I first walked into the cottage," she says. "It was so out of date and a disaster, really, but when I walked through the front door for the first time, I just had this feeling about the place. It just felt like I belonged there." She gives me that incredible smile of hers. "I had the exact same feeling when I walked through your front door."

"I lo . . ." I don't get the rest of my words out before my cell phone rings. Whoever said love doesn't wait must not have a cell phone.

"Hey, Heath," I say then mouth to Mae that he's my agent, in case she'd forgotten. It can be hard for me—let alone anyone else—to keep up with who's interfering in my life these days.

I listen to him tell me that the pictures of Mae at the airport are already hitting the tabloid sites. He's talking a mile a minute, wanting to know how I want to play it. I tell him to do nothing, to say nothing. I know he doesn't agree with that tactic. He's more of the mindset that you should give the press a little nibble to keep their craving for more under control. Normally, I agree with him, but if Mae's not ready, then I support her one hundred percent.

Listening to Heath drone on, I watch Mae wandering around my place, her fingers grazing the fabric of the sofa. I don't know if she's redecorating in her mind, or trying to picture Christmases here with me. Either way, I can't wait to start christening the place with her.

I've never lived with a woman before. That's not to say that past girlfriends haven't slept over in this house, but no one has ever lived here, left stuff here. In fact, I don't know that I've ever spent more than a couple nights in a row with a woman, unless we were on vacation somewhere. I plan on changing that. I've got four nights here with Mae.

If all goes well, my plan is that she'll never have to bring a suitcase to come here again. I'm not expecting her to uproot her life and move to Malibu. I know that's not going to happen, and I wouldn't want it to. But she can certainly have one of the closets, a dresser, a few drawers in the bathroom. Both our jobs are flexible enough that we can split our time between our houses. They're totally different lifestyles, but that's okay. As long as we don't have to spend huge amounts of time apart. I don't want that.

Maybe I'm getting ahead of myself, but I've just seen too many relationships go south because of distance, because of work. It's the curse of acting. You can be gone shooting a movie for months on end, sometimes thousands of miles away. That's hard on any relationship, and it's not something I want for me and Mae. I want to be with her.

I'm at a place in my career where I can be picky about the projects that I take, so I'm not worried about never working again. That's not going to happen, and even if it did, I'd be fine financially. Plus, I've got my own production company in the works. I'm hoping that keeps me home a little more, or at home *with Mae* a little more.

Malibu, New York, Haven's Point? I don't care where we are as long as she's next to me. I'll do what it takes to make that happen.

"You have everything set up for tomorrow?" I ask Heath, glancing at Mae. When he confirms, I say, "Thanks for setting that up."

Ending the call, I shove the phone in my pocket. "What's tomorrow?" Mae asks.

"A surprise."

~

I've had Mae out on the balcony for a good hour while her surprise was set up in the house. Yesterday, we laid low. After the surprise attack at the airport, I figured Mae needed some time to decompress.

The house is set high up on a cliff with enough hedges that the paparazzi can't get very good shots of us. There's always ongoing debate about the beaches here. Landowners want them to be private, but the fact is, most beaches are public areas. So while I'd love to take her for a walk on the beach, broad daylight might not be the best time.

So far, the stuff with the press is manageable. Her job identity is still a secret. She looks adorable in the photos, and while the press is clamoring for more details about Mae, it's all positive. Apparently, me dating a "normal" girl is very appealing to the American public, not that I give a shit about their opinion.

Mae seems to be handling things well, too. The best advice I could give her was not to look at stuff online. Even though it's sometimes brought to my attention, it doesn't need to be brought to hers. She wants things to stay as normal as possible, and looking at pictures of yourself online is anything but.

CHAPTER TWENTY-FOUR

Mae

From Knox's balcony, the Pacific Ocean stretches out before me, endless. The blue water meets the blue sky, and the world seems vast, which is ironic since Knox lives under a microscope. I guess now I do, too.

His arms tighten around me from behind as we stare out to the horizon. It's been about twenty-four hours since news of my relationship with Knox broke. I'm not going to lie. What happened at the airport scared the crap out of me. Maybe if I'd been prepared, my reaction would have been different, but being blindsided like that really shook me.

I've stayed away from all media since. I don't want to read whether people think I'm pretty enough for Knox, or hear what they think about our relationship. Their opinion isn't important. The danger is not what the public thinks. The danger is when we start to *care* what they think. I had a blackout on Knox Merrick for years, pretty successfully. I'm going to do the same thing now.

The only thing I really care about is that I don't get linked to Mother Superior. And so far, from everything I've heard from Knox, my secret is still safe. And no friends, family, or business folks are hitting up my phone to say I've been discovered. I did give a call to my bosses at the station, and, while not thrilled about the media attention, they were okay for the moment. They basically reiterated that my future is in my own hands.

Knox kisses my shoulder, leading me back inside the house. I know Heath is there to talk to him, and Knox is cooking up some surprise for me. Knox makes a quick introduction before Heath disappears into Knox's office to wait while Knox leads me toward the bedroom.

The door opens, and a beautiful woman steps out, giving us a bright smile. My eyes go to Knox, having no idea what to think. "Mae, this is Brynn. You two have fun!" he says before kissing me on the cheek and turning to leave.

"Wait!" I call out.

But Knox doesn't stop. He simply smiles back at me and says, "You're in good hands."

What is going on? Knox left me here with this gorgeous woman who could make any supermodel feel self-conscious. I look back at Brynn, who's grinning ear-to-ear.

"I wish my boyfriend looked at me like that," she says.

I look her up and down; the woman is stunning. "If he doesn't, you should dump him."

Brynn laughs. "Knox said you were a firecracker in a small package." She motions for me to walk into the bedroom. "Let's get to work."

"I'm a little confused."

"That chicken shit didn't tell you?" Brynn asks, shaking her fist in the direction Knox that disappeared.

"No."

"I'm your stylist, sugar."

I'm really not in Haven's Point anymore. "Knox!" I scream, half smiling, half annoyed.

Knox doesn't come back in. "He knew you weren't going to like it. He told me you like simple things, not a lot of fuss or money spent."

"I have clothes. I don't need . . ."

"A dress for the movie premiere," she says. "That's why I'm here."

I haven't even agreed to go to the premiere. I know it's getting close, and I have to decide, so I guess I do need a dress, just in case.

"No one is going to care about what I'm wearing."

Brynn opens her arms, motioning around the bedroom, the walls lined with racks and racks of dresses. "Who do you think gave me all this?"

"I assumed Knox . . ."

"These were all given to me by designers who want to dress Knox Merrick's girlfriend—that's you."

"But . . . I mean, how . . . the public only found out about us yesterday!"

"Things happen fast in Hollywood," she says.

I run my fingers over a box, and Brynn lifts the lid, a pair of diamond and emerald earrings inside. "This is so weird."

"I know, but this is your life now. Knox is the hottest male actor in America right now. This all comes with the territory."

"So you're doing this for him, too?"

"He's a little easier, suits and tuxedos."

I sit down on the bed, overwhelmed. "I know most girls probably love this, but I feel like everyone is going to judge me. It feels like the whole world will be critiquing me."

"My job isn't to make a new you. It's to make everyone else want to be you."

***

I've always wanted to walk into some fancy salon where highbrow people go, sit down with a hair dresser who charges an exorbitant amount of money, and let him cut my hair any way he wants—to see what an artist would do with the mop on my head.

Being with Brynn is kind of like that, but with clothes. Quickly sizing me up, she eliminates half the dress options simply based on colors. She cuts another third because they are, in her opinion, hideous.

"A designer label does not make it stylish," she says.

After her cuts, we are still left with a ton of dresses. "Valentino?"

she asks, holding up a little black number. I wrinkle my nose. "You're right," she says, strolling around the racks. "It's not the Oscars, but this is like a debut for you. The first time the world will be introduced to the woman Knox Merrick loves. Hmm!"

Loves? Surely, he didn't tell the stylist he loves me before he tells me.

"If you could wear any designer in the world, who would you wear?" Brynn asks.

"Target," I say with a smile.

I'm joking, but her eyes totally light up. "Yes!" She starts moving around the racks, searching, clearly on a quest for something, but I doubt she's got a dress from Target in there. "Remember in the nineties when Sharon Stone wore that Vera Wang skirt paired with her husband's shirt from The Gap?" I just look at her like she's insane. "Oh, no, you wouldn't remember that. You were like one."

Brynn isn't much older than me, but this is her business, her life, so I guess her knowledge of fashion trivia is better than mine.

"Anyway, it was a total fashion moment. We need a moment!"

"You want me to wear Knox's shirt?" I ask.

She stops and stares at me. "Vintage, maybe?"

That word makes me think of Gigi. And while I love old things, I don't like the idea of wearing a priceless vintage dress that I could rip or spill something on—at least not my first time out of the gate. So I throw out my own random idea. "What if we do the opposite?"

"What do you mean?"

"What if I wear something from an up and coming designer? Or a student? Someone whose career could be helped by me wearing their dress?"

Her eyes light up. "I know just what to do." She pulls out a dress from one of the racks she initially eliminated. "I've been trying to get someone to wear this dress for over a year. The designer is from Colorado, so that makes it extra perfect. I was a visiting lecturer at a design school, and I saw her sketches. I love them, but I can't get anyone to pay attention because everyone wants to wear Gucci or

Prada."

As soon as she holds the dress up, my heart starts racing. It's not a dress. It's a full, ball gown skirt, paired with a crop top. It's blush pink and beautiful, but still a crop top.

"Bare midriff?" I ask, my nervousness evident.

She holds it up in front of me. "Finding the perfect dress is like finding the perfect man. When you know, you just know."

Softly, I knock on the office door before peeking my head in to let Knox know that Brynn is leaving. Whatever Knox and Heath were talking about has left the air in the room feeling heavy with stress.

"Did you find something?" Knox asks, getting to his feet and walking toward me.

I nod, and thank him for setting it up, but he barely smiles. He seems off all of a sudden, not the Knox I know, and walks past me out of the room. The man I know has a killer smile, which he uses quite frequently to get what he wants, charm my panties right off, or just let me know how happy he is.

I start following him when Heath holds his arm out. "We haven't really had a chance to talk, to get to know each other," Heath says. "Join me in here."

Leaving the door open, I walk inside, taking a seat opposite him. He crosses his leg in a relaxed pose. He looks every bit the part of Hollywood agent—tailored suit, flashy gold watch, not a hair out of place.

"It's been hard for me to get Knox to tell me anything about you. What do you do?" he asks.

That makes me smile. Knox is keeping my job a secret even though I know that's hard. "I have my own radio show."

"*The Breakup Bible*," he says with a smug smile.

"If you already knew, then why did you ask?"

"I was wondering if you'd tell me the truth." He cocks a sideways grin at me. "I needed to know if you'd be honest with me."

"I was."

"Half honest," he says.

"How did you find out?" I ask, giving him my own smirk. "*Honestly.*"

"Just made a few phone calls. Radio is part of the entertainment business."

I hate to think discovering my identity is as easy as a few phone calls, but I hate it more to think I'm part of the entertainment business. I don't think of myself as an entertainer. Entertaining, I hope so, but not an *entertainer*. There's a difference.

"I've listened to a few of your shows online," he says. "I can see why Knox likes you so much."

Brynn used the word "love," and this guy uses the word "like." Does Knox love me? Like me? I hope it's both.

"Is that a compliment?" I ask.

He laughs. "Of course. Look, I can see you trying to figure out whether or not I'm on your side. The answer to that is, I'm on Knox's side."

He's the paycheck! Of course, this guy is on Knox's side, but that doesn't mean he's on mine. This Heath guy is talking out of both sides of his mouth. He must think I'm an idiot.

"Knox and I have worked very hard on his career, his brand," he says. "His brother hasn't always made that easy."

"Ryder is a good guy," I say defensively.

He ignores my comment and continues. I get the feeling he likes the sound of his own voice. "Knox's image is very important. No trips to rehab for drugs, alcohol, or sex. No gambling debts. Aside from being a bit of a ladies' man, he's squeaky clean."

"I'm not going to do anything to dirty his reputation," I say, "if that's what you're worried about. I've known him forever."

"Talking about him on the air will reduce him to a damn reality TV star," Heath snaps.

"You're out of line, Heath," Knox says, appearing out of nowhere. "Mae's career is none of your concern. I asked you to stay out of it."

"You don't pay me to stay out of it," Heath says.

"I have no plans to discuss my personal life with Knox on-air," I say.

"You already have," Heath says. "He's been on your show twice."

"And both times *he* called *me*," I say.

Knox flashes me a grin. "Smartest thing I ever did was calling your show that first time."

Heath rolls his eyes. "Look, as soon as the public realizes you're the lady on the radio, every show you've ever done is going to be analyzed. All the things you've discussed before. The press will speculate whether the guy who gave you the mind-blowing oral sex was Knox."

Yep!

"Or whether the guy who took you to meet his mother on your first date was Knox."

Nope.

"Or if . . ."

"Enough!" Knox barks. "Just like any story, it will all blow over in a few days."

"Why do you think you get to have an opinion about our relationship?" I snap at Heath. "It's not your business, just like it's not the business of the public or press."

"She's naive," Heath says to him. Knox starts to object, but Heath cuts him off and pats his shoulder. "You know I'm right. Your reputation can bounce back, but ask yourself this. Can hers?"

Knox's blue eyes glance my way, and something tells me he believes Heath. My stomach twists into a hundred knots. I trust Knox, and if he's worried, I should probably be worried, too. But I don't give a crap what Heath thinks.

"I'll be fine," I say, more to Knox than Heath.

"Who knew she was coming to California?" Heath asks.

"*She* is standing right here, and *she* would appreciate it if you'd stop referring to her in the third person," I snap.

Knox glares at Heath, telling him, "Dial it back and be respectful." Heath rolls his eyes and nods curtly, and Knox looks my way, asking, "Who knew about your trip, baby?"

I consider the question briefly before answering, "Some friends, my grandmother, why?"

"Heath confirmed that Vincent asshole from the Denver paper was the one that tipped off the tabloids here. Gave them your flight information. But someone had to give it to him," Knox says.

"Everly and Timothy would never, and Gigi would probably give them the wrong information out of spite," I say. "No one I know would betray me like that."

"It's a hard lesson to learn, but not everyone you know is trustworthy. Most can be bought," Heath says, getting to his feet.

"The reporter could've followed me," I say. "Trying to get shots of us together. Saw me go to the airport. I have seen him hanging around."

"When?" Knox asks. "Why didn't you tell me?"

"Because it wasn't a big deal. You weren't even in Haven's Point when I saw him," I say. "He was parked far away the day of Gigi's birthday. I guess he thought you'd be there. I ignored him."

"You should've told me," Knox says, his eyes growing wide. "The pile of shit on your porch."

"What about it?"

"Wasn't that the night of the birthday party?" Knox asks.

"You don't think that reporter guy would . . ."

"A pile of shit? Isn't that what you called him that first night he showed up?" Knox says. "Christ, Mae, he was at your house. On your porch. So fucking close to you."

"We don't know that," I say.

"I guarantee there's a pair of my size twelve leather shoes in his closet!"

"Naive," Heath says again, giving Knox a look before heading for the door. "I'll clear your schedule the next two days. Let me know if you change your mind and want me to make a statement about your relationship. I'll see myself out."

I get to my feet, taking Knox's hand, trying to reassure him. "I know why you've been spending so much time in Haven's Point recently," I say. "This whole place is crazy."

"You don't know the half of it," he says. "That's what worries me."

"Then show me," I say. "Spend the next couple days showing me how crazy your life can get. Let's walk down the street and let those pests snap thousands of photos of us. Let them chase us. Let's not hide. Bring on the crazy."

Before I know what's happening, he tosses me over his shoulder, smacking my booty. "Let's start in the bedroom."

CHAPTER TWENTY-FIVE

Knox

After your first love, you're never the same. Your heart never trusts so blindly, so completely again. They say you never know love like your first love, and that's true. Because prior to your first love, you've never known heartbreak, the feeling of losing the one you love, so you're totally open, totally free. You allow yourself to fall completely without any fear because you believe it will last forever. You don't know any differently.

After Mae, my heart was never the same. I was guarded. Losing her was second only to losing my parents. The pain was so deep, so raw, I never wanted to feel it again. My heart protected itself from ever feeling that kind of pain. From the outside, to the press, my fans, even my friends, it looked like I was just a player.

But the truth was, I never wanted to know the pain of losing a woman I love again.

So I never loved another woman.

It was always Mae. She's it for me.

Mae stands in my closet in her bra and panties. I hung up the few items of clothing she brought next to mine. It's a little habit of mine. When you travel as much as I do, you can literally live out of a suitcase, so sometime early in my career, I made it a habit to unpack. It doesn't matter whether I'm going to be in a hotel for one night or twenty, I always unpack. It is the one thing you can do to immediately make a place seem more like home, so I took the liberty of unpacking her things for her.

I've been dressed and ready to go for at least thirty minutes, but we aren't ever going to make it out of the house if she keeps standing there half naked. My cock is getting other ideas about how he wants to spend the day, and those plans don't include being tailed by paparazzi while touring Los Angeles.

"It's just a normal day," I say. "You don't need to change what you wear just because you'll be all over the tabloids."

"I don't care about that," she says.

"Then what is it?"

She points to a shelf in my closet, a certain old shoe box. Our cassettes are inside, each one labeled with the dates of the first and last entry. They fill the box, some sticking out of the top, stacked one on top of another.

"I haven't seen them in so long," she says. "There's so many of them. There must be close to a hundred hours."

"I've never added them up," I say, wrapping my arms around her waist.

"They're our own version of love letters," she says quietly.

"Would you like to listen to some of them?"

She turns around in my arms. "I'd love that."

Cassette

Mae to Knox

Age Sixteen

Sorry this cassette is late. I hope you weren't worried. I'm fine. Grounded for the rest of my life, but fine.

I had to wait until both my parents were gone to record this. They said my grounding included sending tapes to you. I'll happily sit my butt at home, but I'm not going to not send tapes to you. I'll find a way. Hopefully, this all blows over soon.

I'm sure you're wondering why I'm in trouble. You know my dad has rules. One of them is that I'm not allowed to take public transportation by myself. It's stupid. I'm sixteen. I'm allowed to drive a car. I don't have one, but still.

Anyway, there was this exhibit I wanted to see, and my parents were both busy, so I took a bus there myself. It should've been a non-issue, but the bus was really crowded, so I had to stand. Forget I said that part. Just know that my parents found out, and I got grounded.

I can picture your face right now. I know what you'd say. You'd remind me that we don't lie to each other. But we don't tell each other every little detail of our days, either. That would take too long.

My dad is so angry. My mom keeps telling me he's angry because he was scared, and it's easier for him as a man to be angry than admit fear.

Please allow me this one pass. Please. I don't want you to be mad at me, too.

❧

Mae crosses her legs on my bed, like we did in grade school—criss-cross, applesauce. I push the button on the cassette, stopping it.

Of all the tapes to listen to. It was a random selection, but I would've preferred a sweet one or a flirty one.

"You gave me a pass," she says, smiling at me. "Didn't make you tell me why I was grounded."

"I don't think you would've been as understanding if the tables were turned," I say, tackling her down to the bed. I twirl the curly strands of hair around my finger.

"I definitely would have demanded to know why you were grounded," she says with a giggle.

"I think your pass has expired," I say.

She scoots out from under me, sitting up. I do the same, rubbing her hand a little. That tape is ten years old, no way would I be mad about something that happened so far back, but Mae doesn't look so sure of that.

She takes a deep breath. "The bus was crowed, standing room only. People were bumping into each other. I was holding on to a pole to keep my balance and holding my bag in front of me. I didn't want to get pickpocketed. I thought I was protecting myself. I was using my head. Or I thought I was."

"Sounds smart to me," I say. She gives me a small smile, like the kind of smile you give an idiot—someone who doesn't have a clue.

"Someone standing behind me touched me."

I feel my heart pounding in my chest, my blood skyrocketing through my veins. She doesn't tell me where or how, but it doesn't matter whether it was her ass, her chest, between her legs or her fucking elbow! No one is allowed to touch her without permission. No fucking one!

"I turned around, but there were three men behind me. I didn't know which one did it. They were big guys. I was scared to get off the bus, scared they would follow me. I was so worried about my bag, the small amount of money I had, I hadn't considered anything else. I was only sixteen. Nothing like that had happened to me before."

She gives me that same smile. She was young and naive. Most men don't have to worry about being groped on crowded public transit. But her dad knew to worry. I guess that comes with having a daughter. You live imagining the worst of the male population.

"A nice woman on the bus saw me. She didn't see what happened, but she knew I was upset and scared. She stayed with me and made sure I got home. That's how my parents found out." Mae must see my face turning red and places her hand on top of mine. "Knox, you look so pissed off."

"I am!"

"It was a long time ago. Don't be mad at me about . . ."

"I'm not mad at you. Why would I be mad at you?"

"Because my parents had told me not to ride the bus alone, and I did it, anyway."

"What? I don't care about that. This has nothing to do with your parents and their rules," I say. "The fact that a woman can't ride the bus or the subway without having to worry about some asshole touching her is what pisses me off!"

She places her hands behind my neck, leaning in. "Was my mom right? Are you angry because you're scared?"

Her mom was always too smart for her own good, and I guess Mae inherited that trait. There's not much that scares me. The only time I can remember being truly frightened was when my mom died, and I was six. Cancer took my mom slowly. Or at least it seemed slow to me at the time. Looking back, she was dead within nine months of the diagnosis. Now, that seems fast, but to a little boy watching his mother get thinner and thinner, it seemed like an eternity. Losing my mom was scary, but watching her suffer scared me more.

"I'm about to take you out into a crowd of paparazzi," I say softly. "Anything can happen."

She gives me another smile, a different kind this time, one that doesn't say I'm a clueless idiot. It's for a totally different reason.

"And whatever happens," she whispers, "you'll be beside me this time."

❧

Mae asked me to give her the "full Hollywood experience," as she put it. She thought that meant paparazzi chasing us from here to there, being photographed eating our lunch. That is part of it, of course, but I plan on showing her the perks of my life, too. That means spoiling her rotten.

When we left my house today, there were even more paparazzi outside than usual, thanks to my relationship with Mae being front page news. They've been following us since. We've actually had a steady stream of them all day. You'd think they'd get bored, but they never seem to. I guess there's always a new picture to post.

It's strange. I usually don't mind my fans approaching me, taking pictures with them, but these paparazzi assholes are a whole other story. There should be certain times when I'm allowed to just be a person. If I'm eating a meal or with my girlfriend or family, a decent person would know not to interrupt, but you'd be surprised how many people don't care.

"Can't believe you still have this car," Mae says, running her hands along the leather interior of my restored blue convertible. "It seemed like every cassette you sent me that summer talked about this car."

"Back then, I was too young to drive it," I say, remembering how much Ryder ragged me about that. Even now, I don't drive the convertible much, but I always take it for a spin on my dad's birthday or other special occasions, like today. On those days, I usually have the top down, but not today.

I pull the car in front of a high-end boutique in Beverly Hills. "Time to fill my closet with things for you when you're here."

Mae turns to me. "You aren't serious?"

I stop the car, and a flood of cameras press against the windows of my car. This is exactly why the top is up. The cameras start to click away.

"We can sit in the car and make out while they take pictures of us," I say with a grin. "Or we can go inside and shop. Besides, I'm taking you to a party tonight. You need a new dress."

Her eyes bulge. "A party?"

"The director of my new film is having a thing at his house."

"And you want me to go with you?"

"Full Hollywood experience, remember?"

"Right," Mae says, putting on her wide brim sunglasses, reaching for the door handle.

I place my hand on her knee, stopping her. This is just one of many lessons she needs to learn about my life. You can't just open the car door.

"I'm going to get out first," I say. "Then I'll get your door and escort you inside. No matter what questions they scream, just ignore them, keep walking."

"Okay," she says, not sounding very confident.

"One more thing," I say, yanking the hem of her dress down a little. "Make sure you hold your dress down when you get out, so it doesn't fly up or . . ."

"They'll get a panty shot," she says, squeezing my hand. "I got it."

She releases a deep breath and nods, and then I open my door. I've done this enough times that I know it's best to move quickly and with authority. Otherwise, they'll eat you alive. I'm not someone who likes to travel with security. I know Mae would hate that, as well. Like me, she values her privacy too much. So I'm going to be her bodyguard for now, until we see how things go.

It seems like an eternity before I get to her car door, the crowd bigger today than most days. Opening her door, I reach for her hand, pulling her up and out of the car, then I place one arm around her waist, using the other arm to part the crowd.

"Come on, guys, give us a little room," I say.

Cameras flash in our faces. Questions fly at us. *How'd you meet? How about a kiss? Mae, are you hoping to score a role in his next movie?*

We only have about ten feet between the car and the store, and I manage to get us in without incident. We're met at the door by the store manager, who shoos the vultures away, then leads us to a private room in the back.

As we make our way, I look over at Mae. She's taking deep breaths, but no trembling this time. I'm not opposed to fucking her in the dressing room if she needs it, but it looks like she's handling the craziness much better this time.

The back room is set up specifically for high profile clients. It's got a couple dressing rooms, a nice waiting area with a sofa and chairs, mirrors, and a bar with drinks and snacks. Mae looks up at me, a little crease between her eyes. "How are we supposed to shop from back here?"

Usually shopping involves looking through racks and racks of clothing, which is just one of the many reasons I hate it. But we don't have to go through the hassle of that. "The store's personal shoppers will pick things out for you from the front of the store, and then they bring them back here to you."

"Where's the fun in that?" she asks. "I think half the fun of shopping is going through the racks, finding the incredible deal."

"You don't need to find deals," I say, and her eyes widen at me. "I've got it covered."

"Knox, I don't . . ."

"I want to," I say, not letting her object further. "I can have them close the store for us, if you'd prefer. Cover the windows. That way, you can roam around and look yourself."

"So I won't ever be able to just walk into Target and browse again?"

My heart breaks a little for her. She just wants "normal." But my life is the farthest thing from normal you can get. This is supposed to be fun. I hadn't considered that even shopping would be so different and overwhelming for her.

"They have really cute clothes at Target," she says, flipping over one of the price tags, her eyes going wide. "And their jeans don't cost five hundred dollars."

This isn't about the money, I know that. And this isn't about the jeans or the store, or even about her wanting to browse or find a deal.

This is about her freedom. She still wants to be her. I want that, too.

"We'll hit Target up after this," I say.

Her entire face lights up. "Deal."

Mae's in the dressing room. Frankly, I'm not sure what I'm doing here. She won't even show me the clothes when she tries them on. The store's stylist keeps bringing in and out various items of clothing. I've got my ass parked on a chair outside, but it seems my opinion isn't important.

"The black dress," I whisper to the stylist as she heads back out to grab some more pieces.

"Hey, I never agreed to letting you dress me!" Mae yells over the door, obviously having heard me.

"Then let me *undress* you," I tease.

She peeks her head out the door. "The sizes in this store are wrong!"

"I'm pretty sure sizes are universal."

"No, they're not!" Mae says. "I'm like two sizes bigger here than I am at . . ."

"I'm coming in there," I say, reaching for the handle, but Mae quickly closes the door, leaning against it.

"No, I'm not dressed."

I can't help but laugh. Suddenly she's shy. "You have five seconds to put something on." I start to count. "One . . .Two . . ."

I hear her shuffling around inside. She's belting a dress when I get to five and open the door. My jaw drops to the floor. Damn, she looks beautiful, the silk of the dress clinging to her curves. I don't care if she's a size two, twelve, or twenty-two, she's stunning.

"We're buying that dress."

"Really?" she says, turning and looking at herself in the mirror, smoothing out the fabric.

I step up behind her, letting her feel the hard length of my dick. "Cock approved!"

"Your penis is going to pick out my wardrobe?"

"No better man for the job."

Mae laughs, pushing me out of the dressing room. I plant a quick kiss on her lips before leaving. I lean back against the wall as the stylist passes a few more items to her. Honestly, I'm not sure how we're going to handle a Target run. We'll be dealing with fans and paparazzi both, but for Mae, I'll give it a try.

Mae opens the door again, now dressed in a pink sundress. She does a little twirl before me, ready for my penis scorecard.

"A semi," I say, grinning.

CHAPTER TWENTY-SIX

Knox

"I hear you, Heath," I say into my phone.

Mae's in my bedroom getting ready for the party, and I'm on my balcony trying not to fire my interfering agent. I like the guy, and he's served me well, but he interferes. And we talked about all this in my office yesterday. I know there are some things I need to discuss with Mae, but we've had a lot thrown at us, and I'm looking for the right time.

"I'll talk to Mae."

"Knox," he says, "the women you dated long-term before were in the business. They knew the drill. Had their own teams to advise them. Mae has you. That's it. You can't avoid these topics just because they might be unpleasant."

"I'm not avoiding them," I say, looking out to the ocean. "The press literally just found out about us."

"And she should've already had security in place, so that shit at the airport never would've happened. She should've been on a private flight."

"She didn't want a private plane."

"And the guard?" he asks.

"I haven't had a chance to bring it up to her," I say. "She's with me now. I can handle things."

"And when she goes home in a few days?"

I look down at the cliffs below. I'm on a ledge. One shift in the ground below me, and this could all come tumbling down. "I'll talk to her."

He exhales. "You have someone else to worry about now."

"Don't you think I know that?" I bark.

"Look, I don't want to piss you off. That's the last thing I want. I'm just trying to keep you informed, so you can make the best decisions possible," he says. "We've actually gotten some more letters. Disturbing letters."

"Thank you notes again?" I ask.

"Same M.O.," Heath says. "Seems like the same person. They sound obsessed—like if they can't have you, no one will."

"Did they say that?"

"Not in so many words."

"Christ," I say and pull at my hair. "But haven't we gotten this kind of stuff before? I don't want to scare Mae for no reason. To have her think someone is after me, when this type of shit happens all the time."

"Yeah, here and there over the years, we've received these threats. You've seen them before," he says. "But this just seems different, the tone, the frequency, the timing of it all. And it's my job to take it seriously."

"Fuck," I say, as several hairs stand up on the back of my neck. I don't spook easily, but Heath is right. We need to take it seriously, and I do have Mae to think about now.

"Let me look into it a little bit more," Heath says.

⌇

"Raging boner," I whisper in Mae's ear as we step into the party. She lightly elbows me in the stomach. Thank God, she didn't aim lower, but there's no helping my current situation.

She's wearing this red dress. It's not tight or incredibly short, hitting her right at the knee, but it's the brightest color red, bringing out the natural highlights in her brown hair, which she has pulled up in a high ponytail. She looks gorgeous from the front, but it's the back that's got me panting. The straps cross in the back, leaving a peekaboo opening right at the small of her back, just the spot I like to run my fingers down as I take her from behind.

She hasn't said it, but I know she's got to be nervous walking in here tonight, especially wearing that dress. It was her choice, but there's no blending in looking like she does. She's about to dive headfirst into the deep end, which is full of sharks. But I have no doubt that Mae can handle anything. She's smart, beautiful, funny. This should be easy for her. My biggest concern is what she'll say if someone asks what she does for a living. I guess she's handled that question before, in Haven's Point and beyond. Still, she's just going to have to be careful not to give away too much information, or have a response that elicits too many follow up questions. If she does get into trouble, I'll be there to rescue her.

This place sits on a few miles of precious real estate in the Holmby Hills area of Los Angeles, and it's massive. I guess that's why it has three kitchens. You could get hungry trekking from one side of the house to the other. This area has been home to some of the greats. Aaron Spelling, Walt Disney, and Frank Sinatra, just to name a few.

"You're poor!" Mae jokes as she takes in this monstrosity of a house.

I guess compared to this, I am. It's all relative. There are houses, there are even mansions, and then there are estates. This is an estate—an expansive compound of pools, tennis courts, the main house, and the guest houses.

"Knox!" someone calls out, and I wave to a person I don't know.

Mae squeezes my hand, and I whisper, "I won't leave you."

She doesn't know a soul here, so it's my job to make sure she's comfortable and having as good a time as possible. We spend a few minutes making the rounds, working our way deeper inside the party, which is being held in the den of the main house, extending outside under the patio. This is a small get-together by Hollywood stand-ards—about one hundred people or so, mostly from the movie set to premiere soon.

A group of four women descend upon me, and suddenly, I'm lost in a sea of tits and ass, each one's dress shorter and tighter than the next. It's not uncommon for women to throw their arms around me, or even sit on my lap unsolicited. I doubt any of these women actually want the real me, but are more interested in what I can do to advance their careers.

I see Mae rolling her eyes. She knows me—all my flaws. Being an actor doesn't make you a god. Mae wants to be with me for me, despite the fact I'm in the public eye, not because of it. That's the key.

Time to shut this shit down! I don't want to give Mae any reason to be jealous or have doubts. Pulling Mae to my hip, I coil my arm around her waist. The four women stare daggers at Mae. With a grin, I introduce her as my girlfriend, and that causes them all to scatter. Thank God.

"Sorry," I say to Mae.

She leans up, planting a sweet kiss on my lips, letting me know she understands it's just a side effect of my work. "I hate these circles," Mae whispers, looking around. "You know how everyone is always huddled in these circles."

"Me, too," I whisper back.

"You're not *in* the circle," she says. "You're the sun everyone is orbiting around."

Smiling, I roll my eyes. What she fails to realize is this is just a moment in time. It just happens to be my moment. But tomorrow it could be someone else's turn. I always remember that.

A new group approaches and strikes up a conversation, and Mae gives me an *I told you so* look. She makes small talk when she can, and I do my best to include her. I know this can't be easy, walking into a room of people who know one other and feeling like the odd man out.

That's the thing about Hollywood, it's a pretty small town. When I go to a big awards show, like the Oscars, I often wonder how many people have slept with each other in the room. I mean, you've got divorced people, ex-lovers, random one-night stands. It can get pretty awkward, which is why I should've been prepared for the woman walking toward me.

Mae and I haven't delved too deeply into each other's sexual pasts. Perhaps it was just easier that way, because neither one of us wanted to think about it. But if I'd known Mae was going to come face-to-face with someone I used to share my bed with, I would've warned her, or avoided the party all together.

"Knox, so good to see you."

Shit, crap, fuck! Things happen on movie sets, and not all of it is in front of the cameras. My trailers have seen just as much action, and well, this woman had a bit part in a film of mine two years ago. She's hot, but not a very talented actress. But hot can take you a long way in this town, and in my trailer. She wasn't the first. Maybe the third? Or fourth? Just to be safe, let's call her Trailer Woman Number Five.

Trailer Woman Number Five leans in to kiss me, but I turn my face, forcing us into an awkward, weird side hug.

I'm not sure why she's here. She's not in this movie. She's not attached to anyone in the movie that I can think of. Trailer Woman Number Five's eyes go to Mae, waiting for an introduction, which I regrettably have to make. The best I can hope for here is that Mae doesn't pick up on anything. I know she never really followed my career. That still bothers me, but at this moment, I'm thankful. If I'm lucky, she missed this rumor, which certainly had some truth to it.

Seeing her and Mae next to each other, I'm not sure what I ever saw in her. They are complete opposites. Mae is brunette, blue eyed. Trailer Woman Number Five is blonde with brown eyes. Mae is smart and funny, and this other woman is . . . well, you get the idea.

The women exchange a polite hello, and Trailer Woman Number Five starts talking to me about some upcoming project she thinks will be good for my production company. Ugh! Sometimes it seems everyone is always looking for a piece of me. Still, there is a familiarity that exists between ex-lovers. It's hard to hide. It's small—the way she looks at me, touches my arm, how she leans into me when she laughs. I'm doing my best to hide it, to move away, but that's telling, too.

"I think I'm going to go outside and get some fresh air," Mae says.

"I'll come with you," I say, giving my ex-trailer companion a small smile before walking off.

I see Mae is already stepping out onto the patio. I try to catch up, but keep getting pulled into a handshake or hello.

By the time I get outside, Mae's a good twenty feet from the house, staring up at the moon. She's beautiful, but the look on her face makes my stomach churn. I know that look. She's thinking. Correction, she's overthinking. An overthinking woman is a dangerous thing.

CHAPTER TWENTY-SEVEN

Mae

Staring up at the sky, I remind myself it's the same sky in Colorado, but clearly, I'm not in Haven's Point anymore. We don't have parties like this. Our parties are small watch parties at The Tune Up, or involve the Silver Sirens singing to my Gigi at the lake as everyone swims and hangs out. We eat on paper plates, not fine china. We grill, not cater. We don't have to buy new dresses, and our cutoff jean shorts work just fine.

If someone follows you in Colorado, that's called stalking, and you call the police and have them arrested, but that's an everyday occurrence for Knox. He lives amidst ongoing threats and doesn't seem to blink an eye. It's a complete warped sense of reality out here, but this is Knox's life, full of money, glamor, women. My life is more coffee shop, lake house, simple.

"I miss you," Knox says, wrapping his arms around me from behind.

"How many other women in there have you slept with?" I ask, pulling away from him. Does he really think I didn't pick up on that?

"How did you know?"

"I knew as soon as she approached us. The way your hands landed on her arms when she leaned in to kiss your cheek, like you didn't want her any closer."

"It's over. It was a long time ago."

"You forgot the *it's nothing*," I say, raising an eyebrow at him.

"I have a past. So do you," he says. "Let's . . ."

"I don't fit in here," I say softly. "This isn't who I am. Not at this party. Not in fancy stores."

"This isn't who I am, either. I'm the same guy who made you cassettes," he says.

"Are you?" I ask.

"Yes, you know that." I nod my head in the affirmative, because I do, in fact, know. "This here," he says, pointing back to the house, the party, "it's just part of my job."

"Please," I say with sass, "you're Hollywood royalty. As for me, I'd be more comfortable in the kitchen, talking to the staff than whoever these people are."

"There are some good people in there," he says. "You just have to weed through them, just like with anything else."

I look up into his handsome face, those blue eyes of his, the ones I've known almost my whole life, and I realize none of this other stuff really matters. What matters is that we are together. The size of the party or the house? Designer clothes or cutoffs? At the end of the day, he's the boy that talked me through my childhood via cassette. Strip away everything else, and that's who we are.

"I'm sorry," I say, taking a deep breath and holding my hands up to indicate the massive real estate before us. "It's a bit overwhelming."

"I know," Knox says. "Why don't we go?"

"No," I say quickly. "I just needed a breather. I asked to see your life, and this is part of it."

"In the future, we can navigate this however you want. There are plenty of spouses that . . ."

"Spouses? Future?" I ask, my eyes popping out of my head. Is that where his head is? That's the direction he sees this heading?

"I just meant there are husbands and wives that don't walk red carpets with their spouses. They don't do interviews or any of that stuff. It works for some couples. They want as normal a life as possible for themselves and their kids. We will have to see what works for us. For you."

"And our kids?" I ask, teasing him.

"Yes," he says, teasing me back. "All twelve of them."

"You're *insane*."

He kisses me lightly on the lips. "This is a lot. I know that, but now that the public knows about us, we have to make some changes. Be more careful."

"What do you mean?"

"I mean, when you go back to Haven's Point, I'm sending you with a security guard, since I can't be with you all the time."

"No," I say, shaking my head.

"Mae, what happened at the airport is just the tip of the iceberg."

"I can handle the press."

"It's not just press. It's crazy fans, too. Stalkers," he says. "I won't take any chances with your safety."

"Knox, this is a non-starter for me. I won't have a guard."

"Mae, listen, please. Just hear me out."

"No," I say again.

"I get crazy letters."

"I'm sure you do."

"Some celebrities have had break-ins, attempted kidnappings, and . . ."

"No, I won't have a guard."

"You're not listening to me," he says, taking hold of my hips.

"No, you're not listening *to me*," I say. "At the station, I get fan mail, too. Some of it is weird. Some of it is crazy ex's thinking their partner broke up with them because of something I said. I get it. I do. But I need my life to be mine. I need to be as normal as possible."

It's early Sunday evening and I have a radio show to get back to. I stayed as long as I could, wanting every minute with Knox, but now I have to get on a plane back to Colorado. This trip has been a whirlwind.

Knox made me call just about every person who knows about us back home to make sure there haven't been any paparazzi sightings. Apparently, that's why a lot of celebrities choose to live in cities outside of L.A. and New York; the paparazzi must not have a lot of frequent flyer miles. From what Gigi and Everly said, things are calm, and I should be fine in my little neck of the woods. And if a few stragglers decide to show up, it won't be like it is here in Los Angeles. Knox also put out a few feelers to get me security and bodyguards back home. Like I already said, I'm not having any of that. I need my life to be mine. I think he understands that. But I can tell it's killing him to let me leave without him, even though he himself doesn't travel with protection.

Things are different now, different than just a week ago when he was visiting me. The public knows we are a couple. So far, that only means they know my name, that I'm from Knox's hometown. But now, I won't be able to go to the grocery store without seeing some picture of me and Knox on the cover of some rag magazine. If that's the worst of it, I can live with it. I'm sure I'll be old news soon. And they will go back to reporting on secret babies, affairs, and alien abductions.

I hate saying goodbye to him. Goodbyes don't usually bother me. I grew up saying them, but saying goodbye to Knox has never been easy.

"I'm not going to cry. It would be stupid to cry," I say, as Knox wipes my cheeks with his thumbs, grinning at me. The more time we spend together, the harder the time apart becomes.

But it's time for me to leave California, to go back home to my normal, simple life, and my anonymous radio show. That part, I'm looking forward to.

"Ten days," he says, looking over my shoulder at the private plane waiting to whisk me back to Haven's Point.

Knox didn't want me to have to deal with LAX paparazzi again, so he arranged for me to fly home in style. I didn't object this time. And I have to say, not having to remove my shoes or liquids to go through security is a perk.

Knox and I were escorted back to a private room to wait until the plane's ready. It's pretty nice. No crowds, my own bathroom, no lugging my bags around. So this is the celebrity life? A girl could get used to this.

"At the most, ten days," he adds.

I'm definitely not going to miss Los Angeles, but I am going to miss the man in front of me. Everything about him. His smile, waking up next to him, the way he looks at me. Everything.

"Ten days," I whisper back.

His movie premiere, I'll be back for that. It will be a last-minute decision whether I attend or not, but either way, I want to be here for him. Whether I'm on his arm walking down the red carpet or at his place waiting for him in bed, I want to support him.

He's very busy promoting the film until the premiere, but he promised to try and sneak in a trip to Haven's Point. I don't want to add any more pressure, so at the longest, we will see each other in a week and a half.

"I'll be looking at your picture on my phone," he teases. "You know the one."

I laugh, but bury my head in his chest as he runs his fingers through my hair and kisses the top of my head. We stand quietly for a few minutes, holding each other. I wonder what he's thinking. I'm thinking I don't want to let go.

Finally, I look up. "I'm going to have to figure out how to do my show remotely."

He grins, but I see the worry in his eyes. "You talked to Gigi and Everly?"

"Things are quiet in Haven's Point," I say.

"You call me, day or night," he says, "whenever you need me."

"I will."

"I wish you'd stay at Gigi's," he says.

"Not going to happen."

"If you get scared staying alone . . ."

"I'll call you or go to Gigi's," I say.

"Please be careful," he says. "I have some crazy fans."

I roll my eyes. "They hate me for bagging you, so what?"

"Bagging me," he says, tickling me a little. "I think *I* bagged *you*."

Looking at the clock on the wall, I know I have to go. As it is, I'm going to have to go straight from the airport to the radio station.

"Ms. Sheridan," a cheerful voice says behind me. "We're ready for you to board." Knox intertwines his fingers with mine, heading toward the door. "I'm sorry, Mr. Merrick," the woman says. "Only passengers are allowed on the tarmac."

He gives her a polite nod. But I can tell Knox wants one more minute, so I pull him to me, kissing him sweetly on the lips. Then I turn and follow her out the door toward the plane.

A few tears roll down my cheeks. It feels silly to cry. It's only ten days, but Gigi always says there are no silly tears, just ones that need to be shed. Promising myself I'll only look back one time, I wait until I reach the top of the stairs of the plane.

I make it to the top and turn around, but he's not there. I thought I'd wave, blow him a kiss, like something out of a movie—*our* movie.

But he's not there. He just left.

～

I don't care how short the flight is—flying always makes me tired. And I'm not one that can sleep on an airplane. So I'm not as peppy as I usually am before my show. It's times like these I wish I liked the taste of coffee.

Even though the press hasn't put together that Mae Sheridan is Mother Superior, the higher ups at my station know about my relationship with Knox. For now, they are content to let things play out—which is the best I could hope for. I'm good business for them. They should just chill and be patient. No need to do anything rash at the moment. And I'm grateful for that, too.

I could use a shower, but instead, I go straight from the plane to the station via a private car that Knox arranged. Amy sees me pulling my suitcase down the hallway of the station and opens the door for me. It looks like she's been here for hours, and there are all kinds of papers scattered around. She looks like she's ready to do the show for me.

"I know you were busy," Amy says, talking quickly. "So I jotted down some ideas for tonight's show."

"That's sweet," I say. "But I had the flight to prepare."

"Oh," she says. "Of course."

I didn't mean to sound dismissive. It's not that I don't want to hear her ideas. It's more that I don't want to have to turn them down if they're bad. Still, I like that she's eager, and if no one had ever given me a shot, then who knows what I'd be doing. That's a scary thought! What would I be doing if it wasn't this? I hope I never have to find out.

Anyway, I believe we have to pay it forward—especially women helping women. So I smile at Amy and say, "Let's go to lunch this week and look at some of your ideas."

"Really?" she asks with a huge smile, and I give her a nod. "How was your trip? From the pictures all over the internet, it looked fantastic."

My smile fades. Amy knows me. Well, she knows me a little bit, and she's still looking for information online. She's curious. It's no big deal. Still, it's unnerving to think that people all over the world now know my name, care about my life, envy me, or hate me all because of a few photos. All because of the man I'm dating.

"Things are good," I say then make a quick switch of topics. "How's the apartment search?"

"Oh, fine," Amy says, waving her hand dismissively. "Are you going to the premiere? Because this one entertainment channel is reporting that . . ."

I managed not to listen to any of that while I was with Knox. I didn't read one online report. But apparently, Amy read and watched them all.

"There is this poll on Twitter about how long your relationship will last," she says. "Want to know how I voted?"

I laugh. "It better have been forever!"

"Forever, huh? Sounds serious."

My smile says it all, but I don't want to share too much. I don't want to jinx anything, plus I've never been the kiss and tell type. I guess that's good because I have to be even more careful about who I trust now. I don't like feeling that way, especially among friends.

Is that how Knox feels about people, even those close to him in his business and personal life? Like he never knows who to trust? Heath certainly thinks that way—he believes someone in my circle sold my flight information to the press. But that's ridiculous. No one close to me would do that.

After all, this isn't just about me. It's about Knox. I could accidentally say or do something that could make him look bad, cause horrible stories to be written, damage his career. That's what Heath was explaining to me. I didn't like what he was saying, and I definitely didn't appreciate his tone, but I suppose he's right.

God, I'm tired. Rubbing my temples, I disappear into the booth. I'm giving myself a headache. Overthinking tends to do that.

And I did that the whole flight home. I lied to Amy when I said I was working on show prep. Really, I spent most of the flight overanalyzing the last few days, including what it meant that Knox just left like that.

Right now, I have a show to do, so my own neurosis will have to wait.

~

"Mother Superior," a female caller starts, "I've never called before."

"A blessed virgin," I say with a laugh.

Probably burning in hell for that little comment.

"In more ways than one," she says.

Of course, sex gets brought up quite often on my show. It's a natural part of any romantic relationship.

"If you've listened long enough, you know my position on this. If he's pressuring you, then he's not the one."

"He's not," she says. "But I know he wants to."

"And what do you want?"

"I'm twenty-five," she says. "I've waited a long time."

"Nothing wrong with that," I say. "I've talked to thousands of women on this show. In all those calls, I've never had a woman call and say she wished she'd had sex with a man. But I've had plenty call and say she wished she hadn't."

"I've never thought about it like that," she says. "Thank you."

She hangs up, and I send the show to commercial break. This is a shorter one, not the longer one that happens on the hour. It's not enough time for me to go to the bathroom or anything, just long enough for me to take a deep breath.

I'm still bothered by how Knox left me at the airport. Normally, I'd bring something like this up on the show: *Has your man ever not waved goodbye to you at the airport? Just disappeared into thin air? How did that make you feel? Confused? Like shit?*

It's my job to raise these kinds of topics, but I said I wouldn't discuss Knox on-air. And I don't want to talk about my situation, either—he might be listening and call in out of the blue! I don't need that right now. Still, I need to get this off my chest. Amy points at me, indicating that we are back on the air, and I decide to go for it— but to change the story up a little, so the feeling is the same, but the circumstances are different.

"I'd like to know how you feel about something. Let's say you have a long-distance relationship, and you fly out to see your boyfriend. Keep in mind this is a new relationship, you haven't been married for years. Would you expect him to park and walk in to pick you up? Or would him picking you up at the curb be okay with you?"

The phone lines light up like a Christmas tree. I can see Amy struggling to keep up. Apparently, I've touched on a hot button issue. Some callers say it's more practical to wait at the curb or just drop off—airport parking can be expensive, too. Others say there is something inherently romantic about rendezvousing at the airport and wanting to spend each possible second together. I guess I fall into the hopeless romantic category. By the time the show ends, I think I've started a war of the sexes. The women overwhelmingly wanted their man to escort them in and out, and the men didn't care one way or another. Was Knox leaving the way he did simply part of his male DNA?

It's late when I wrap the show, and I just want to get out of here. I'm anxious to get home, shower, get in my bed, and dream about Knox. I quickly make my way out of the station, and find another car service waiting for me. I insisted that I could have Everly pick me up, or even take an Uber back to Haven's Point, but he wouldn't hear of it. When I think back on how generous and considerate he's been, it's possible I read way too much into the whole airport non-goodbye. Things are obviously fine with Knox. The man is devoted to me.

"Fancy?" Amy says, stepping out of the door behind me.

I force a smile and keep walking. But I find myself triggered again, the trust issues rushing back. I can't help it. Knox and Heath planted the seed in my head. Someone had to give my flight information to the press, and I am supremely confident it was not Gigi or Everly. That leaves Amy, and I'm tempted to say something.

Ugh, I'm tired. I don't want to get into it with her, not now.

Perhaps she mentioned something to the wrong person on accident. Or maybe someone called the station and asked for me, and without thinking, she said I was in California. I want to believe the best of her. I don't want to mess up our relationship.

Suddenly, I can't walk another step, the weight of it all bearing down on me. I stop in my tracks. I have to know.

"Amy," I say, playing with the handle of my suitcase. "When you were at my house for Gigi's party, I was wondering if you remember seeing a pair of Knox's shoes on my porch?"

I'm totally fishing for information. The shoes hadn't disappeared at that point. I'm just trying to gauge any sort of reaction from her.

From handling thousands of calls on the radio, I've learned that there are things people just don't want to reveal. Tactic number one is usually to dodge, obfuscate, get defensive. An innocent person doesn't do that. An innocent person laughs it off. If I accused Everly of something she didn't do, she'd jokingly call me a bitch and say I owe her a drink.

Amy laughs a little. "His shoes? Not that I can remember. What did they look like?"

Her response seems genuine. Knox is probably right. It was most likely the sleazy reporter who left me that little present on my porch.

"Oh, it's not important," I say, before continuing as delicately as I can. "There's something else I was wondering about. I don't like having to ask you this, but did you tell anyone about taking me to the airport?"

Lightly, she places her hand on my shoulder. "I wouldn't do that. I know getting slammed by the paps the minute you walked out of the airport must've scared the crap out of you—to be blindsided like that."

Another genuine response.

"Sorry, I had to ask. I just thought maybe something slipped out."

"No worries. After everything you've done for me, I only want you to get everything you deserve," she says, winking at me. "Including the Hollywood hottie!"

Smiling, we say goodnight and go our separate ways. So glad I cleared the air, I head to the car. The driver steps out, getting my door and taking my suitcase. I sink into the backseat and look up at the driver as he pulls off.

In these situations, I never know whether or not I should make conversation. Does the driver just want to be left alone? Do they like talking? Am I rude if I don't talk to him? How much talking is too much? I've been talking for the past two hours, so I hope this driver is the biggest introvert in the world. I really could use some peace and quiet.

I check my phone, which I keep turned off during the show, and find a couple messages from Knox. The first one is wondering whether I arrived safely. I guess I should've texted him a while back on that, but I was in such a rush when I landed. The second is that he's listening to my show. Good thing I didn't get into the waving goodbye bit. And the last text is a series of question marks followed by one word.

Airport.

He knew I was talking about him. Crap. I guess I wasn't so discrete and clever after all, or perhaps Knox just knows me too well.

I need to reach out to him. A phone call would be best, but this isn't a limo. There's no privacy screen to raise. I don't want the driver hearing my business. He might sell me out, too. God, I hate thinking like that. But that's my new reality. I decide to text Knox rather than call.

Me: *Sorry, I should've let you know I landed safely. It was a bit of a scramble to get to work. Thanks again for the car! Both cars!*

Knox: *You're welcome. Did your airport segment tonight have anything to do with me?*

Thinking about how I want to respond, I break my vow of silence and make small talk with the driver—thanking him, confirming he knows my address, that sort of thing. He's polite, but he keeps his answers short and concise, a sure indication he's not one for idle chit chat, at least not at this hour.

Me: *Maybe!*

Knox: *I felt like our goodbye at the airport got cut short. I needed a few more minutes.*

Me: *Me, too.*

Knox: *I couldn't stand to watch you get on that plane.*

That's why he left! It hurt him to watch me go! My brain needs to stop assuming the worst.

Knox: *There was something I wanted to tell you, to say before you left.*

My heart starts to thump in my chest. It's been a long time since I've heard Knox say he loves me. Could it be that?

Me: *Tell me next time you see me.*

~

Everyone in my life knows not to call me early on a Monday morning, so why does my phone keep ringing? It may not be early for everyone else, but it is for me. After letting it ring a few times, I put it on vibrate and wrapped pillows over my ears, but nothing's working. It's just a constant stream of calls and texts.

No more sleep for me today.

Groaning, I grab my cell phone to see who I need to politely remind that sleep is important. There are multiple calls from Knox and a bunch of numbers I don't recognize, and even more texts. Clearly, I need to change my number, get an unlisted one.

Casually, I hit the button to return Knox's call. He answers before the first ring is even over. "I'm sorry, baby! God, I'm so fucking sorry. I'm at the airport now, heading to you."

I bolt up in bed. "Knox, what's going on?"

"You haven't seen it? You don't know?"

"Know what? I just woke up."

"I'll be there in a couple hours."

"Knox?"

"My phone . . . My phone was hacked."

"That's terrible," I say. "So I guess that's why everyone is calling me. The press has my number now. Assholes."

"No, baby," he says, pausing, the brief silence a warning. "Pictures."

I don't know what happens first—my heart stopping, or my breathing taking off like a rocket.

I hear Knox saying my name over and over again, but it's not computing in my brain.

I'm completely frozen thinking about my ugly underwear pictures minus the underwear.

Oh my God! Oh my God!

I reach for my television remote, turning to a national morning show. The headline story is about Knox's phone hack. And my naked photo flashes across the screen, my private areas covered up with blurry blobs.

No! This can't be happening. Not to me! Dear God, please!

I drop my phone to the ground. It doesn't shatter, but it doesn't matter.

My life just went to pieces.

CHAPTER TWENTY-EIGHT

Knox

A baseball cap and dark glasses are anyone's best friends in times of crisis. That goes double when you live your life in the public eye. As I walk out to meet my plane, I'm donning both. It's not that I expect no one to recognize me, though I always hope for that. It's more to deny those assholes a decent shot and to protect my tired eyes.

It was barely light out when I got the phone call from Heath about the photos of Mae. I didn't go online and look at them. I didn't need to. And the fact that Mae's face wasn't showing didn't do anything to protect her identity. My phone was hacked. They had my text streams, my email. It was easy enough to piece together.

I haven't talked to Mae since her phone went dead this morning, but I've spoken with both Everly and Gigi. Having to tell the grandmother of the woman you love there are nude photos of her granddaughter all over the world was only slightly easier than breaking the news to Mae. Gigi promised me she'd get Mae somewhere safe. She told me to go to The Tune Up and wait there when I land.

I work with some of the best writers in Hollywood, and I don't think they could give me the words to describe what I'm feeling. It's a combination of heartbreak and rage all rolled into one big ball of shit. I keep trying to call Mae, but there is no answer. I wonder if Everly and Gigi got hold of her.

Of all the times for something like this to happen! I'm over a thousand miles away from Mae.

I have to get to her. I told Heath to clear my schedule, for however long is necessary.

Stepping onto the plane, I realize things are not so private. Heath is aboard, with a laptop beside him. "Thought I would fly with you, and we could talk."

I'm not in the mood, and I don't need an escort. But I know Heath is trying to help. And frankly, the company might be good for me. Being alone, I have too much time to think. Too much time to wonder what Mae's thinking. What kind of state she's in. Why she hung up. How to convince her not to dump my ass over this.

"How's she doing?" he asks.

"Not good," I say. "I actually haven't talked to her again. I think her phone went dead or something. I'm worried."

"We will be there soon."

"Any luck on having the pictures taken down?" I ask.

"Can't purge the internet entirely, but we've made some progress," he says.

I take a seat opposite him. Because we have a total passenger count of two, it doesn't take long for the plane to be ready to takeoff. There's one flight attendant on board who offers us drinks and food, but I politely wave her away. I'm not one who likes someone to wait on me when I'm having a good day, so I really don't want the attention when I'm having the worst fucking day of my life.

I can't even imagine what Mae is feeling right now. It's hard sitting here with Heath, knowing he must've seen those pictures, even if he hasn't said so. She must be a complete mess. She has to wonder if every person she knows has seen her naked. And how many strangers have downloaded the picture to view over and over again later.

"Who's responsible for the hack?" I ask as we taxi out to the runway.

"The authorities are looking into it," Heath says.

"They need to work fucking faster. Find out who did this. Bring charges against them, and all the motherfuckers who posted those pictures."

It's the worst when you're upset, and the person you are talking to is calm—trying to "handle" you. I don't want Heath calm. I want him to go nuclear, to be as pissed off as I am. That way, I can be sure he'll fight to the death to bring down the assholes who did this to Mae.

Some asshole reporters are speculating that this whole thing is a publicity stunt to create buzz around my upcoming movie premiere. Can you imagine that? How completely fucking stupid. I've told Heath that anyone who breathes that shit will never get an interview with me again.

"The funny thing is—it was just you. Normally, these hacks take down a handful of celebrities, but it's like they specifically targeted you."

"Did they hack anything else from me besides the pictures?"

"Some financial information. A few scripts," he says. "I've already handled all that."

"I don't give a shit about that stuff," I say. "Just the pictures. No one knew about those pictures but me and Mae."

"Perhaps they were just fishing, looking for anything. But you were definitely the target," Heath says. "I've turned over the letters you've been getting to the authorities."

"You think there's a connection between the letters and the hack?"

"I'm not sure, but it's possible."

"You don't actually believe I have another stalker? This is not the way they usually operate. Those fuckers show up at your house, try to break in, go through your trash. I've had none of that."

"That's what worries me," Heath says. "Whoever did this isn't out of control. They're the opposite—calculated. The thank you note was very calculating. I find that concerning. But we need to let the police, FBI, whoever, do their jobs, and you need to focus on yours."

"Seriously?"

"The movie is coming out in a little over a week. You have . . ."

"You can't expect me to continue doing press. You know all everyone is going to be talking about is those pictures."

"We can control that."

"No," I say, feeling the plane increase in speed, waiting for the tires to leave the pavement.

"Knox, you have a responsibility to the film."

"Do you really think I can do press junkets and walk the red carpet while these perverts are holding online polls about how fuckable my girlfriend is?"

"I think you've enjoyed living in this little secret fairytale with her," Heath says. "But that's over now. Shit just got real. The only thing we can do now is move forward."

"By working?"

"Yes, but also figuring out if you want security for Mae. How she feels about that? Do you want to make a statement about all this? Does she? Do you want to do an interview? Does she? Do you . . ."

"Fine, I get it."

"Look," he says, leaning forward slightly. "I've always got your back, and I've seen a lot of this crap over the years. It always seems like the end of the world at the time, but it will pass."

"I doubt Mae feels that way," I say, looking out the window, the world speeding by. "What do you think is best? Address it head on, or lay low?"

"I think that's going to depend on Mae," he says.

"I need to be able to give her advice," I say.

"I think it's best to address it," Heath says. "Those were private photos, meant only for you."

"She was just trying to be cute and sexy while we were apart."

"You should say that, too," he says. "How would these fuckers feel if it was their wife or girlfriend? Their sister, friend, or daughter?"

"I know in a lot of ways I'm a brand, a product," I say. "But Mae's not. She should be off limits."

"Unrealistic, but I think it would be very powerful if you looked in a camera and said just that." He relaxes back in his seat. "We can make this work in our favor."

"Heath, I'm not looking to capitalize on . . ."

He waves me off. "I'm not talking about money. I'm talking about spin." He pats me on the knee. "You are Hollywood's leading man. Mae is the perfect girl next door. Your old high school and college girlfriend. If that doesn't sound like a perfect movie, then I don't know what does."

"You're suggesting I make a movie of my relationship?" I ask, rolling my eyes.

"No, I'm saying the public will eat that shit right up. If we handle this right, Mae will be adored by the public."

"It doesn't change what happened," I say.

"No, but we can change how everyone sees it."

I look out the airplane window, Los Angeles now thousands of feet below me. I'm not sure what to do, or what Mae wants to do. Without hearing her voice, having her input, I feel stuck.

But I do know that if we are going to do something, we need to act fast. We need to get a handle on this story, change the narrative. I can't allow what's happened to linger.

I have no idea if it's the right move or not, but I give Heath the go-ahead to get my team to spin this her way—now. It's not an easy call for me. She's the victim in this whole mess, but I want the public to see the strong woman she is.

∽

My first stop is The Tune Up. When Timothy sees me coming in, he flips the store sign to closed and ushers out the handful of customers that were inside. It isn't much of a hideout, considering the number of photographers outside. As soon as the pictures of Mae hit the internet, all the vultures flocked to Haven's Point like it was the next big gold rush.

This is the shitty price of fame. I only wish the shit would've landed on me and not Mae. I'd have gladly paid the price.

I still haven't heard from Mae, Gigi, or Everly. I keep trying to call Mae, but it goes straight to voicemail. I want to see her, hold her, tell her we will get through this.

"Where's Mae?" I ask Timothy as I take a seat in a booth.

"Don't know," he says.

"Did you see her? Or talk to her?" I ask.

He shakes his head. "Everly shot out of the house like a bat out of hell."

Out of nowhere, Gracie heads my way and scoots into the booth across from me, sliding a picture to me. "Earlier today, Mommy was yelling about some bad pictures. She said Auntie Mae was crying. So I made her a new one. Can you give it to her?"

She's colored a picture of a St. Bernard, complete with the barrel around its neck. "I will," I say, feeling a huge lump in my throat. "It looks really good."

"Daddy printed the picture for me to color. St. Bernards are Auntie Mae's favorite."

The lump gets even bigger.

"Hey, Gracie, I think I have some stickers in the drawer in my office," her dad says. "Why don't you go look? Maybe you can add some to Auntie Mae's picture."

My phone rings in my pocket, and I rush to answer. Leading Gracie away, Timothy asks me, "Is it Mae?" I shake my head.

"How's Mae?" Ryder asks, skipping any pleasantries.

"I don't know. She's gone MIA," I say, keeping my voice low, wanting to avoid any detection from the assholes' high-powered microphones outside. "You saw, huh?" My voice gives way slightly at the thought of my brother seeing Mae naked.

"I heard," he says.

If he's lying, I appreciate it and love him even more for it. "I don't have any idea where Mae is," I say. "I flew to Haven's Point, but she's gone into hiding somewhere. I'm waiting to find out where she is. I guess I should be grateful she's away from the cameras and chaos. You should see Haven's Point right now. It looks like a red carpet on steroids."

"You need me?" he asks, ever the big brother. "I was coming to your premiere next week, anyway. I can come earlier."

"Thanks, Ryder, but I need to focus on Mae, finding her, making this better."

"Okay, then. I'll see you in a few days," Ryder says before hanging up.

Mae doesn't want or need this craziness. She's private. She likes her solitude, living alone on the lake. She likes the anonymity of her radio show. She doesn't want a life in the limelight. She prefers the natural sunlight.

She's crushed right now.

I haven't seen her, but I know it. I feel it because I'm crushed, too.

What I'm feeling is different than what she's feeling. I know that. I've never been so fucking angry in my life. Angry that I ever asked her to send me that picture. This isn't the first celebrity hack in the history of the universe, but it is the first for me. Still, I should've known better. I was selfish. My first and only thought should have been protecting Mae and her privacy. I should've anticipated it. It's my job to protect her, first and foremost. I didn't do that. I failed her. I let her down.

I don't even want to consider it, but I know I could lose Mae over this.

The front door to The Tune Up opens, startling me. Cameras flash, and the noise from the photographers outside fills the place. I see Gigi pause in the doorway, turning back around to the herd.

"You want a quote?" she asks them.

I brace myself. No telling what will come out of Gigi's mouth. Could be a fuck you. Could be a Bible verse.

"Betty White once said, 'Why do people say "grow some balls"? Balls are weak and sensitive. If you wanna be tough, grow a vagina. Those things can take a pounding.'"

Well, the paparazzi doesn't hear that every day! I get what she's trying to convey, though. Mae is a tough woman. This won't destroy her. It can't. I won't let it.

The door closes behind Gigi, and the noise and flashes fade away. Her eyes land on me like a laser. Getting to my feet, I head toward her. "Where's Mae? Is she alright? Is Everly with her? I need to see her."

"She's safe," Gigi says. "Can you even imagine what she's feeling right now?"

"I know it has to be . . ."

"No, you don't know shit. There aren't nude photos of you all over the world. Someone can't Google your name right now and see you naked. For the rest of her life, everyone she will ever meet will be able to see that. How would you feel if you had to wonder whether every person you looked in the eye had seen your penis?"

My eyes close. I don't want to think about how many people are seeing the woman I love this way. And it's all my fault.

"Everly tried to get Mae to come here to meet you. But Mae didn't want to face Timothy, even though Everly swore to her that he hadn't looked at the news today. Mae still didn't want to see him. She's mortified. You have no idea."

"I need to be with her, Imogen, please."

"We had a deal," she says, arching her brow. "I say the word, and you leave."

"Gigi, *please?*" I beg.

She releases a deep breath. "Come with me."

CHAPTER TWENTY-NINE

Mae

"How are you?" Everly asks.

How the hell does she think I am? Completely and utterly destroyed. My whole body hurts. My heart is broken. I cry. I pray. I cry some more. I'm sure the radio station is freaking out. Sleep is impossible. I want to crawl in a hole, but Gigi's house will have to do.

I feel so stupid. I am not a teenage girl. I should've *known* better. This topic has come up on my show many times before, and I always advise my callers not to send nude photos to anyone, not even their spouse, because you just never know. I should've heeded my own advice.

My phone has been turned off since this all started. It's kind of nice—no dinging of my email, no calendar notifications, no phone ringing.

Blocking the outside world feels like the only thing to do. I don't want to logon to the internet and see a story about me, and I definitely don't want to see those pictures. I'm not longing to find out what else is going on in the world, either. It's probably just more bad news. I've had enough bad news today for my whole life.

I hear some ruckus coming from outside—yelling, just some general noise. The front door comes flying open, Gigi and Knox hurrying inside. Everly meets them by the door.

"Get me a bat and some iced tea," Gigi tells Everly. "Think I need to have a nice long sit on my front porch."

That brings a smile to my face. Gigi is crazy, and even those slime balls won't want to deal with crazy.

Knox's eyes frantically search the house until they land on me, sitting on the sofa, wrapped up in a blanket. "Mae," he cries out, rushing to me and pulling me into his arms. "God, baby, I'm so sorry."

I simply cling to his shirt and cry. He holds me closer, tighter than I think he ever has in his life. My chest heaves as the tears come faster and harder, the magnitude of what has happened hitting me in waves. The embarrassment and humiliation, followed by how stupid I feel, topped off with how violated I feel. It all swirls around inside, my body unable to process and contain it all. We must sit like this for hours, with Knox holding me, letting me cry. There's nothing he can say or do to fix this or make it better, so he just stays with me.

Finally, I look up at him, his blue eyes holding back tears of his own. "Thank you for coming," I whisper, wiping my cheeks.

He runs his fingers through my hair. "I was so afraid I'd lost you."

"Knox?" I say, placing my hands on his face, feeling his stubble beneath my fingers.

"So many relationships would end over something like this," he says softly. "You have no idea how sorry I am."

He's afraid of losing me. I've been so upset I hadn't considered what he was feeling. And I get why some women would leave if this happened to them, but I've lost Knox before. I know what that means. What that feels like. I never want to feel that again.

"Don't you know I'm a badass?" I tease. "It's going to take more than some nude photos to scare me away from you."

He pulls me to him, kissing me hard on the lips. "I fucking love you."

I can't help but laugh. One's first declaration of love isn't usually preceded by a cuss word. "I fucking love you, too," I say, giggling.

His hands on my cheeks, he kisses me again—slower, longer. When he pulls back, he twirls the hair around my face with his finger, studying me. Knox knows me well. He knows I'm not over this, not by any stretch of the imagination. This has fucked up my world. But he's here with me now.

That doesn't fix everything, but it does make it a little easier.

~

We spent much of the afternoon cuddled together on the sofa. Gigi kept guard out on the front porch, and Everly left to go back to The Tune Up. Knox and I both know we can't stay locked away inside my grandmother's house forever.

The front door opens, and Knox gets to his feet. "The old woman with the bat on the front porch is a nice touch," Heath says, giving us a grin.

I was surprised to discover Heath flew in with Knox. I'm not sure why, but I guess all this attention is going to take some getting used to.

"That's Gigi," I say, "and I don't recommend you refer to her an old woman to her face."

"We met," Heath says. "And after she told me that I suck at my job, and to do better, you don't have to worry about me referring to her as anything other than ma'am."

"How'd you respond?" Knox asks, inviting him into the den to take a seat.

"Stayed out of swinging distance while telling her she'd be out of a job soon," Heath says. "A security team is on its way."

"What?" I cry out, looking at Knox, wondering if he knew about this.

"Heath, I never agreed to guards. I told you . . ."

Heath holds his hands up to Knox then directs his words to me. "Mae, before you say anything, I need you to listen. Because God knows, Knox doesn't."

"Okay," I say, looking over at Knox, who gently takes my hand.

Heath reaches into his briefcase, pulling out some papers. He proceeds to tell me how Knox was the only celebrity hacked, how unusual it is for only one to be targeted at a time. Then he shows me some letters.

They're creepy, talking about how much they love Knox, how they are meant to be together, how he'll soon realize what's right in front of him. My stomach turns. I knew Knox got this kind of mail, he told me as much, but reading it makes my skin crawl.

"The police have these?" I ask.

Heath nods. "The running theory is that whoever sent these is the same person who hacked Knox's phone." Knox's eyes dart up. "We are dealing with a pretty savvy individual."

Knox gets to his feet and peers out a window, my Gigi's yard covered in camera crews. "This is my doing," Knox says quietly. "None of this would've happened if I'd stayed away from . . ."

"Knox," I say, getting to my feet and lightly kissing his shoulder. He turns, looking down at me, and for a fraction of a second, I wonder if he's considering leaving me—to protect me. But then he pulls me into his arms, hugging me tightly.

"Another thing," Heath says, interrupting our moment. "The police tested the letters. No fingerprints. No DNA."

Goosebumps cover my arms. This isn't just a crazed fan.

"Knox," I whisper. "Please keep security with you. It will ease my mind."

Heath leans back, seemingly happy I agree with him. But all we get from Knox is a single, quick nod of his head. He's only doing this for me. I know that.

"I want security on Mae, too," Knox says.

Before I can object, or tell them Gigi's protection is enough, Heath chimes in, "I think that's a good idea. Whoever this is has already proven they'll use Mae to get to you."

Security, phone hacks, nude photos, reporters trampling Gigi's lawn—I'm fully indoctrinated into Hollywood now. It's hardly what I wanted, but I want Knox.

So I'm willing to pay this price. I just hope the stakes don't get any higher.

∾

"I can't believe Gigi's letting us sleep in the same room," Knox says, slipping in beside me.

My old room only has a full-size bed, but Knox pulls me so close, it doesn't matter.

"She knows I need you," I say quietly, a tear rolling down my cheek.

"What can I do?" he asks, playing with my hair. "It's killing me that I can't make this better for you."

"I feel so dirty," I say. "Like all these eyes are on me."

"We are doing everything in our power to get those pictures taken down."

"I know, but it's like . . . When the security guys showed up to-day, I couldn't look them in the eye. All I could think about was whether they'd seen me naked." I look up at Knox, the moonlight peeking through the curtains. "It feels like it will always be that way, now."

His eyes close.

I don't have any idea what this is like for him, knowing other men are looking at me. It's hard for me to watch him in a pretend sex scene. This has to be killing him, too. He's protective. I know he blames himself for my life being turned upside down. And it's not over.

In a moment of bravery earlier, I checked my messages. The station heads want a conference call with me in the morning. I'm not expecting good news. What happens on that call will probably determine whether we go to California or stay in Haven's Point until the premiere. Knox wants me at his house because he thinks it's more secure, but I feel I need the security of my friends and family right now.

"It's hard on you, too," I say.

"Don't worry about me," he whispers, his eyes roaming my face.

"What?" I ask.

He answers by kissing me sweetly, his tongue slowly massaging mine. "I love you," he whispers, his fingers grazing my neck. "My eyes on your naked body, my hands, my mouth—try to think about that instead."

I look up into his bright blue eyes. "Knox, I . . ."

"Don't worry, I'm not interested in being on the receiving end of Gigi's bat tonight," he teases before he turns completely serious. "I know you can't possibly be in the mood tonight, but I want you to know that nothing will change how I look at you. Ever."

CHAPTER THIRTY

Mae

Once those photos leaked, any and all information about me was a hot commodity, far beyond even what happened after I was blitzed at the airport. And even though the number of people who know the truth about my job could probably be counted on two hands, it didn't take long before my identity as Mother Superior became public. I've now been suspended from my show. Upper management feels there's too much publicity surrounding me, and think it's best that I take a few weeks off. When things calm down, they will "reevaluate."

I guess I understand. The suits want Mother Superior, the mysterious, anonymous voice on Sunday nights, not an amateur Playboy centerfold. It doesn't seem to matter to them that those photos were only meant for one person, not the world, or that they were obtained illegally and published without my knowledge or consent. They care about their image, the brand. So like I said, I guess I understand.

"Screw 'em," Everly says, holding her glass of wine up to Gigi. A little while ago, she came over in a show of support, making her way through the paparazzi still camped outside.

We're all sitting in Gigi's den—me, Everly, Gigi, and Thomas. It's sweet they are here, especially because Knox is off with Heath somewhere working on press releases and a plan of action on how to deal with all this, whatever that might be.

Gigi dings her glass with Everly then turns to Thomas, who gently squeezes her hand. Gigi is beautiful, but there's a sadness behind her eyes today. She's still acting tough, of course. She and I have always had that in common. But on the inside, I know she's heart-broken. Not because she's ashamed of me, but because she knows I'm hurt. I think that's why Thomas came by. I really don't want a lot of visitors, but I couldn't deny Gigi. She needs support right now, too.

"Your father called again," Gigi says, leaning into Thomas a little. "Checking on you, Mae."

I haven't spoken to my dad since I broke the news to him a few days ago. That was a hard phone call for me to make, telling my father about those photos, knowing how disappointed he would be in me. He didn't say that, but I know that's how he must feel. I wonder what it must be like for him to know his military buddies can see his daughter naked with a simple internet search.

If he could get leave, I know he'd be here right now, but I'm kind of happy he's not. It was hard enough facing Thomas, so I don't know how I'm going to look my father in the eye ever again. I'm honestly not sure how I'll look anyone in the eye again without wondering whether they've seen me naked.

"You know, I have a daughter," Thomas says, causing me to look up at him. "And nothing could ever change the way I feel about her. Nothing."

He said a great deal without saying a great deal, and I barely manage a somewhat tearful thank you when my new security guard, Floyd, comes through the front door. "There's a woman out front says she works with you. Says her name is Amy."

I groan inside. I really don't want to see her, or anyone else, but she drove all the way here, so I feel like I have to. "It's fine."

He waves Amy inside, and she walks in, motioning to the guard. "He's new." I just nod, and she comes over, pulling me into a hug. "It's crazy out front. I think a hundred people took my picture!"

"That's one reason Knox and I both have security now," I say, thankful that at least they aren't hanging out in front of Everly's business anymore. At least if they know where Knox and I are, they focus on us and not on bothering our loved ones.

"I'm sorry to bother you. I know things are . . . I tried to call, but there's something I need to talk to you about."

"Maybe we should give the girls some time to catch up?" Thomas suggests to Gigi.

Gigi looks at me, and I nod that's fine, and they all disappear into another room.

"I'm gonna head out, too," Everly says. "Timothy has Gracie at work. I'm sure he needs some help."

"I miss her," I say. "What I wouldn't give to be eating some cheeseballs and fishing with Gracie right now."

"It's sweet you're so close to her," Amy says.

"Couldn't love her more," I say, thinking of how she makes me smile.

"She misses you," Everly says, giving me a hug, and saying her goodbyes.

Amy takes her spot on the sofa beside me. "I guess you heard about my suspension," I say. "Do you know what they plan to do for the show Sunday?"

"That's why I'm here," she says, looking away. "They asked me to fill in. Just temporarily until things get sorted out, of course."

"Oh!" I say, wondering why they aren't just broadcasting previously recorded shows. When my mom died, they rebroadcast popular segments from our backlist. I guess these current circumstances are much different.

"I told them I had to think about it. I wanted to talk to you first—friend to friend," she says. "I've been going back and forth about it. It feels weird. I don't want to betray you. You've done so much for me. But then I don't want them to bring in someone else, either. Someone gunning to replace you."

This stings. I've never had someone fill in for me on my show. Not once.

"Trust me, I won't do it if you don't want me to," Amy says. "That's why I came here. I had to talk to you."

I pause for a moment to consider. God, this sucks. But as much as I hate it, Amy's right. They could put someone else in the seat, someone who isn't my friend. They also could simply fire me now and find a permanent replacement.

"I think you should do it," I say, forcing a smile. "You always had a ton of ideas."

"Wow, thanks," she says. "But actually, I'm not sure I'm ready to talk about my personal life on-air. My divorce. It's still too raw."

I have no idea what happened in Amy's marriage. We've never talked about it, and it's not my place to snoop. But whatever it is, she's still torn up about it. I can see the sadness in her eyes.

"You don't have to talk about anything personal if you aren't ready," I say.

"You're absolutely sure you're okay with this?" Amy asks.

I give her a little nod, afraid if I speak much more, my voice will let on how much this hurts. I'm not ready for my reign as Mother Superior to be over, even for a few weeks.

"Is it worth it?" Amy asks.

"What?"

"In the past couple days, you've lost your privacy, your freedom, possibly the show. Is any man worth all that?"

My mind drifts to all those cassette tapes, all the years spent apart, and the answer is easy. "Yeah, Knox is."

CHAPTER THIRTY-ONE

Knox

Heath has been hard at work getting the pictures of Mae removed from the internet. And he's been pretty successful at it, while working with the police and FBI. After sending cease and desist letters from fancy lawyers, and personal threats from certain investigators, he's managed to get most of the pictures taken down.

Still, every few days a new, sketchy website pops up posting the photos, and we have to go through the process all over again. The cycle seems never ending. And I know none of this solves the problem of the thousands of people who took screenshots of the pictures.

Heath's also set up a team to do image control for Mae, releasing stories about how successful she is, a self-made woman. It's all great, but good news doesn't ever get as much traction as bad. What people really want is to hear from me, from Mae.

Of course, early on, Heath issued a statement on my behalf, condemning the hack, asking for privacy—the standard bullshit. But it doesn't feel like nearly enough. It's been days, and all the news outlets are clamoring for an interview with me, with Mae. But she's not anywhere near ready to do that. She hasn't even left Gigi's house yet.

I can't even really consider the possibility of an interview with her right now. The last thing I want to do is drag her further into the spotlight, if that's not what she wants.

On the rare occasions that I leave Gigi's house to go into town, when one of those assholes sticks a camera in my face, it's so hard not to say something. It's all I can do not to completely lose my shit.

The only thing stopping me is that I don't want to do anything else that could hurt Mae in any way, and going on a rampage for the whole world to see is simply feeding the beast.

So Heath continues to work behind the scenes, slowly trying to turn the tide in our favor. I'm sure he's hoping for some other scandal to break the news cycle, which seems to go on without end.

The world now knows that Mae is the host of *The Breakup Bible*. I thought that might help her. She has millions of loyal listeners, and millions more who don't listen, but have still heard of the show. Her popularity rating is through the roof. People overwhelmingly love her show. Her fans almost broke the internet in support of her, threatening to blacklist tabloid sites that published and continue to capitalize on her photos.

There's even an online thread devoted to advice for Mae. Things like *hold your head up, and hold your breasts even higher*. Others recount how their boyfriend showed their private photos around, how it crushed them, and how they got through it. Others suggesting that Mae, as Mother Superior, do penance in the form of *three fuck you's* and *two who gives a damn*.

All good advice, but it didn't make one bit of difference with her bosses. She can't seem to catch a break, hit from every direction.

"The premiere is only a few days away," I say. "I think we should go back to California. Even if you don't want to attend with me, I still think it's safer there."

A knock on Gigi's door interrupts what I'm sure was going to be a litany of reasons why she'd rather stay here, all of which I understand. Floyd opens the door, and Heath comes walking in. He's even more anxious to get back to California than I am. There's not a bone in his body that likes small town living. I think he's allergic to fresh air and nice people.

It's after eleven at night. This man earns his money, seemingly never off the clock. But showing up at this hour can't mean good news.

"I know it's late," he says, coming in and sitting down. I've never seen him look like this. He's always dressed in a suit or slacks, always polished, always together. Now he's in sweatpants and a t-shirt, like he was ready for bed. "I need you to look at something for me."

"You could've texted or . . ."

"Are these your shoes?" he asks, holding out his cell phone for me to look at a picture.

Mae is a few feet away, but I can feel her eyes on me. "Why?" I ask Heath.

"A package was delivered to my office today with these shoes," he says, "mailed from the Denver post office. They came with a note that said, '*Look how close I can get.*' Does that mean anything to either of you?"

Every muscle in my body tightens, my fists clench, my jaw clamps shut. I want to hit something—hard.

"Knox, what is it?" Mae asks.

"These are the shoes that disappeared off your porch."

"Pile of shit shoes?" she asks.

"Yes," I say.

Heath raises both eyebrows. "What?"

I quickly bring Heath up to speed, how we assumed it was an animal. "How long ago was this?" he asks.

My heart is pounding, my head hurts like a bitch. This has been going on much longer than we thought. "That motherfucker was on her porch, at her front door, while she was there alone and fucking scared!"

"And she's fine," Heath says, trying to be the voice of reason.

I look over at Mae, a concerned look understandably plastered on her face. How much more of this will she tolerate? I don't want to put her through anything else, but I can't let her go, either.

"Whoever this is, isn't interested in Mae," Heath says. "They're trying to get to you."

"And they're using her to do it!" I bark.

I can't begin to describe the all-consuming rage I'm living with, every damn day, that me being directly targeted has had such horrible repercussions for Mae. I have no idea why some people do what they do. Come after me, fine—I'll deal with it. But there was simply no reason for my hacker, stalker, whoever the fuck he is, to release the photos, to bring Mae into this, to hurt her so publicly.

"She has security now," Heath says. "No one will get within twenty feet of her."

"I just don't understand what they want," Mae says.

"There's no point in trying to understand what motivates a crazy person," Heath says.

"Remove my security," I say.

"Knox!" Mae cries out.

"No!" I say. "If they think they can get close to me, then they will leave you alone."

"That's crazy," she says. "I'm *not* going to let you do that."

"She's right," Heath says. "Mae, could you give me a minute with Knox?"

"Sure, I'll go check on Gigi," she says reluctantly, then adds before walking out, "Heath, don't let him do anything stupid."

As soon as Mae is out of earshot, Heath leans in close to me and asks, "Is she worth it?"

I bristle at the question and resist the urge to punch him in the face. "What?"

"I'm asking you to think about whether or not this woman is worth it."

"What the hell kind of question is that?"

"A good one," he says. "If this is just a fling, then maybe it's time to end it. Why put her through this if it's not going to last?"

"I love her," I say firmly.

"Does she love you?"

"Yes."

"Enough to put up with all this?" he asks then pats my shoulder before heading for the front door. Before putting his hand on the knob, he turns back and says, "And your security stays."

The door shuts behind him, and I close my eyes tightly, fuming. I take a few breaths and open them to find Mae staring at me.

"He's an asshole!" she says, having obviously heard everything Heath said.

"I remember you that night," I say. "That night with the shoes. The kitchen knife next to your bed. You were so scared, you were shaking."

"I'm still scared," she says. "Of something happening to you. Of losing you."

"I'm not going anywhere," I say.

"I'm not, either," she says. "I promise."

Mae's strong. She's been incredible through all this. But everyone has limits. The realization that I do, indeed, have a stalker seems to be the straw that broke the camel's back, despite her previous reassurances to the contrary.

Mae's been quiet, withdrawn, all day. It's close to five in the afternoon, and she's barely said a dozen words since breakfast. But there's still so much we need to talk about.

The premiere is just a few days away, and I really should be back in L.A. already, doing promotions, press. But Mae is more important. Still, I'm contractually obligated to go back, and I can't imagine leaving without her.

Mae's been standing in front of the bathroom mirror for I don't know how long, putting her hair up in a ponytail over and over again. She gets it up, considers it, then rips it down and tries again. I'm not sure what's wrong with it each time, but she seems to be taking out all her emotions on her hair.

Walking over to Mae, I wrap my arms around her from behind, lightly kissing her hair. She glances at me over her shoulder, giving me a small smile, then starts in on her hair again. Gently, I take the brush from her, placing it on the bathroom vanity. Placing my hands on her waist, I lower my head to hers.

"California," she whispers.

"It's safer. All the letters have come from Colorado. The shoes were mailed from a Denver post office. They were on your porch. Whoever is out to get me, probably lives in Colorado. It makes sense to go back to California."

"I know," she says. "I just don't know anyone there except you, and . . ."

"Ask Gigi to come with us," I say. "It could be like a little vacation, just for a few days. Hell, she can walk the red carpet with you at the premiere if you decide to go."

That makes her laugh. I haven't heard that in days. It feels good to hear her laugh again, if only for a moment.

"Dear God, could you imagine Gigi on a red carpet?" she wonders.

"I think it's her natural habitat," I say. "She'd steal the spotlight from us."

Her fingers run through my hair, her lips softly landing on mine. We haven't had sex since those pictures leaked. I miss her, but I doubt she's going to want a mid-afternoon romp with her grandmother just downstairs. Another reason to go back to California.

My phone rings in my pocket, and she lets out a long exhale. Planting a quick kiss on her lips, I pull out my phone.

"It's Timothy," I tell her and answer the call, placing him on speaker, since he's probably calling to talk to Mae.

Before I get a chance to say anything, I hear frantic wailing from a woman, like her heart is being ripped out of her chest.

"Everly!" Mae screams, recognizing the cries from her friend.

"I need Mae," Timothy chokes out, sobbing.

My eyes lock on Mae. What could possibly be happening now?

"Timothy, Mae is here with me. What's going on?"

"Gracie," he cries. "Gracie is missing."

CHAPTER THIRTY-TWO

Knox

I've done plenty of action flicks, stuff with police and FBI, but nothing prepares you to actually see police tape covering the entrance of The Tune Up, the police lifting fingerprints off tables and chairs, doors and windows, detectives questioning your friends, emergency personnel on standby.

Mae and I stand quietly in the coffee shop, silently supporting Everly and Timothy, both of whom are beside themselves.

Mae and I managed to get out of Gigi's house without being followed. It took some maneuvering, but we did it. We had the security guys pull their SUV as close as they could to Gigi's side door. Then they held up sheets, blocking the paparazzi from seeing us climb in. Only it wasn't Mae and I that got inside, it was Gigi and Thomas. The windows in the security firm's SUV are way darker than what's probably legal, but provided the cover they needed to pull off the switch. I breathed a sigh of relief when the paparazzi dutifully followed them wherever they were going. When the coast was clear, Mae and I made a break for it and raced over here.

Timothy is kneeling by Everly, who is sitting in a chair answering questions from the detective. She's still crying softly, but not screaming anymore. I think they probably gave her something to calm her down, so she'd be able to give them information. The first few hours are crucial. Apparently, the longer the child is missing, the less chance they have of being found alive.

Everly looks up at the clock. I know she's keeping track in her head. I overhear that it was around four thirty, when they closed the coffee shop for a few minutes to make the transfer to bar, that Gracie went missing. She was coloring at her usual table, Timothy was due at the shop any minute, and Everly went to use the bathroom. When she came out, Gracie was gone. Just like that. It happened so fast.

"It was only two minutes, and I had the damn bathroom door open," Everly sobs, looking at her husband for forgiveness, and he gently pats her hand.

They've already given a description of Gracie's clothing, been questioned about possible places where she might go. At this point, no one knows whether she wandered out of the shop or if, God forbid, she was taken.

"She knows not to go off alone," Timothy says, certainty in his voice. "She knows our phone number and address. We know that having Down's makes her a little more vulnerable, so we've been extra cautious with her. She wouldn't wander off."

"Why would anyone do this?" Everly cries out.

"They will find her," Mae says.

"She loves everyone," Everly says. "She trusts so easily. I should've . . ."

"Everly," Mae says, leaving my side and going to her friend. "You're the best mom."

"I just had to pee," Everly says, breaking down once more.

"What if she's hurt? What if someone has her?" Everly looks up at the clock. "It's been sixty-one minutes!" she cries out then hunches over and vomits on the floor.

Mae holds her tightly as Everly dry heaves over and over again. Timothy takes hold of Everly's hair, but that's all he can manage, rightly consumed with his own grief. Some emergency personnel come over to assist Everly and clean up the mess.

God, this is awful. And outside of offering up our security team to help in the search, which I've already done, there's nothing I can do to help. I hate feeling useless. Then something occurs to me. "What if I go on television and offer a reward," I say, looking at one of the hard-nosed detectives for approval.

Everyone in the room just stares at me. I'm not sure if they are stunned, think I'm crazy, or just don't like the idea. And I don't care if they say a million, five, ten, or twenty. Gracie is priceless. I'd give every last cent I have for her safe return.

"Just tell me the amount," I say then catch Mae's glance, her eyes filled with gratitude.

Steadying herself a bit, Everly wipes her face and says, "That could work. Yes, if someone has her, they might let her go for money. They'd have to. And we don't even need to wait for the local news. The paparazzi are always following you. You could just go tell them. It would spread like wildfire."

"It could also lead to a lot of false leads and chaos this early on," the detective says.

"She's my baby!" Everly screams at him.

The detective kneels in front of her. "I assure you, we are doing everything we can to find her, and a reward might work, but it's my job to weigh the pros and cons."

Tears stream down Everly's face as she grabs his forearms. "Please find her. Please, please, bring her home to me."

The more she begs, the more tears come—from her, from Timothy, from Mae. I'm trying to hold it together for them, but this is a nightmare. It's worse, actually. There's no waking up from this. There's no going back. Even once Gracie is home—yes, I have to believe that, the alternative is not a consideration—none of us will ever forget these moments, these heartbreaks, the fear.

Fear lives forever. I can remember the fear I felt when my mother died like it was yesterday. It hasn't dulled over time. And neither will this.

Suddenly, the detective reaches into his pocket, pulling out his phone. The room goes silent as we all collectively hold our breath. For some reason, the detective's eyes land on me. Mae, Everly, and Timothy all see it. Why is he looking at me? Does this involve me, too?

The detective doesn't give anything away. He's not asking questions. He's simply listening. Whoever is on the other end is doing all the talking, has all the information. Each second is like a year. I wonder if he's stalling, trying to figure out how to give us bad news.

He lowers his phone, and the detective's eyes land on me once again. It's eerie the way he is looking at me. My heart starts to beat against my chest like a battering ram.

"They found Gracie."

CHAPTER THIRTY-THREE

Mae

"Gracie is alive, unharmed. Our officers found her not far from here," the detective says.

"Where?" Timothy and Everly both say, jumping to their feet.

The detective glances at Knox again. I really wish he'd stop doing that. Knox had nothing to do with this. "She was found at the cemetery. By the graves of Mr. Merrick's parents. Someone had taken her there, and left her."

Knox moved, clearly anticipating her next move, but not quickly enough to avoid Everly's punch landing squarely on his jaw. "You fucking bastard!" she screams as Timothy steps in to hold Everly back from landing another blow, now thrashing around in her husband's arms.

Knox holds up his hands, then massages his jaw a little. "Everly, you know Knox didn't do this," I say. "He would never."

"Not him!" she screams. "Don't you get it? *His life*. He brought this down on us, just like he brought those pictures down on you. He may not have taken her, but he's responsible!"

The detective intervenes and directs his voice to Everly and Timothy. "Your daughter is being taken to the hospital. Just routine. And she'll need to be questioned. One of our officers will take you to her."

They nod, heading toward the door. "Everly?" I say softly.

Everly turns around. "As long as you're with him, I don't want you anywhere near my family."

My breath catches like someone just sucker punched me. Knox's arms go around my waist, like he expects me to fall.

"She didn't mean it," he whispers. "She's been through hell. Give her time."

~

I can't get the image out of my mind—sweet little Gracie all alone at Knox's parents' graves. It sends shivers through my body. We haven't been able to see her. She went straight to the hospital. She was only gone for a little over an hour, and we were told there's not a scratch on her. Just some smeared chocolate on her cheek. Apparently, her abductor brought chocolate cupcakes. I'll never be able to eat chocolate or cupcakes again. The detectives told us she wasn't even scared, that she was her usual happy, smiling self.

Knox and I are still at The Tune Up. The police have questioned us. Heath is here now, too. I'm having a hard time focusing on anything being said, Everly's words ringing in my ears. She's never going to forgive me for bringing Knox back into her life if Gracie's abduction has anything to do with him. And it clearly does. It can't be a coincidence that she was left at his parents' graves.

Here come the goosebumps again. What kind of sick, fucked up person leaves a little girl alone in a graveyard? What kind of message are they intending to send?

I have no idea what time it is. Is it late at night or early in the morning? I can't tell. At this point, my leaked photos seem like years ago, like a distant memory. They're not, of course, but kidnapping trumps everything. And now the world seems even heavier, like gravity is working overtime, holding us down, preventing us from moving.

It's funny how tiring worry is. Worry makes you more tired than running a marathon ever could. The mind running is way more exhausting than your feet moving, or most anything you can put your body through physically. Not that I'm going to take up running as a hobby or anything.

"Can you tell us anything about what happened?" Knox asks. "Anything about the person or . . ."

"I'm more interested in what you can tell me," the detective says.

The detective takes out an evidence bag, sliding it across the table to Knox and me. Heath is looking over our shoulder. He tried to insist Knox have a lawyer present, but Knox didn't want or need one. We have nothing to hide, and that would only waste time.

"Gracie's abductor asked Gracie to give this to you," the detective says.

The typewritten note isn't signed. It's only one question.

Knox, did you really think a few security guards could keep me away?

"Fuck!" Knox whispers, looking over at me. "Everly was right."

"What do you know about this?" the detective asks.

Heath goes into action, explaining that Knox has an active stalker, filling the detective in on all that's happened, suggesting that Gracie's abductor and Knox's stalker are one in the same. Heath wraps up by saying, "Don't bother testing for prints or DNA on the letter. You won't find any."

"This person targeted Gracie because of me," Knox whispers.

"Appears so," the detective says. "As the note says, you have security. You're harder to get to."

"Me, too," I say. "I now have security, too."

"So they went after someone else close to you," the detective says, "someone innocent, easy to get to. Any idea why Gracie was left at your parents' graves?"

Knox shakes his head. "I have no idea. I guess it's just part of their game, trying to rattle me."

"Did Gracie give a description of the person?" I ask.

"I really can't comment on an active case, but we've found that someone as young as Gracie isn't always a reliable witness. They tend to be easily confused, influenced."

"Okay for them to fly back to California?" Heath asks. "Movie premiere in a few days."

"Fine," the detective says, getting to his feet. "We are continuing to investigate and actively look for this person, and we will follow up with you all if we need to."

With that, the detective and a few other officers exit the shop. Heath heads toward the door as well, leaving Knox and I alone. We stay seated together, our hearts still pounding, the weight of this so heavy we can't seem to get up. The door closes behind him, and we sit in silence for a few moments. I don't know if there's press waiting outside. I guess it doesn't matter. Gracie being taken makes those pictures of me seem like amateur hour.

Knox's hands slide to mine. "We should leave for California immediately. This person is still around. We need to get you out of harm's way."

I slide my hand away, and my chest starts to rise and fall quickly. My heart knows what it has to do before my head can even compute it. And my heart knows the pain that's coming, but my head won't hear of it. "I'm not going."

"Mae," he says, reaching for me again, but I get up out of my chair, moving away from him.

I can't let him touch me. His touch weakens me.

Taking a deep breath, I muster enough strength to lie. "I need to be here for Everly."

Knox stands at the front door of my cottage. A car waits out front to take him to the airport. He gathered his stuff from Gigi's house and mine, slept a few hours, and now is heading back to California.

Alone.

I look out my window, the sun shining on a new day. But the damage of the past few days is evident. I see my beautiful wildflowers have taken as big a beating as I have, now trampled to the ground by spying paparazzi. Some of them are dead, but others are fighting to stand tall. I know how they feel. The struggle is real.

The police are still looking for Gracie's abductor, trying to piece everything together. I don't know why things are taking so long. Haven's Point isn't a big place, and Colorado isn't a big state. The person couldn't get far. Why haven't they found this crazy person already? For that matter, why hasn't anyone found out who hacked Knox's phone? If it's the same person, then hurry up and figure shit out!

Holding his duffle bag, Knox turns back to me. His blue eyes beckon me. Rushing to him, I hug him, wrapping my arms around him, feeling his hard muscles underneath my fingers, memorizing the way I feel in his arms. I know he's worried about leaving me behind, even with security. But he's worried about the wrong thing. He'll find out soon enough.

As his lips lightly land on mine, I slip a cassette in the side pocket of his duffle bag.

Cassette

Mae to Knox

Age Twenty-Six

Knox,

It's been two decades since we met. Twenty years. You've been in my life more than half the years I've been alive. I don't have many memories before you. My memories after you . . .

After you?

There will never be an after you. There is only you.

But I can't do this. It's one thing for me to be followed around and harassed. It's quite another to have my friends and family hurt.

You tried to warn me. I should've listened. Then neither of us would be hurting right now. I wouldn't be hurting you.

I hope one day you can forgive me. I hope you can try to understand.

I can't.

I don't know how else to say it. I just can't.

I'm sorry, Knox.

I don't want things to end badly between us like last time. I didn't want to fight, to argue about this. I wanted to be brave, try to do this in person, but I just couldn't.

I wish I could do this without any tears, but that's asking far too much. My heart is breaking, Knox. But I can't have my family hurt. Little Gracie . . . When I think about what could have happened?

All because of me. Because I love you.

You told me that being with you has a price. I thought I could do it, but the price is too high. If it were just me, I'd pay it. I'd figure out a way. I think I proved that with the photos, but the people I love are off limits.

As long as there is danger to them, I just can't do this.

Loving you costs too much. I knew that as soon as the detective showed us that letter from Gracie's kidnapper. I knew in that moment I couldn't share this life with you.

In another life . . .

CHAPTER THIRTY-FOUR

Knox

Opening the front door to my own house is depressing as fuck. I'm tired. Pissed. Worried. Heart-broken. Exhausted. I don't want to face a life without Mae, and walking inside alone feels like that's exactly what I'm doing. It feels like this is the beginning of my life without her.

I can't.

That's what her cassette tape said. It didn't say she didn't love me anymore. It just said she "can't."

I found the cassette in the side pocket of my duffle bag just seconds after landing. I reached for my sunglasses and felt it. As soon as I did, my heart stopped. I didn't wait until I got home to listen to it, making the driver stop at a big box electronics store and purchase a cassette player and earbuds. In the car, watching the California landscape pass by, I listened to her goodbye.

I don't flick on any lights in my house. There's natural light coming in through the huge windows, but the house is covered in shade, like a shadow, or ominous dark cloud, is hanging over it.

Of course, I tried to call Mae. Of course, she didn't answer. I'm getting the same silent treatment from Gigi, and I don't dare bother Everly and Timothy with this.

Gracie.

Sweet, precious Gracie—hurts my chest to think about what happened. Thank God, she seems totally unaffected by the whole thing. Nowhere in my mind did I fathom something like this happening because of my fame. It's unusual, to say the least. Most stalker situations involve the celebrity, occasionally the immediate family, but that's just usually because they are in close proximity. But never the daughter of a friend of an actor's girlfriend. It's so far removed that it never occurred to any of us.

I left security with Mae. The police are watching Gracie's house, and if they need more protection, I'm happy to provide it. It's the least I can do. I walk into my bedroom, considering whether I should call the security team and have them put Mae on the phone. That seems a bit drastic, and I doubt Mae would go for that.

My suit for the premiere hangs in a garment bag in my closet. Sitting down on my bed, I stare at it, knowing in forty-eight hours, I have to be smiling, waving, taking selfies, and giving interviews like my life hasn't just fallen apart.

Hanging up next to my suit is Mae's dress. I haven't even seen it. She wanted it to be a surprise. Dammit, she should be here. She should be on my arm when I step out of the limousine at the premiere. Instead, we are in the middle of this nightmare.

Losing her this time feels even worse than it did five years ago. I know how bad this will hurt. There is no moving on from Mae. There is only trying to move forward. Endless days of work, going about the business of life. Endless nights of sleeplessness, the bed now too big.

This time, I know that no one can fill that space. Last time around, I quickly tried to fill her spot in my bed, but I know now, more than ever, that no other woman can.

If it weren't for the premiere, I would still be in Haven's Point. After it's over, I'm going back. I have no other choice.

I pull out my phone. I'm not sure why I even check. She's not calling or texting, and she won't respond when I do. My finger runs over her name on the screen. She insisted I change it from Mae Sheridan to something else. I'm Scooby-Doo in her phone, so I toyed with the idea of making her Shaggy. But while Mae is my best friend, she's so much more than that.

I look down at her contact name on my phone, changing it to the only thing that makes sense. The only thing she will ever be to me.

The One.

CHAPTER THIRTY-FIVE

Mae

Gigi walks to the curtains of her den and peers through. She does this every few hours or so, periodically checking to see if she needs to grab her bat, I guess—even though Knox's security team is still posted out front. I came back to her place after Knox left, thinking the company would do us both some good.

She tilts her head. "Is that? It can't be!" she says.

My back stiffens. "What now?" I ask, my nerves on edge from the past week's events.

Gigi shakes her head, saying, "I think that's Ryder Merrick."

"Huh, Knox's brother? What would he be doing here?" I ask, getting to my feet to take a look. Pulling back the curtain slightly, I peek outside. No reporters are lurking around, but a huge tour bus is parked down the street.

The only soul outside is Ryder, standing in the empty lot where his childhood home used to be—right across the street from Gigi's house. He doesn't look at it the same way Knox does. The house may be gone, but the ghosts that haunt Ryder are still very much present.

There are some men you can't help but love. You know it's a bad idea. You know they've got issues and it's not healthy, but you get sucked in by how damn cute they are.

That is Knox's brother, Ryder, in a nutshell.

Nothing about the man is runt-like—he's actually pretty buff. It's on the inside that's he's stunted. He's so damn cute, though, you just can't help but love him. Thank God, I don't love him in a romantic way. He's so closed off. I pray for the woman who falls in love with Ryder. She'll have her hands full knocking down all his walls.

Without thinking, I walk to the front door, opening it. My guards immediately come to attention, but I hold my hand up, indicating that everything is okay. The sun feels good on my skin, the fresh air filling my lungs. Barefoot, I head across the street, the hot pavement making me walk faster. It's a welcome relief when I reach the grass on the other side.

"Knox send you?" I ask.

"Knox doesn't know I'm here," Ryder says, turning to me and smiling. "I took a little detour on the way to his premiere."

"Lots of memories," I say, and he just nods. "You haven't been back here since . . ."

He waves his hand, not wanting it all brought back up. "There's nowhere I wouldn't go for Knox." He shakes his head, grinning at me. "Little Mae Sheridan!"

There's no hesitation in his voice, no pity, no looking at me like I'm anything other than the little girl who used to visit her grand-mother across the street, the girl his brother loves.

"Ryder," I say as he wraps me in a hug. "I have all your albums on my phone."

Ryder and Knox look a lot alike. They're both tall, both have those killer blue eyes, but Ryder's always looked a little more dangerous, rougher somehow than Knox. Maybe it's because he's older, so he understood more when their mother was dying. Maybe it's because he had a very strained relationship with their father. Maybe it's the other heartbreak he suffered, the one that sent him running from Haven's Point. I can still see that Ryder has a big heart, no matter how guarded it is.

"Come inside," I say.

He shakes his head again. "I just came to pick you up."

I have no idea how he knew I was here, or whether he knew at all. Maybe he simply was visiting the spot of his childhood home, and I interrupted him. It doesn't matter. He's here now.

"I guess you haven't talked to Knox. There was this whole thing with pictures and my friend's daughter. We broke up. I'm not going."

He sticks his hands in the back pockets of his jeans, his eyes boring into me, like he's trying to figure me out. "Very first time I met you, we were right in this spot," he says.

"It was the same day I met Knox. I remember it like it was yesterday."

"Me, too," he says, a certain sadness in his voice. Their mother had just died. I'm sure the memories are burned into his soul.

He reaches over, flicking my brown hair. "You had half a pigtail," he says. "Whacked all your hair off to make Knox feel better."

Playfully, I pull at my locks. "Been having a bad hair day ever since."

He squats down a little, catching my eyes. "You were just a little girl. You weren't scared of your parents punishing you. You weren't afraid of what anyone thought of you."

"This is different."

He wraps one arm around me, leans down, and whispers, "No way does that same girl stay home, miss Knox's premiere, lock herself away. No way. Not that girl."

~

It's Sunday night. I'd normally be getting ready to broadcast my radio show, or, before things went to hell, maybe even taking the night off to attend Knox's premiere.

Instead, it's come to this: No boyfriend, suspended from my job, best friend not talking to me. If what they say is true about karma, I must've done some seriously bad shit that I'm not aware of.

I've lost everything.

I'm a twenty-something girl, mostly holed up at my grandmother's house, living in sweatpants and sweatshirts. Gigi calls it my heartbreak wardrobe. I guess she's right. Crying is easier in an elastic waistband.

I haven't seen Everly in a few days. We'd never fought before, at least over nothing bigger than who gets the last glass of wine. I miss seeing her. I miss Gracie and Timothy, too. What I wouldn't give to walk into the coffee shop and see his beanie loving head! To have a cup of whipped cream and listen to Gracie chatter on about something.

It's simple. But I don't even have that now.

Still, I had to do what I did. I had to end it with Knox. I love him. I won't ever love another man the way I love him.

When he first came back, I was concerned about losing my freedom, my privacy, even my job, but those seem like small things when compared to what happened with Gracie. My friends and family shouldn't have to lose anything for me to have love. They shouldn't have to be scared or worse because my heart belongs to a movie star. I can't do that to them. I only hope Everly will forgive me.

It's been a few days. I've tried calling her and Timothy, but they won't answer. I've left a dozen messages of apology. I don't want to go over to their house or the shop and risk upsetting Gracie, but if I don't hear from them soon, I will. I've lost too much to lose them, too.

And I'm desperate for information, to find out what, if anything, Timothy and Everly know about the person who took Gracie and what exactly happened. There hasn't been any news coverage, either. I suspect the police are holding what they know close to the vest. I'm totally in the dark.

I gave up Knox to keep them safe. The thing is, there will always be another target. If this psycho hadn't chosen Gracie, they could've gone after Gigi, or anyone important to Knox and me. Maybe even our future children. So I did the right thing. I did what I had to do. I know that, but it doesn't make it any easier on my heart.

Gigi told me that all love is about loss. The loss was just too great this time.

News of our breakup has already hit the airwaves. I don't know how the media found out. I certainly didn't tell them, and I can't imagine Knox did, either.

Most of the paparazzi left town with Knox. He's the star, not me. Gigi's heard there are a few stragglers, but for the most part, Haven's Point is quiet again. Somehow, they managed to keep Gracie's kidnapping being tied to Knox's stalker out of the press. Not sure how Heath pulled that off. I guess he's good for something. Everly would've flipped her shit if Gracie had become a tabloid story.

Gigi takes a seat beside me on the sofa. I haven't slept at my cottage since Knox left, mostly because Gigi wants me close. She's not convinced that just because I broke up with Knox, his stalker still won't target me. That's why I haven't dismissed my security guards, either—not that Knox would let me. He writes their checks, so they report to him. Still, it eases Gigi's mind to have me here, so I've stayed. For me, it's nice not being alone. Doesn't matter how old I get, I still need my grandmother. I always will.

And who knows how long it will take to find this crazy person. They seem elusive. I remember hearing somewhere that most crimes are committed by people we know, but that's not the case for celebrity stalkers. The list of suspects is literally the whole world.

"The premiere is tonight," Gigi says, patting my leg.

"It's funny," I say. "After our last breakup, I totally blocked him out. Wanting never to see him again, but now I want to watch. His movies, the premiere—those are the only times I'll be able to see him, so . . ."

My voice trails off, cracking, and I lower my head, my hair covering my face.

"Then we'll watch with you," I hear Everly say from the doorway.

I look up, seeing her holding Gracie in her pajamas, but she still gives me a sleepy smile and little wave. It's the first time I've seen Gracie since she was taken, and my emotions get the better of me, tears streaming down my face. I'm so thankful she's alright. There are no words.

Everly takes a seat beside me, and Gracie reaches up, wiping my face. "Why you crying?"

"I'm so happy to see you," I say, pulling her and her mom into a hug.

"I couldn't let you be alone today," Everly says. "I know tonight is going to be hard on you."

"Thank you," I whisper, holding her closer. "I'm so sorry." She shakes her head, glancing down at Gracie, smooshed between us.

"Gracie, why don't you come with me?" Gigi says. "We can get pillows and blankets, snacks. Make a pillow fort."

"Like a sleepover?" Gracie asks.

"Yep, just like that," Gigi says, taking her hand, and giving me and Everly a look, knowing we need some time.

"Did I hear that Ryder Merrick showed up at your house?" she asks.

"He stopped by to . . . encourage me to talk to Knox. I guess he was just doing what big brothers do," I reply.

"Good. I was worried for a minute that you were going to lay claim to both Merrick brothers, and that would be a shame for some lucky woman," she responds jokingly.

"God help the woman that lands Ryder Merrick," I reply, thinking back on how hard it was to turn down his request to accompany him to Knox's premiere.

"Though I guess both Merrick brothers are technically up for grabs?" she questions as she grabs my hand.

Everly and I sit in silence for a minute, holding each other's hands. "Everly, I can't tell you how . . ."

She shakes her head at me. "You broke up with Knox because of what I said."

"I broke up with Knox so the people I love could be safe."

"The other night," she says, "I was out of my mind. I said things that . . . Things I'm sorry for. I needed someone to blame, someone to hate, to lash out at. I wasn't thinking straight. I never thought you'd break up with him for me."

"I'd do anything for you, for Gigi, Gracie," I whisper.

"Oh, Mae," she says.

Clearing my throat and shaking away my tears, I say, "Let's just get through tonight."

CHAPTER THIRTY-SIX

Knox

My name is being screamed from every conceivable direction.

Wave.

Smile.

Wave.

Smile.

Stop for picture with a fan.

Cameras and lights everywhere.

This is life on the red carpet.

It takes forever to walk the five hundred feet into the theater. Normally, you could walk the length of it in a few minutes, but this will take me close to an hour to maneuver.

The early reviews on the movie are through the roof, calling it summer's big blockbuster. There's even been some Oscar buzz, but everyone in the business knows that summer movies don't get the nod from Oscar. It doesn't matter to me either way. I don't need a gold statue to validate me as an actor. I have one already.

And frankly, I hate the whole award show season, going from show to show presenting awards. No other profession in the world feels the need to congratulate itself on a job well done—at least not the way we do. It's ridiculous and pompous, if you ask me. We are all paid handsomely for our part, we don't need an extra pat on the back.

I'm directed to one of the many interviewers waiting on the carpet. My co-stars have already been down the line. That's the way it works. The bigger the star, the later you arrive. Tonight, I'm the last to arrive.

Smile for the camera!

The interviewers ask the standard questions. *Who are you wearing? Tell me how you prepped for this part. What drew you to this project?* It's most always the same drill—and certainly tonight it is by design. Heath made sure of it. The evening has all been perfectly orchestrated, even more than usual. They all know I'm not answering questions about my personal life.

And they better not even ask.

Normally, an actor doesn't walk the carpet alone. You are flanked by a couple handlers, your publicist or agent. Heath has that role tonight, but he's hanging back. He's here to usher me along if someone tries to slip in an uncomfortable question. Then they will be blackballed for life.

So far, so good. It's the same questions over and over again as I make my way down the carpet. I'd rather spend my time with the fans, some of whom have been waiting here for hours just to catch a glimpse of me and my co-stars, so I make sure my attention always returns to them.

I don't ever want to lose sight of the fact that going to the movies is expensive for the average person, especially when there are so many streaming options. Stopping and taking a selfie is the least I can do in return.

"Where's Mae?" someone from the pack of fans yells out.

It's amazing how I can hear her name over everything else. Cameras are flashing, people are screaming, but it's her name that has my full attention. I have at least a thousand cameras on me at the moment, so I can't react.

Ignoring the question, I move down the row, shaking hands, taking pictures, giving hugs. I never get used to this. I'm just a guy from Haven's Point, Colorado. I haven't cured cancer. I'm not God. There's really no reason for people to scream when they see me, yet they always do.

"Is Mae coming?" another person yells.

Smile.

Wave.

Ignore the gaping hole in my chest.

There are so many things wrong about what happened, it's hard to wrap my mind around it. The pictures, her job insecurity, Gracie, her leaving me—it's all gut wrenching and enough to drive a man to the brink. She's gone.

That's hard to swallow.

I can't say that I really blame her for leaving me. How's she supposed to trust me to take care of her, watch out for her, when I failed so epically? I have no one to blame for this but myself.

Smile.

Wave.

Smile.

Wave.

Just a few more feet to go, and I'll be inside the theater. The lights will go out, and I won't have to smile anymore. I know Ryder is already inside, having gone in a back entrance to avoid all of this. Perhaps he had the right idea.

For a moment, I close my eyes, the past five years of my career flashing before me. I stood on a carpet similar to this one and lost Mae the first time. Now here I am again, without her.

Fuck it! I don't care about the script we have planned for tonight. I don't care how much Mae pushes me away. I'm not going without a fight, and that starts right now. I motion to Heath, who's not far away. He steps toward me, and I lean over, whispering what I want him to do.

Five years ago, I lost her on a red carpet. Tonight, I will win her back.

CHAPTER THIRTY-SEVEN

Mae

Gracie's asleep in her pillow fort, her hand still in the bowl of chips she was snacking on. I'm on the sofa with Gigi and Everly flanking me. We've got my laptop on the coffee table, open to an entertainment news outlet that is broadcasting the premiere.

It reminds me a lot of that fateful night five years ago, when I sat surrounded by college girlfriends, waiting to catch a glimpse of my man on his first red carpet. I was so excited then.

Here I sit again, surrounded by women that love me, only this time, the breakup already happened.

I've come full circle.

Only the circle is broken.

We've seen all the interviews with his co-stars. We've heard from the director. They've broadcast some early reviews of the film, all glowingly positive.

Then I saw him.

Handsome as ever, stepping out of a limo, waving to his throngs of fans, smiling wide.

I know it's not real. I broke his heart less than forty-eight hours ago. He's doing his job.

Everly and Gigi both move closer to me, and I smile at them as we watch him saunter down the carpet. I watch every step and move he makes. I love him. That will never change.

Not long ago, we talked about me being beside him tonight. Even though I'm not there, I hope he knows I still love and support him. I hope he doesn't hate me and can understand why I did what I did. It's what I had to do.

Finally, he reaches the last interviewer before entering the theater. They ask him the same basic questions about who designed his tux and how he prepped for the part that he's answered numerous times already. Knox smiles and answers, charming as ever, but then . . .

"Reports are swirling that your relationship with your hometown girlfriend, Mae, has ended, and that you are once again single. Care to comment?" the interviewer asks, sticking the microphone in front of his face.

Knox looks directly into the camera, like he's looking right at me. "I am very much taken," he says. "Mae is the love of my life. The one. Always will be."

My hands fly to my mouth, trying to capture a broken sob, but it escapes anyway. I want to hug my laptop, hop on a plane tonight, and rush to him. But I can't. The very reasons I can't surround me— Gracie, Everly, Gigi. Nothing has changed.

Sometimes love isn't enough. Perhaps that's what hurts the most. My heart feels like it's breaking over and over again, and there's nothing I can do to fix it. The pain of losing him again isn't going to go away. Knowing it's for the best doesn't make it any easier. Even being confident I'm doing the right thing doesn't make my heart hurt any less.

Gigi and Everly are both talking to me, but I can't focus on them, my eyes glued to the screen, lost in my feelings, watching Knox disappear into the theater.

Five years ago: "Very much single."

Tonight: "Very much taken."

Gigi reaches over, closing the lid of the laptop. "Guess he doesn't hate me," I say. "That's a positive."

"Maybe you should talk to him. You know, in person. Not over a cassette," Gigi says, and I can hear the scolding in her voice.

Yes, I know it was a chicken shit way to break up with someone, but I wasn't strong enough to do it face to face. "Let's talk about something else," I say.

"Any word from the radio station?" Everly asks. "About when you can . . ."

"No, and that reminds me," I say, my eyes going to the clock, seeing it's almost ten. "Amy should be doing the show in a few minutes."

"No offense to Amy, but you are irreplaceable. The station will figure that out soon," Everly says, getting an evil little glare in her eye. "Should we listen?"

"I don't know," I say.

"Come on," Everly says. "Might be good for a few laughs."

I look at Gigi, who nods, elbowing me slightly.

"Okay, maybe just a few minutes," I say half-heartedly, opening the radio app on my phone.

It's easy enough to find, but I hesitate for a moment before I push play. Do I really want to hear someone else on my show, my baby, the nationwide broadcast that I built? The answer is no.

But my hope is to be back on-air soon, so I guess I need to know how things are going. Plus, I'm curious how Amy will do, what topics she will raise, whether she gets into her own personal life. I hit the play button, and the intro comes on, followed by Amy's voice.

She starts by giving a very brief explanation that she'll be filling in for a bit, but doesn't offer any details. It's obvious corporate told her what to say at the outset—they had her read from a prepared script. Nothing on my show has ever been scripted, but that was probably a good idea for Amy at the start. Having the words in front of her probably helped calm any nerves she may be having, allowed her a little time to find her footing. I know I was nervous my first show. I still get nervous sometimes.

"She's calling herself Reverend Mother," I whisper, a bit annoyed, but also admiring how clever that was.

I truly hope my friend and co-worker does well. She's been loyal and good to me the past few months. And who knows, maybe soon we will be neighbors in Haven's Point. I wonder where her apartment search stands.

After the script, Amy segues into an overview of the topics she wants to cover tonight and, of course, invites any and all to call in and discuss.

Gracie wanders out of her makeshift pillow fort, rubbing her eyes. "Sorry, baby, were we being too loud?" Everly asks, cuddling her close.

Her lips in a little pout, Gracie points to my phone and says, "The cupcake lady."

CHAPTER THIRTY-EIGHT

Mae

I lower the volume on my phone and ask, "Who's the cupcake lady?"

"That's what Gracie calls the woman her took her," Everly says, a confused look in her eyes.

"A woman?" I cry. "The police never gave us any details. They wouldn't. And you and I haven't spoken since, so I had no idea what actually happened."

"Apparently, it was a woman with black hair, wearing sunglasses," Everly says. "She opened the door of The Tune Up, finding Gracie alone. It's unclear if this woman knew the shop is briefly closed at that time. She didn't come all the way inside. She called Gracie by name, then asked Gracie if she knew Knox. Gracie said she did."

Everly turns to Gracie and asks, "Is that right, baby?"

"Yes, Mommy."

I guess they've been over this a thousand times already—at home and with the police—but I'm struck by how calm Everly is while relaying this information. She's not freaked out, trembling, just recounting the facts. My head is spinning just thinking about it all, trying to process a child's kidnapping. I still can't get over that someone targeted Gracie because of Knox.

"The woman said she had a cupcake in the car waiting for Gracie," Everly continues. "Gracie remembers the car was dark blue and had four doors."

"And, and . . ." Gracie interrupts, excitedly, "she let me sit up front. Like a big girl. No car seat."

My eyes catch Everly's. "Apparently, that was the best part," Everly says, a certain tone in her voice.

Gracie leans closer to me, whispering, "I think Mommy is mad I sat up front with no car seat."

I can't help but grin at her innocence, so thankful this whole thing hasn't scarred her for life. The rest of us will happily carry those scars.

"Gracie, how long were you and the lady together?" I ask.

"I don't know," she says.

Everly jumps in. "She doesn't know how long they were in the car or the cemetery. Mae, can you turn up the volume on your phone?" I do, then Everly takes her daughter's little hand. "Now, Gracie, honey," Everly says. "That's Miss Amy on the radio. She works with Mae. You met her at Gigi's birthday."

Gracie just shrugs. "She's the cupcake lady."

A chill goes through the air. We all feel it. This feels wrong, but maybe right at the same time. Everly's eyes go to me. Gigi's hand lands on my shoulder. "The lady on the radio is the lady that took you from the coffee shop and left you at . . ." Everly's voice gives way. "You're sure?"

"Yeah," Gracie says, hopping back into her pillow fort.

"Gracie is really good with voices," Everly says quietly. "She knew Knox was the voice of the bear from her movie immediately."

I get to my feet, grabbing my keys. Gigi takes hold of my elbow. "Mae?"

Looking down at Everly and Gracie, I whisper to Gigi, "Call the police. Call Timothy. Now."

"Where are you going?" Everly asks.

"The station," I say.

~

It's a good forty-five minutes from Haven's Point to the radio station in Denver. By the time I pull into the parking lot, the show only has a few minutes left.

On the drive, I confirmed with Everly that Timothy called the police. I've also listened here and there to the show. If I'm being honest, I'd say Amy did a pretty good job tonight for her first time—if I hadn't also been debating whether she is a fucking deranged kidnapper.

I keep going over what Gracie said. I still can't believe it. Surely Gracie is mistaken. I mean, I've worked with Amy for a while now. She was always hardworking, eager. I was helping her apartment hunt.

Crazy lunatics don't dress cute and show up at work every day with a smile on their face!

Amy was at Gigi's party. I know Gracie had to see her there. Wouldn't Gracie recognize her and tell the police? Gracie said the woman who took her had black hair. I guess Amy could've worn a wig and sunglasses. That would explain why Gracie couldn't identify her. And Gracie is only five.

But Amy? Knox's stalker?

That doesn't make sense. I hired her a few weeks before Knox called my show that first time. Unless she did some major sleuthing and discovered I was his old high school girlfriend and that's why she applied for the job. Still, that seems farfetched. I guess it could be a coincidence that she worked for me and was obsessed with Knox, but I don't believe in coincidences.

Maybe the obsession started after she knew about us, but that seems quick. Don't these crazy stalker things develop over time?

I've thought about calling Knox almost a dozen times, but he's probably still watching his movie, or celebrating at a party afterwards. If he even picked up, I'm not sure what I would tell him. I don't have any real answers. All I have is the word of a five-year-old.

I look up at the radio station. I don't know why I'm here. It's not like I'm going to storm the building myself. And it's certainly not smart to confront someone in a parking lot in the middle of the night. But if Amy actually did this, I want to be here if and when the police show up. I want to see the look on her face. Most of all, I want some damn answers.

But maybe I'm getting way ahead of things. I'm assuming that the police will show up, take her in tonight for questioning. I'm also assuming that things would move quickly, and then I'm not going to get any answers directly from Amy. I don't know if any of this is true, but right or wrong, these are the assumptions I'm working under.

I sense my window of opportunity is closing. This is my chance.

My mind is racing. All the weird and terrible things that have happened lately. I mean, was it Amy that initially told that Denver reporter that Knox was at my house? Was it her that gave my flight information to the press in L.A.? Then there's those compromising photos that were leaked. She wouldn't? I mean, could one woman really do that to another woman?

But she does have the background for that. Her technical knowhow was a huge part of why I hired her. She's a computer whiz and handled all the social media platforms, website updates, and technical programming for the show.

Picking up my phone, I glare up at the window, the one closest to the booth I know she's sitting in. Screw it!

Luckily, the call screener who answers knows who I am, and patches me right through to Amy. My call is next to go on-air with Reverend Mother, A.K.A. Amy. A.K.A. kidnapper.

My heart pounds against my chest. I can't remember being this nervous on-air since my first night. Then it felt like I was being fed to the wolves. Now, I'm the wolf, and I'm about to slaughter the wolf masquerading as a lamb.

"Welcome, caller," I hear Amy say. "What's your name?"

She's not using my standard line of, "*How can we break you?*" She might be a kidnapper, but at least she's not a thief.

"Hello, Reverend Mother," I say, almost vomiting in my mouth. "This is Mother Superior."

She laughs. "I think the cat's out of the bag. Alright if I call you Mae?"

"Sure," I say. "I wanted to call in and wish you luck. So happy I got through before the show ended."

"That's so sweet," Amy says. "You've been listening."

"Of course," I say, the bile rising again. "Great show. I can't thank you enough for taking over for me. I also wanted to let the listeners know that I plan on being back very soon."

"I'm sure they're happy to hear that," Amy says. "Thanks again for . . ."

"That's not the only reason I called," I say, staring up at the window, wondering if she's smiling or squirming in my chair. "I actually have a problem. I'm so used to talking about stuff on-air, I thought you could help."

"I'd be honored," Amy says. "Of course, we all know about your latest breakup. How can we help?"

My heart squeezes a little. Knox? If his stalker is Amy, and she gets locked up, then maybe he and I can . . . Ugh, I miss him so much, but I push that aside for the moment. "Actually, this isn't really about a boyfriend. It's about a friend."

"Okay," Amy says. "I'm intrigued."

"I'm afraid this person betrayed me," I say. "I suspect she went after my man."

"Juicy," Amy says. "What did she do, exactly?"

"First, she was sending him letters. They were anonymous, so it took me a while to figure out who was sending them."

"Hmm," Amy says. "He showed you the letters?"

"Not all of them, but yes," I say. "The first one was more of a thank you note."

"That doesn't sound inappropriate," Amy says, without hesitating one bit.

"No, it wasn't," I say, "But then I suspect she was the one who leaked our relationship to the press."

"Why would she do that?" Amy asks.

"I'm not sure. Maybe she wants him all to herself."

Amy laughs a little, and suddenly I feel like I'm way off base.

"Maybe you're being jealous. I mean, you were dating a famous actor."

"Believe me, there's nothing this woman has for me to be jealous about."

"That's harsh to say about someone you said is your friend."

"A friend doesn't come to my house in the middle of the night, scare me half to death, leave shit on my porch then steal my boyfriend's shoes!"

This time Amy hesitates. I hear her breathing on the other end of the line. My blood runs cold. It's the first time that I'm truly confident she did this, that she is capable of doing this. And I don't think she had a clue how much of the puzzle I put together.

"That sounds . . ." she pauses. "What proof do you have that your friend did those things?"

"I'd rather not reveal that," I say. "She's listening."

"Why would your friend do all this?" Amy asks.

"That's what I'd like to know," I say. "Knox never did anything to this woman. Any theories?"

"I'm afraid I don't have a criminal mind," she says, and I swear I can hear the smile in her voice, taunting me. "Perhaps it's time for me to take another caller. Best of luck to you, Mae."

"One more thing," I say. "Are chocolate cupcakes your favorite?"

The line goes dead.

But I don't leave. I can't. I need to see her. I want to look her in the eye. From a distance, I hear sirens approaching.

My heart thunders in my chest. Any remaining disbelief I had melts away. This is happening. But I still need to know why. Why would Amy do this?

Watching the officers enter the building, I get out of my car. The chill of the night air rattles my bones, and I wrap my arms around myself. The door to the radio station opens, and I watch as two uniformed police officers escort Amy to their squad car, apparently taking her in for questioning. Amy's eyes find mine through the darkness—cold and hard. She looks so different. It's like I'm not even looking at the same person.

Voices have changed my life.

I fell in love with Knox listening to his voice over old cassette tapes.

I made my living using my voice.

And Gracie solved a crime that way.

The sun rises on a new day. I haven't slept. I just hung up with the police and walk out to the field of wildflowers around my cottage.

It was always so hard for me to believe Amy was Knox's stalker.

That's because she wasn't.

She was mine.

CHAPTER THIRTY-NINE

Knox

Five years ago, I knocked on her door after a red carpet, and I quickly had my ass handed to me. This time, this morning, I'm hoping she hands me back her heart. I'm ready to do whatever it takes to get her back. I don't care how long it takes, who is stalking me, or how many times she shuts me down.

I'm not giving up on her, on us.

In movies, there are always these epic lines about love. I've had some good ones in my films, though I'm not sure they compare to those in *Jerry Maguire* ("You had me at hello") or *As Good as it Gets* ("You make me want to be a better man") or *The Fault in our Stars* ("It would be a privilege to have my heart broken by you.")

The thing that makes those lines great is truth.

I feel that way about Mae. I don't have a line to use on her, but I have the truth.

I love her. I've always loved her. I always will.

The sun still coming up, the plane touches down in Denver, and I don't wait for us to stop before I pull out my phone, considering calling her again. But I don't call this time. She never answers, anyway. And I need to do this in person.

My phone rings. I wish it was Mae, but am even more surprised at who's on the other end. My heart rate spikes. All I can think is that something else has happened. That something has happened to Mae. Why else would she be calling?

"Everly, is Mae alright? Gracie?"

"Have you seen the news?" she asks.

"No, I just landed in Denver."

"The police just arrested Amy for stalking and kidnapping," she says.

"Amy?" I ask. "Amy is the one who's been stalking me?"

"No," Everly whispers. "She was stalking Mae."

Turns out, it was never about me. It was always about Mae.

Amy hates her. Everyone just assumed it was about me, and that's what Amy was counting on. That everyone would assume the Hollywood actor was the intended victim, not the anonymous radio personality from Small Town, U.S.A.

So Amy sent me the letters, took my shoes, and hacked my phone, but it was all designed to slowly destroy Mae's life.

Mae was always the target, and Amy was intent on fucking up her life. It was Mae that got scared at her house that night. It was Mae that had compromising photos spread across cyberspace. It was Mae that got suspended from her job, with Amy taking her place. It was Mae who saw Everly suffer when Gracie was kidnapped. It was Mae that broke up with me.

At the police station, Gracie wasn't able to identify Amy out of a lineup, even when she wore sunglasses and a black wig. But as soon as the cops made her speak, Gracie knew exactly who "the cupcake lady" was.

We were all left with the same question – why? When all roads led back to Mae, the police started considering the possibility that maybe this wasn't about me at all. After all, Amy came to work for Mae before she and I were back together.

The police ran down a theory that perhaps Amy was a crazed fan who discovered I was Mae's ex, and was using Mae to try to get closer to me. But that was soon dismissed when the police contacted Amy's ex-husband.

Low and behold, he had once called Mae's show. Phone records confirmed it. The radio station sent the police an archived copy of the show. He called in asking for advice because his wife had cheated. It was a brief call, right before a commercial break, and she quickly gave him her standard cheating advice. Mae couldn't forgive that betrayal, but more power to you if you want to try.

He ultimately filed for divorce. The police talked to a few people who knew them before the divorce, and it was widely suspected that he cheated on Amy first. Of course, he never offered that information to Mae, and Mae never asked for any other details on the call. Apparently, he made out fine in the divorce, but Amy was left in bad shape—no house, no job, no money.

So, that was Amy's motive for all this – revenge, wanting to get back at Mae for her "bad" advice, offering baseless opinions without all the facts, wanting Mae to lose everything just like she did. She took the job at the station to get close to Mae, to dismantle her life from the inside out.

And it almost worked.

She scared the shit out of Mae, threw her to the paparazzi, exposed her private photos, took her job, and then—worst of all—kidnapped a little girl to stoke more fear and panic, to torture and torment Mae with the notion that her loved ones were in danger, which eventually led Mae to break up with me.

What kind of fucked up person does all of that? Amy appeared perfectly normal. She never gave any indication that she was capable of doing what she did.

As I pull up to Mae's house, I see her sitting among the wildflowers by her cottage. Her hair is down, blowing in the breeze, and her head is resting on her knees. Fuck, she's beautiful.

I wonder how long she's been sitting there, alone. Women are softer by design—their skin, their hair, their hearts, so their strength is often missed, overlooked. But that doesn't mean it's not there. Mae is the perfect example. She's strong enough to withstand those pictures, figure out this whole mess—all on her own.

I'm just hoping she realizes that we're stronger together.

I'm barely out of the car when her head turns to me. Her blue eyes look so sad. Tears are flowing down her cheeks. Shaking her head, she cries a little. "How can you be here already? The police just arrested Amy a few hours ago."

"I was coming back to fight for you," I say, kneeling down beside her. "I didn't know about Amy until I landed. Everly called me."

"She was never after you," Mae says, looking out to the water. "It was me."

"I know."

"The police think when you called my show that first time, she saw an opportunity and took it. She could make everyone think it was about you, while destroying me."

"I hope she rots in hell," I say.

Mae begins to sob. "You know why I left, right? You understand? I thought I was protecting my family, my friends. That's the only reason why I . . ."

"Mae, baby, I listened to your cassette," I say, wiping her tears. "I understand."

"I made so many mistakes. I trusted Amy."

"You had no reason not to," I say, playing with the hair around her face. "I'm sorry."

"I broke up with you," she sobs, a small smile breaking through. "By cassette! Shouldn't I be the one apologizing?"

"I don't need you to apologize," I say and hold her face in my hands. "I just need you to take me back."

"No," she says softly, leaning in closer. "I need you to take me back."

Right before my lips land on hers, I whisper, "I never let you go."

EPILOGUE

TWO MONTHS LATER

Knox

"Did you hear that caller tonight?" Mae calls out to me, walking into her cottage on the lake.

"Which one?" I yell to her, not coming out of the bedroom.

Waiting for her to come to me, I look out the window. The moon is out, the lake is calm, the flowers are in bloom, and everything seems right with the world.

For starters, Amy is behind bars. She pled guilty. No one ever said she was dumb. No way was she going to win a jury trial if they put Gracie on the stand against her. Since Gracie was missing for only an hour or so and the kidnapping didn't involve a weapon, she pled down to five years. Not long enough in my opinion, but it wasn't my call.

The radio station was practically begging for Mae to return. Mae played some hardball with them, though, making them grovel, getting a new contract and more benefits.

"Some guy called in talking about how testicles have taste buds!" she says, laughing. "Have you heard anything like that before? Apparently, if you put orange juice or soy sauce on your balls, you can taste it!"

"I can't believe some dude actually tried that," I holler back.

We've been splitting our time between California and Colorado for the past couple months. It's working out fine. The longest period we've spent apart is about one night a week. Not ideal, but not terrible. My team has done its best to purge the internet of those pictures. It happened, and Mae has come to some sort of peace about it, or at least acceptance, and she knows I'll do my best to shield us from the ugly side of fame.

You lose some freedom doing what I do. And, in turn, she loses some, too. There is a cost, but we're not going to lose each other. That's too big of a price to pay.

"I'm waiting for you. What are you doing?" I call out to her. "Come to bed."

"Always trying to get in my pants," I hear her laugh, her voice growing near.

"Is it working?" I say.

"It's . . ." She stops mid-sentence when she sees me on the bed, a great big surprise waiting for her. She bursts into a giggle.

"What did you do?" she cries.

Letting go of what I'm holding, the big ball of fur runs towards her. "Your dream dog," I say.

"A St. Bernard!" Mae bends down, the dog kissing all over her face. At barely four months, the puppy already weighs close to fifty pounds. "I love him!"

"Her," I correct, getting to my feet. "She's already trained and everything."

Mae leans over, planting kisses all over me. Apparently jealous, the dog now gets in on the action, jumping all over us, sending Mae into laughter. "What's her name?" she asks.

"Brandy," I say, trying to hold the puppy still and showing her the classic St. Bernard barrel around the dog's neck.

Mae laughs. "You know that's a myth, right? The breed didn't actually transport booze in their barrels."

"Maybe you should open the barrel, just to check."

She gives me an odd look and unhooks it, finding a little black velvet box inside. Her face lights up. "Oh my God!"

Taking her hand, I get down on one knee, pulling out the twenty-carat emerald cut diamond on a platinum band—twenty carats for the twenty years I've known her.

Her mouth falls open, just as I hoped. She tries to settle herself and draws a deep breath, attempting to clear her head so she never forgets this moment.

I don't have an epic movie line scripted by a team of Hollywood writers. But I only need two words.

"Say yes!"

"Yes!"

ALSO BY PRESCOTT LANE

Ryder (releasing September 2020)

Just Love

A Gentleman for Christmas

All My Life

To the Fall

Toying with Her

The Sex Bucket List

The Reason for Me

Stripped Raw

Layers of Her (a novella)

Wrapped in Lace

Quiet Angel

Perfectly Broken

First Position

ACKNOWLEDGEMENTS

I need to thank everyone! Everyone who waited for me to release while the world was turned upside down with a virus. Everyone who understood that I wasn't comfortable talking about my book when the world was suffering. My whole team for seeing me through this process—no matter how long it got!

Nina Grinstead, (Valentine PR), Nikki Rushbrook (editor), Letitia Hasser (cover design), Michelle Rodriguez (beta reader), bloggers, Instagrammers, anyone who even mentioned this book, thank you so much.

Readers! Thank you for sticking with me book after book. And if you are new to me, thank you for taking a chance.

2020 has been a heck of a year. But here's to hoping it ends with a HEA!

Hugs and Happily Ever Afters,
Prescott Lane

ABOUT THE AUTHOR

PRESCOTT LANE is originally from Little Rock, Arkansas, and graduated from Centenary College in 1997 with a degree in sociology. She went on to Tulane University to receive her MSW in 1998, after which she worked with developmentally delayed and disabled children. She currently lives in New Orleans with her husband, two children, and two dogs.

Contact her at any of the following:
www.authorprescottlane.com
facebook.com/PrescottLane1
twitter.com/prescottlane1
instagram.com/prescottlane1
pinterest.com/PrescottLane1

Made in the USA
Monee, IL
11 August 2020